The
Best
Intentions

All Saints Book Three

For Sarah Clements.
The wind beneath my wings, and the end
to my cup.

PROLOGUE

Silence.

Was it silence?

He could hear an odd ringing in his ears, and his body felt as though it was being dragged along the rough ground.

Alex opened his eyes and saw two men above him, and they seemed to be shouting, but he couldn't hear anything except the persistent ringing.

These men were on the security team. He didn't know their names, but he recognized their faces as they shouted at each other.

Why were they shouting?

The ground beneath him shook, and both men dropped his arms and fell over him, knocking out his breath.

"Brad?" he tried to speak, but he heard nothing though he felt his lips move and the vibration in his voice box, but white noise prevailed.

He'd been talking to Brad. He remembered that much. But then…what?

The security team got off him, and one of

them turned their faces down towards him and spoke.

"I can't hear," he spoke, trying to communicate and taking it on faith that they still had hearing.

The man nodded. He then clasped his hands together, and flowered his fingers apart rapidly, his lips forming a single word: Boom.

Had there been an explosion?

Alex raised his head, instantly dizzy, but he determinedly took in the scene.

Fire. The car had been on fire before. Had that exploded? The fire seemed more intense now.

Jesus where was Tim? Alex remembered pulling him from the car. He'd been unconscious, and bleeding from a head wound, but he'd been alive.

"Tim and Ernie?" he asked, still not hearing his voice, but he didn't even care about himself right now.

The security man shook his head.

"Oh God are they dead?"

Another headshake.

"Where are they?"

A gesture behind him made his head whip around to the left. Two prone figures and several paramedics and firefighters were working around them. A warped sheet of metal seemed to be pinning down a leg. Whose leg?

Oh God, it wasn't just pinning the leg, it was *in* the leg.

Cool hands turned his head.

Brad. Handsome as always, but looking worried, and speaking frantically to him.

"I can't hear."

He clearly saw Brad relax, but then his eyes strayed to where the emergency workers were busy, and the tension returned, along with an unheard shout of panic.

Alex watched Brad hurry over to the emergency and took charge.

Clearly Alex was fine, as far as the lack of necessity for emergency care was concerned, and the security team seemed to realize this as they stopped pinning him down.

Taking their hands, he got to his feet slowly, and nodded his thanks.

Firefighters were tackling the flames, and now that he was upright, he saw that the car was in several pieces.

Facing Brad, he watched with horror as the metal was pulled away, and the leg looked oddly disjointed. Almost too long.

He stepped closer to identify the wounded party, but it wasn't necessary. His gut knew.

Because life seemed to be an ongoing shit storm right now, who else could it be but Tim.

Having just buried their father, Tim had stormed off. At the time Alex had thought his brother-in-law was guilty of shirking his duty to Christina, but he didn't deserve this hellish punishment.

Brad was tightening a tourniquet around Tim's thigh and giving rapid instructions to the emergency workers who were issuing chest compressions.

Shit!

Was Tim dying?

No. It couldn't be.

A greyness began to sap his vision, and he felt his legs buckling under his weight.

This couldn't happen to Christina.

No.

A strong pair of hands suddenly gripped his upper arms and steadied him. Hunter stood in front of him, his blue eyes meeting Alex's with a stern assessing look. He could see the man's lips move and thought the words might be 'are you okay?'

Alex nodded, "I can't hear," he told the man he despised.

Hunter lifted a hand and ran it under Alex's ear, coming away wet with blood. He showed

7

Alex.

Alex wasn't concerned by the blood, but he was astonished at Hunter's blasé attitude towards it. This man knew he was HIV positive, and he wasn't repulsed or concerned about touching his blood. Maybe he wasn't such an arrogant prick after all.

There was a moment, where Hunter seemed to understand that Alex was surprised by his actions, and his cocky facade was nowhere to be seen. Hunter gave Alex a nod, and pointed to an ambulance.

"I'm fine, I can't go to hospital." Didn't Hunter understand that he couldn't possibly leave with his brother in law in peril, and a mad shooter on the loose.

With careful enunciation Hunter spoke. "You are going. You need to be checked out."

Alex thought he heard something faintly. A mumble. But the ringing persisted.

But Tim…

Hunter seemed to anticipate the objection. "You can't help him."

It was true.

ONE

Alex didn't like his new Captain. A formidable figure named Janet Markson.

She was a woman, though that wasn't the source of his dislike. She was white, and middle aged, but they weren't the issue's either. The problem was Alex himself, and it was very obvious that she viewed him as such.

He was bi-sexual and HIV positive, and nobody wanted to partner with him.

Upon joining his new district's department, it was clear that people either viewed him with polite distance or open hostility. The partner he'd been initially paired with was a middle-aged Caribbean man, who disliked anybody of the 'not straight' persuasion, and when he'd found out that Alex was HIV positive too, he'd requested an immediate change of partner.

"Alex, I'm not sure how I can put this delicately," she began with an involuntary wince.

Alex shook his head, "you don't need to tiptoe around me, I already know what everyone thinks."

She winced again, "and what do you think everyone thinks?"

9

"That I have HIV, and I'm bisexual. Not only am I gay, I'm dirty. Nobody wants to partner with someone who they may have to entrust their life to, and who is themselves a danger." Alex fought down his anger. "I know you've been given the job of pacifying me, or appeasing the others, but I'd rather work alone than be forced into a partnership with someone who despises me."

Markson actually smiled a little. "I can see we've made a great impression with you so far. But I can tell you that no, I haven't had that kind of feedback at all, simply conflict of personality grievances."

Alex gave her a skeptical glance, but knew she had to tread very carefully here. If she acknowledged that he was correct, she was admitting that she had bigoted officers working for her.

"It can be difficult for anybody to find a partner they work well with. The chemistry has to be right, and that can't be forced."

He acknowledged the truth in that with a nod.

She leaned back in her chair and clasped her hands in her lap. "Do you think you will have any problems working with a woman?"

He snorted, "of course not."

She nodded at that, "good. As of Monday I'm partnering you with Kathleen Fuller. I'll tell her to meet you at Joey's at 9am."

He nodded, but wasn't thrilled to have been partnered again so soon. He actually did want to work alone. But Alex acknowledged to himself that he had been blue since returning to his hometown and leaving his old precinct. He'd been happy there, and had founded bonds of real family and friendship during his time, but had to admit to himself now that he'd only done so to somehow substitute for the real family he'd hidden himself away from here.

The bond was now reformed with his family, and since the death of his father earlier in the year, he felt it was more important than ever to be close to home.

"Enjoy your weekend," Janet said by way of dismissal.

Alex bid her goodbye, and felt a heavy sigh escape him as he left her office.

It should be a relatively good weekend. He'd be seeing the family on Saturday, and had actually offered to babysit so that Eric and Jeanie could attend a charity dinner.

His niece Lily, and her newly adopted brother Ben were no problem, and in fact spending time with them seemed to revive Alex in some essential way. Children were a joy and a blessing, but of course as a single male, he could make that bold statement.

No doubt he'd see little Alvin too. The now six-month-old baby was an infant giant, and as Christina and Tim were still residing with Eric and Jeanie, he had no doubt that he'd be getting baby cuddles too on Saturday evening.

He collected his jacket from his desk and checked his phone as he left the building and headed for his car. No calls, but it was quite late. There was one message a few hours ago in his families chat group, and it had been posted by Brad.

The message was a short video clip of Brad's girlfriend Misha supporting Alvin in the bathtub, and the infant was giggling at the bubbles he was making with his tiny butt.

He couldn't help the laugh that escaped him but couldn't help but be sad too. Little Alvin had no way of knowing that his parents weren't doing so well these days.

Tim had not adjusted well to being a father. That fact coupled with the life threatening injury he'd sustained at his father's funeral, had pushed Tim into a depression where he rarely spoke or showed interest in anything.

Christina was physically recovered from

Alvin's difficult birth, but it had been necessary for her womb to be removed, and so had left her without the ability to have any more children. This added to Tim's distant behavior and his lack of support had pushed his sister into her own depression, and nobody seemed to know how best to help either of them.

For now, they all helped to nurture Alvin as he grew. Christina did her best, but caring for an infant alone was never easy, and thankfully it didn't have to be an option with the family intact once again.

He climbed into his car and debated briefly whether to work out tonight. It was late, but he preferred his local gym when it was late. No douchebags of either gender tended to workout at 11pm, so he immediately voted in favor of a workout before he went to his small apartment.

When he'd decided to return to live back in his hometown, Eric and Jeanie had immediately offered him house room, as had Brad, who had assumed tenancy of the old family home. But Alex needed his own space, and they respected that need for independence, and insisted that he take keys for both properties and demanded the verbal assurance that should he ever need or want to use them, he would.

He'd found an apartment in central town,

above a shoe store that catered to women with large feet and drag queens. The store owner took comfort in knowing that his business was protected overnight by a cop in residence, and offered Alex a free fitting whenever he wished to try a nice stiletto.

His workout bag was in the trunk of his car as always, so he drove straight to the gym that was just a block from his home. It wasn't the best part of town, and as he pulled his bag from the car, he heard a drunken couple arguing nearby as he went into the gym.

There were minimal staff this late in the day, so he wasn't surprised to see nobody manning the reception desk. He used his membership card to enter and quickly changed in the locker room. He was pleased to see that there was only one female on the treadmills, and a couple of young men leaning on the Watt-bikes post workout.

Alex preferred to start his workout by lifting weights, so he turned his back on the other patrons and loaded his preferred weight.

"I'm not kidding man, she was so flexible."

He sighed at the monologue that was too loud for social normality. He hated posturing douchebags, and the fact that people who just wanted to better their own physical health with an innocent workout had to endure the constant presence of multiple douchebags at any given time.

"Her right leg went behind her own head!"

Maybe he should invest in some headphones.

He glanced at the two men, who were still leaning against the bikes but showed no intention of actually using any equipment. They were both sporting fake tan and tribal tattoos, and both kept glancing at the female on the treadmills. Shaking their heads disapprovingly as she struggled to keep her balance as she had one arm crossed over her chest.

The female was staggering as she tried to maintain a slow jog on the treadmill. She was wearing oversized sweatpants and hooded top, and she was very red in the face. Not only was she inappropriately dressed, but she was also clearly not used to working out.

Alex was immediately angry at the douchebags for laughing at her, which they openly did as she dropped her arm from her chest and clutched at her falling sweatpants with both hands. She still maintained her pace as she yanked them back into place, but her red face reddened further as she looked at the laughter aimed at her.

"Guys," Alex stepped closer to them and summoned his commanding tone. "Leave her alone."

They both turned and immediately puffed out their chests before they saw the size of Alex and wilted under his gaze. "We weren't doing anything," one of the men said defensively.

"I suggest if you aren't working out you should leave."

"What are you the police?" the same man sneered.

"Yes, I am." He loved moments like this, as with his tattoos and piercings, he looked nothing like a law enforcement officer should to most people. "You guys aren't breaking any laws, but you're being dicks towards someone you don't even know, who is clearly trying to improve herself. It's people like you who stop people from exercising."

The silent man had the good grace to blush.

His verbose counterpart sniffed indignantly, "we were done anyway."

Alex smiled unpleasantly as they left, and looked again at the woman, who looked as though she was gasping for breath, and her legs were about to buckle, but she pushed herself on.

He turned his attention back to his weights

and remembered the first time he'd tried to work out after being attacked, and how weak he had felt. He'd been sure that people had been laughing at him, at how skinny and puny he must have looked and how ridiculous it was that he was attempting to improve himself.

It was hard. His body had still been recovering from the Heroin overdose, and his mental state was less than brilliant. Thoughts of suicide were never far from his mind, and his new obsession, 'getting healthy', was the only thing that had gotten him through.

As he began his reps, idly counting them at the back of his mind, he remembered that he had to partner with someone new again on Monday and tried to ignore the sinking feeling in his stomach.

Try as he might, he always had his defenses up when he met someone new these days. He couldn't help it. Given that he had so many facets to his personality these days that could irritate some or offend others, he tended to start each encounter with a bad attitude, which only furthered the issues of compatibility where it came to finding a new partner.

Perhaps this one would be a good match? What was her name again? Karen? Coral?

Shit, this was a great start, he'd already forgotten her name.

He'd better not mention to his family that his new partner was going to be a female. No matter how many times he told them he was not looking for a relationship, they all wanted to pair him off. And no matter how often he reminded them that he was bisexual, since they'd found out that his viral load was negligible, they were determined to pair him with a female to breed.

That was one thing that frustrated him beyond belief with his family. But it wasn't even just his family, it was all people who were heterosexual. The need to breed wasn't now, nor had it ever been present in Alex and how he viewed a potential partner.

He didn't have the burning desire to spawn any offspring. Not that he hated children, the love he had for his niece and nephews were some of the strongest loves he'd ever felt, and that love continued to grow as the children did.

But when he pictured the future, and the potential for a mate that he committed his life to, he never saw being surrounded by children or being a father. He couldn't picture himself ever being called 'Daddy', or assuming that role with any level of comfort.

Not only could he not tolerate the thought of leaving a life partner with the burden of living with his disease and his almost certain early expiration date, but he couldn't knowingly bring a child into this world with the intention of leaving it fatherless.

But then, the flip side of that scenario was that all parents expired before their children. And Brad's argument for this debate was always the trump card he played the few times he'd been fool enough to engage in a conversation about it; "Nobody knows when their number will be up."

He was right of course. Their own mother had died upon their birth, and their father, who had been flawless as far as paternal figures go, had raised them along with Eric, their senior sibling of almost fifteen years.

He'd been raised just fine, as had they all. He just didn't want to be a Dad. He was fully content with being Uncle Alex.

TWO

He always felt better after a workout. He knew that he didn't need to burn off any junk food as he avoided it on principle, but the sense of satisfaction that came from making his muscles burn was priceless.

As he was putting his gym bag in the trunk of his car he noticed that across the street the woman from the treadmills was shakily exiting the gym, closely followed by the two douchebags who had laughed at her.

They were still laughing now, he guessed at her slow walking speed, and both seemed to be making mooing noises in her direction.

Angry once more, he slammed the trunk shut and ran across the road. "Hey!"

The two men looked over their shoulders at him and quickly looked panicked and broke into a sprint, overtaking the woman who was frozen on the spot.

Alex saw that her reddened cheeks were wet with tear tracks. He hurried to her, "are you okay?"

She seemed fearful at his appearance but nodded.

"Can I walk you to your car? You really

shouldn't be walking around alone this late."

She shook her head, still looking terrified.

He reached into his jacket and pulled out his badge, "I'm a cop. My name is Alex."

She raised her eyes from the badge to his unshaven face, and he saw her looking at the piercings in his eyebrow and upper ear, and the tattoo showing on his neck. Her eyes briefly met his, and she lowered them to the ground once more.

"Where is your car?" he asked, trying to use his soothing voice.

She shook her head again, still studying the ground, "I don't have one," she said quietly.

He grimaced, she really wasn't being sensible. A lone woman walking through any neighborhood at midnight wasn't a good idea.

"Do you live far? Can I drive you home?"

"No, thank you," she turned to resume her walk, but Alex didn't feel good about leaving her to walk.

He fell into step behind her, and so she wasn't alarmed, he told her, "I understand you don't want to get into a car with a strange man. But I'm not okay with leaving you to walk alone. It's not safe."

She stopped again and faced him, searching his features.

21

"I'm happy to walk you home," he smiled.

"It's only a couple of blocks," she shrugged.

"It's no problem," he assured her.

She studied his face again, "you're really a cop?"

He nodded, "I am. I can give you my badge number if you like? Show you my driver's license?"

She almost smiled, "no it's okay. Thank you though, for understanding."

"May I walk you home?"

She nodded, shyly, and wiped at her eyes.

Alex gestured for her to lead the way, and he fell into step beside her.

They walked on in a comfortable silence for several moments, but Alex felt that she was owed an apology. "Those guys were assholes, just ignore them."

She nodded, "I was. Ignoring them I mean."

"I'm sorry that they ruined your workout though."

She seemed uncomfortable, but shrugged a shoulder, "I shouldn't have gone there anyway."

"Why not?"

"It was a silly idea, trying to be better…"

He shook his head, "no, don't feel that you didn't belong there. Those assholes had no right to act the way they did. You're entitled to work out. Don't let them put you off."

"I don't even have the right clothes to wear, I'm a complete fraud."

He scowled at her, "it isn't about wearing the right clothes or looking a certain way. You want to be healthier and you are trying to take steps to look after your body. Right?"

She nodded.

"So that doesn't take clothes, it just takes the right attitude. And you've obviously got the right attitude or else you wouldn't have gone to the gym in the first place."

"Yeah," she agreed, but she still sounded dismayed.

"Please don't let those guys stop you from coming back."

"No, I won't," she didn't sound as though she believed her own words.

"Look I go there most evenings. Not usually this late, but I can if you want some company?"

She immediately shook her head, "I can't go every night. Only Mondays and Wednesdays."

"Okay, well if you like, I can pick you up?"

"No, thank you," she said immediately.

"Was that no to the company or a no to being picked up?"

She hesitated, "being picked up I guess," she

seemed uncomfortable.

"Well on a Monday and Wednesday I'll be at the gym late and I'll keep the idiots away from you and then walk you home again. How does that sound?"

She stopped walking and faced him, "why would you do that?"

He took a moment to think. Why was he offering to be a white knight in this scenario? "I guess I know how it feels. To make a change in your life and start going to a gym can be scary. I used to be a skinny librarian believe it or not."

She smiled, as if she didn't believe him, but she appreciated the lie.

"I have no ulterior motive, I'm not trying to impress you or romance you," he declared. "I'm just being nice because…Well I moved back to town recently and I don't really have any friends. Maybe we could be friends?"

She looked hesitant again, "maybe."

They crossed the road and Alex realized that they were passing a graveyard, and he could see and hear some teenagers partying. He wondered if he should go and stop them.

"They stop by 1am, usually," she commented.

Alex looked at her, "you know that? Do you usually party with them or something?"

She frowned, "no, but I hear them most nights."

He frowned, "so we must be close to your house?"

She nodded, "yes, in fact I should say goodbye now. I can't have the neighbors seeing you."

Alex was amazed, "are you under house arrest or something?" he joked.

"In a way," she agreed in all seriousness. "It just wouldn't be good for me."

He frowned, picturing a jealous husband returning from a late shift. "Are you okay?" he felt like he had to ask this strange woman.

She nodded and straightened her back, "I am. And thank you for helping me, it was very kind of you."

Alex grinned, "you're welcome."

"I'm going now." She turned around and took a step.

"Wait!"

She turned around again, "yes?"

"What's your name?"

"Charlie."

He smiled, "nice to meet you Charlie. I'll see you Monday?"

She smiled too, "see you Monday Alex. I'll be there at about 10."

Alex watched her walk away, still not convinced that she was nearly home, but when she turned to cut through the church courtyard she was out of sight, so Alex respected her wishes and started heading back to his car.

She was a very strange woman, but not in any way that was offensive. She was obviously nervous around strangers, and he could sense that she wasn't comfortable with men.

There was a definite air of loneliness that came with the baggy sweatpants and the un-styled long red hair she had piled on top of her head in a simple ponytail.

He saw no other people as he walked back to his car, and when he reached it he realized that in his haste to help Charlie, he hadn't locked his car again. Thankfully nothing was missing, but he couldn't believe he'd been that careless.

As he fired up the engine he felt his stomach rumble, and knew that he didn't have much food at home.

Eric and Jeanie's kitchen was always well stocked though, and he decided to head over there, feeling only minimal guilt over treating their home as a rest stop. They had told him to do so should he need it, and he'd be there tomorrow anyway, so he may as well spend the night and save himself having to grocery shop for another day.

They'd given him a permanent room as an incentive to make him stay with them long term, but at the time he'd valued his independence over the lavish suite they'd decorated for him.

He still valued his own company but felt that they'd all realized now that he wasn't going anywhere, and so they'd all relaxed into the new family dynamic in a way that had been missing for a long time. In the freedom of living alone, he felt more comfortable returning to the family on a casual basis, and though the logic of that situation were backward, he didn't care.

THREE

When he got to the newly reinforced security gates of All Saints House, he typed in his security code, and waited for verification.

The security had been heightened at All Saints House since a criminal had knowingly targeted Jeanie earlier in the year, and neither she nor Eric had wanted to take a chance that their home was not secure for themselves or the children.

External walls and fences were all raised in height and alarmed. A patrol regularly walked the perimeter and reported back to the security team that had installed CCTV cameras covering the entire property, and were all fed back to the security station, situated in what used to be the old garage, but was now a hub of monitors that was manned 24 hours a day.

Alex couldn't blame them for going overboard in their security precautions though, as he'd seen firsthand the damage that William Straker had done at his father's funeral.

Since that incident there had been several fires at Allen House, all attributed to arson. And one ladies self-defense class had been crashed by an unknown male who had swung a gun around, but thankfully hadn't fired it upon anyone.

Three letters had arrived at All Saints House in the last few months. Alex knew because he'd seen them firsthand, and they had been the main reason for the enhanced security detail.

All three letters had been hand delivered to the mailbox at the end of the long driveway.

The first had simply read; FOUND YOU. Alarms had been installed on all the windows and doors within the property.

The second had read; WATCHING YOU. The CCTV had been installed and a permanent security team had been appropriated.

The last had arrived just last week, and the security team who now opened and read all the mail found; YOU CAN'T HIDE FOREVER. The police had checked all three letters for fingerprints, and there was a match for the prints on file for William Straker.

Every member of the family had a personalized code for the gate, and Alex turned his face up to the camera that he knew was looking down at him, to verify his identity.

The gate started to open, and he ducked his head back into the car and drove along the driveway to park up next to the garage. He knew the security team would want to check his vehicle and himself.

Sure enough as he switched off the engine, two men emerged from the building and nodded to him. One he recognized, the other he did not. He took a crack at the name of the man he recognized, "Simmons?"

The man smiled, "Simons. How are you doing Mr. Steinberg? It's kind of late."

"Yeah I'm good thanks," he handed his car keys to Simons. "I've got a bag in the trunk I want to take into the house, want to check it first?"

"Sure thing," Simons opened the trunk, and the bag was the only thing there.

"Fair warning though, it's got my dirty gym clothes in it, so it might stink."

Simons laughed, but his nameless counterpart didn't seem amused. He just watched on as Simons rummaged through the bag, and then handed it to Alex.

"Any problems?" Alex had no doubt that the security team had everything in hand.

"All quiet."

"Cool. I'm good to go?"

"Sure, you got your key?"

"Yeah. Is the alarm set?"

"It is. But you have your code?"

He nodded. His personalized code was not

only for the outer gate, but the front door as well. The security system installed was state of the art, and it tracked the comings and goings of all individuals that had codes.

As he entered the door, the lights in the entryway were dim, but always lit. The alarm system was in night mode as it was after midnight, so it didn't emit the beep that it would during the day. Instead it flashed incessantly until he tapped his code in, telling the system that he was inside the house and it should return to monitoring the exterior.

He dropped his bag at the foot of the stairs and headed straight to the kitchen. Alex had expected it to be deserted at this time of night but was surprised to see Christina sat at the table, staring at a full glass of wine.

"Hey sis," he said jovially, though he was dismayed at how pinched his sister's face was looking these days. She had little to no appetite these days, and she had lost her baby weight. But the fact that she had lost a little too much weight didn't seem to bother her.

No matter how often she was reminded or chastised to take better care of herself, for Alvin's sake if not for her own, it just seemed to fall on deaf ears.

The sadness she seemed to constantly exude

never seemed to ease, and none of the family could think of a way to help her or Tim in their troubles.

She looked up at Alex, "hey." She forced minimal inflection into her tone, and he established quickly that she wasn't drunk at least. That wouldn't help her state of mind at all.

He decided not to comment on the wine, or her pale drawn face, and he crossed to the fridge. Daisy, the head housekeeper and cook always kept the fridge and cupboards well stocked, and she was amazing at what she did. He saw several containers in the fridge that she had thoughtfully labelled, and he knew the security team frequently cleared out her leftovers, which just made her cook more.

He decided to take the tub labelled Lasagna to the table with a fork, and sat across from his sister, who grimaced as he tucked into the cold pasta. "Don't judge me," he said with his mouth full.

She gave him a small smile, "never."

"How are you?"

The smile fell, and her eyes returned to the glass of wine. "I feel like it's my fault."

Alex frowned, "what is?"

"His unhappiness."

Tim. Alex was more than frustrated with his brother-in-law. He was angry. Brad often defended Tim with the explanation of his Asperger's diagnosis. Autistic people struggled to cope with change, or adapt to new circumstances, and when they were left with no choice but to face change, it was common for them to withdraw.

Alex thought that was a bullshit excuse.

Tim was legitimately Autistic. Nobody would argue with that. But Alex believed that Tim was being a depressive and thoroughly selfish asshole on top of that, and that was the thing he couldn't forgive.

"He's a grown man Christina, you aren't responsible for how he's choosing to behave."

"But is he choosing to behave this way? It's like he can't help it."

Alex had suffered with his own depression issues, and knew he was in dangerous territory when he said, "the only thing a person can truly own and be responsible for, is themselves."

She stared at him for a long while as she considered this. "If that is true, then I don't know if I can stay married to him."

Alex winced, "nobody would think less of you."

She shook her head, "I shouldn't have said

that. I can't turn my back on him now, just because things are tough."

"You haven't turned your back on anyone, and you still exist in your relationship too," Alex said, stuffing another bite of Lasagna into his mouth.

Christina sat forward and put her elbows on the table, knotting her hands together. "Why does adulting suck so much?"

He snorted, "it's life."

She shook her head, "it all starts so simple. You fall in love, you learn to live together, you grow together, you take the good and the bad because the bottom line is that you've chosen that person to stick with, through thick and thin. But then the bad gets really bad, and it's so hard to even remember the good things and the good times. And now all I can think about is running away."

Alex frowned, "I can vouch for the fact that running away is a very lonely business. It doesn't help."

"I didn't mean physically running away, I meant ending my marriage. He keeps talking about it too, on the rare occasions that he talks."

"Are you serious?"

She nodded, "he says now that he should

have never married me and should have definitely never impregnated me."

Alex couldn't believe that Tim was capable of being such a bastard. "He's just down."

"He hates Alvin."

He knew that Tim had only had minimal contact with his son since his birth, and whenever Alex had witness them together, the word awkward didn't even come close to describing it.

Tim wouldn't hold his son, and seemed able to ignore his presence, even when he was crying in distress.

His entire focus was inward at the moment, and nothing anybody did or said seemed to get through to him.

"What do the doctors say?"

"Physically they're happy with the way his thigh is healing, and if he puts in the work there is no reason why he can't start to train for prosthesis."

"I meant about his mental state?"

Christina shrugged, "he has his weekly appointments with the shrink, but I don't know if he even talks. He could just sit there for the hour and stare at the wall for all I know, the doctor would bill us all the same."

Alex didn't know what to do, other than offer

the same thing he had countless times before. "Want me to talk to him?"

Christina shook her head, "he doesn't listen. He just sits at the computer, playing some game all day and night where he can pretend to be someone else, listening to the same song on repeat at full volume while I'm trying to sleep. He doesn't even stop to eat or go to the bathroom, I've found bottles of pee around the desk. They stink."

Alex was horrified, "are you kidding?"

Another sad headshake, "the last time I interrupted him, I pulled the headphones off his head, and he screamed in my face." Christina's tone had flattened, to an almost robotic monotone. "I don't think he even wants to be alive right now."

He was genuinely stunned, and reflexively he said, "end it."

She blinked in shock, "Kill him?"

"No, no, I mean your marriage. It's not healthy for you, or Alvin. Tim has a choice, and okay I may not be Autistic, and I'm certainly not an expert in what that means, but he isn't helpless in this. He is choosing to be a dick."

She smirked, "a controversial stance."

"Well it's my opinion. I love you and I've

seen enough battered women as a cop to know that not all domestic abuse is fists and black eyes. He is neglecting you right now, and I don't want to see it get any worse."

Her eyes filled with tears then, and she lowered her head so he didn't see them fall. "I just feel like I can't cope with him. And I'm so tired. I know now how people go insane with sleep deprivation."

"Yeah and I bet you feel guilty too, like you should be able to cope with all this. But you're not weak Christina. You're a strong woman, and right now you have yourself and Alvin to think about. Alvin is your priority, and it should be Tim's too. If he can't strive to be better for himself he should be doing it for the two of you, but he's not. That's his choice."

Alex could feel himself getting riled up. He had always been slow to anger, but this situation with Tim had been escalating for too long now, and he was furious.

Even worse, was the fact that it wasn't his place to interfere, so it took all of his restraint not to go charging up to Tim right now and beat some sense into him.

Christina nodded, "that's what hurts the most. The fact that he doesn't love me or his son enough to try and adapt. Are we not worth it?"

Alex chewed the Lasagna and pointed the fork at her, "you are. You deserve someone who is going to wake up every day and be thrilled you're beside him."

Her lip trembled again.

"Look, if having HIV has taught me anything, it means I'm grateful for my life. If I'm ever lucky enough to find that one person who wants to stick with me, I'm going to do everything in my power to keep it. Eric and Jeanie are lucky they have each other, and the thing that makes them strong is that they know it and they express it to each other. You can tell by looking at them."

Christina nodded in a confident way, "I thought I had that too, but it all changed when Alvin was born."

"I'm not going to settle for less, and I don't see why anyone should. If Tim isn't making you happy, then find someone who does."

She smirked her old cynical look, "sounds so easy. But if I divorce Tim, I'm then a single mother. Not exactly an attractive prospect to most guys."

Alex shook his head, "don't be negative, you don't know who is out there waiting for you."

She studied him for a moment, "the same is

true for you as well, you know."

He blinked at his sister, "huh?"

"You don't know who is out there waiting for you. I know you said you have no intention of entering into a relationship with your illness, but I think you shouldn't rule it out."

He frowned and was about to object.

"No, hear me out Alex."

He closed his mouth and gestured that she could continue with the fork in his hand.

"I know Brad is always nagging you to find a girlfriend, but none of us care who you end up with, man or woman. Human beings weren't meant to be solitary, we are wired to be communal beings. We're meant to have a companion."

He shrugged, "so what are you saying?"

"I'm saying you should stop actively avoiding looking for a mate."

He frowned, "is that what I've been doing?"

"Seems that way to me. And look, I love you, we all do. Nobody wants to tell you how to live your life. But there is someone out there for you. They're waiting for a big burly tattooed cop who has Lasagna all over his chin, because that's what is missing in their lives."

He'd heard so many iterations of the same lecture from all of his family, but this time he saw something in Christina that he hadn't from anyone else before. Loneliness.

It was easy to dismiss the lectures from Brad and Eric because they had found the elusive unicorns they had been seeking. They were genuinely happy and therefore wanted the whole world to be as happy as they were. But Christina was miserable, and so alone in her relationship.

She had more in common with Alex and so maybe that was why he found himself staring at her so intently.

"It's not like I've been rejecting anyone, 'Stina."

"You exude an air of 'I'm not dating so don't bother asking'. Did you know that?"

He blinked, "I do?"

She nodded. "For a long time after you came back you were very defensive. It's started to get better, but you need to drop all those defenses 'Lex. You used to be such an open person before."

FOUR

When Alex woke in the morning, he knew it was late. The sky was too bright, and he heard children playing in the garden beneath his window. Lily and Ben seemed to be playing some variation of cops and robbers, but Lily was refusing to be either, she was determined to become a secret agent. Ben was trying to arrest her.

Alex smiled. He had a special affection for Ben, especially as he and Brad had been the ones to rescue him from his neglectful father, and Ben had since fully adjusted to life in All Saints House.

Whenever Alex visited, the boy seemed to want to be near him, and he suspected that it was simply because Alex was one of his saviors.

He kicked back the covers and stretched out all of his limbs, enjoying the freedom of the whole bed space. If there were another body in the bed, he couldn't do this.

He felt a pang when he realized that if there were another body in the bed, he'd be spooning it right now. Images and memories of his previous spooning buddies popped into his mind as he forced himself out of bed. Julie,

Mike, Lisa, Adam….

He stopped his train of thought. Damn Christina! He didn't know why she had bothered him, but her words seemed to have planted a seed of doubt within his cast iron resolution to remain single.

Was he unhappy?

No, he was actually happier than he'd been in a long while. Coming back home had been the right thing to do.

But how long had it been…

He gave himself a mental shake as images and flashes of his spooning buddies came back again. Karen, Malcom, Chris…

Yes of course he'd like a companion. A partner. A lover.

But it was too risky.

Brad immediately popped up in his mind, 'we all have an unknown expiration date bro, you can't use that as an excuse to stop living'.

In his mind he slapped Brad and he gave himself a mental shake. Today would be a day of reading child literature and probably getting roped into a game of cops and robbers, or as it sounded, cops and secret agents.

After a quick shower and dressing in his most comfortable jeans and t-shirt, he ventured out into the house.

All Saints House was large, and Jeanie and Eric were generous. They'd given him a suite in the older wing of the house, which was largely unused, but he himself didn't mind, and it still gave him a measure of independence as it was so far removed from the rest of the family.

There was even a little kitchen in the old servant's quarters, but nobody ever went down there. The old space was usually used for storage, but he knew that Jeanie was talking about potentially renovating the space as an apartment for Tim and Christina. Eric had objected saying that they couldn't as the older wings were to be preserved, and not altered in any way.

But Jeanie loved a project, and so she'd just shrugged and insisted they built a little house for Tim and Christina in the grounds instead.

Alex smiled when he thought of his sister-in-law. Back when they were younger, he'd always pictured that Eric would end up with a severe and joyless lawyer, as that was the only type of people he ever seemed to interact with.

He remembered the day that he'd brought Jeanie to the college campus to help Christina, and how surprised he'd been in amongst all the worry that day. This tiny little blonde sprite had such a surprising energy and positivity about her, and it had lit Eric up in a way that was a joy to behold.

His thoughts then ran to Christina again. She'd endured that ordeal, was it fair that she was having to endure again?

Knowing that he was about to feel anger at Tim all over again, he forced himself to focus on other thoughts.

He reached the kitchen and was pleased to see the happiness on Jeanie's face as he entered, "Alex!"

It was a nice feeling to know that people were happy to see you, and he returned her smile, "hey Jeanie." He accepted her hug, careful not to squeeze her increasing girth.

"The readouts said you came in last night," she said as she returned to the table where it seemed she was reading a long document. Every morning the security team fed back any overnight activity, and he was guessing his arrival had been diligently logged.

"Is that what you're reading?" He gave the pages a cursory glance as he poured himself some apple juice.

"Ugh," she turned her nose up at the apple juice. Pregnancy seemed to have turned her off apples. "And no, boring accountancy stuff. My accountant seems to keep forgetting that I pay him to keep my accounts, not chastise me for spending money."

He smiled, "you could always fire him."

She grinned, "I'm tempted, but he means well. He's just telling me off because of all the money I've spent on security, and he's trying to tell me that it's excessive."

Alex could well believe that an accountant wouldn't care for security, all they cared about was the 1's and 0's in a bank balance. But Alex didn't disapprove in the slightest of the security measures. They could afford it, so why shouldn't they protect themselves. He knew firsthand the number of times police procedure had let people down in these kinds of situations.

Alex drank the juice down and quickly replaced it with orange juice, the smell of which didn't seem to offend Jeanie. "How are the twins?" he asked, gesturing to her belly.

She smiled and stroked her stomach, "fighting a lot. At least that's how it feels. One of them keeps getting hiccups."

He shook his head in wonder, amazed that a mother could feel all that going on inside her. "Wow."

"Are you still okay to watch the kids tonight? I know Rosa is always happy to watch them, but I don't like to impose too often."

Alex knew it wasn't a question of imposition, but more the fact that since the explosion that had claimed Tim's leg, Ernie had suffered minor burns and a gunshot wound and concussion. Since then, Jeanie had felt guilty over the endangerment of her staff.

"It's no problem, I was thinking of reading The Hobbit with them."

Jeanie grinned, "you know you will hurt your throat with doing all the funny voices you insist on doing."

He did always have a hoarse throat after reading with the kids, but it was a routine that had quickly become tradition, and he loved it. They would snuggle under a blanket on the oversized couch, Lily to his left, and Ben to his right, and he would read. Sometimes he wouldn't notice that several hours had passed, and a lot of the time, one or both children would fall asleep.

There was something wonderful in reading these stories again, but aloud and to an avid audience. They'd already ploughed through several books, and though Lily knew some of them, she never complained about hearing them again, knowing that to Ben, a lot of the literature was new.

"How are they both?"

"Absolutely fine. Lily has suddenly started saying 'oh crap' a lot, and we're trying to ignore it. The books say it's usual for a first child to start acting out at the prospect of a new baby."

He grinned, "oh crap?"

"It could be much worse, hence we're letting it slide for now. Plus, I think having Ben around has really helped her see we have enough love for everyone."

He laughed, "where is Eric?"

"Had to run to the office for the morning. Are you staying all day? He will be back for lunch I think."

"I didn't have any plans."

Christina came in then, carrying Alvin on her hip. She looked tired as she put him in the highchair that was beside the table, "morning."

Alex smiled brightly at his nephew, who never seemed to be in a bad mood, and clapped his hands together at the sight of Alex. "Hey big guy," he said.

Alvin had the Steinberg brown hair, and his blue eyes were darkening to brown too. Alex didn't think he was wrong to say he was going to be a giant as well, he was already in eighteen month old clothing, though he wasn't even a year old yet.

47

Christina put a colorful bead toy in front of Alvin and then went straight for the coffee machine.

Alex saw Jeanie look at her worriedly, "how are you?" she asked Christina softly.

Christina shrugged and put on a faux smile as she sat beside her son. "What do you want for a snack kiddo? Orange goop or purple goop?"

Alvin dribbled on the beads he was chewing, and Alex interpreted that to mean that he didn't care the color of the goop, but just to make it snappy.

Alex got to his feet again and went to the fruit bowl, gathering a couple of bananas and apples, as was his usual breakfast. He exchanged a concerned look with Jeanie, but then turned to Christina who was spooning orange goop from a jar into a bowl. "Is Tim awake?"

Christina looked alarmed and paused in her action, "yes."

Alex nodded, "okay. I'm going to go and talk to him."

She looked horrified, "I really wouldn't Alex. Please don't."

He should have just gone and done it without consulting her first, "why not? After what we talked about, it really can't make things worse can it?"

Christina actually paled, "Alex, please. What do you think you can say to him that I haven't said already for myself?"

"I'm not going to speak on your behalf. I'm going to speak to him as his brother-in-law. Everyone has been tiptoeing around him since the accident, and maybe it is time to put a stop to that."

Christina seemed to be torn between her desire to keep things as they had been, though everyone involved was miserable, or the potential for upset, which may have a long shot of getting through to her husband.

He held out his hands in a peaceful gesture, "I'm not trying to cause problems, but honestly, can he get any worse?"

"I hope not," she said instantly, then lowered her eyes to the goop she'd been spooning for her son. "Okay, I guess there's nothing to lose."

FIVE

Alex opened the door without knocking, and was first struck by the smell. Sour sweat and energy drinks.

Tim was seated at the computer he'd insisted be put in the bedroom, so that he could work. He was wearing headphones, and his shaggy hair was clearly matted beneath them with his own sweat.

His hands were hammering on a keyboard repetitively while he clicked the mouse to target different 'bad guys' on his screen. Through the headphones Alex could hear something heavy metal and European, that he seemed to be nodding his head in time to.

Alex spotted a litre bottle that once contained water on the floor beside Tim's remaining foot, and it now contained a deep yellow liquid that he knew was piss.

Thoroughly disgusted, Alex closed the door behind him, and stepped further into the room, glancing around. The bed was made, but clearly only one side of it was regularly occupied, it's pillows sagging slightly more than it's neighbor. The side that was facing the baby bed of course.

Angry that Christina had to try to sleep and pacify an infant with that song playing over and over again, he stepped over to Tim and yanked the headphones off his head.

Clearly startled, Tim cried out. Though Alex wondered if it was because of the sudden interruption to his gaming or because of the lack of noise, he was pleased that Tim was distressed. The spiteful part of him was glad that Tim was unhappy with this turn of events.

Tim whipped his head up to see Alex, and he screamed and reached for the headphones, which Alex flung away. He grabbed Tim's arms, and held them while he began to struggle, still screaming.

Alex did the only thing he could think of to shock Tim into silence, and he screamed back at his brother-in-law.

Tim stopped screaming, but whined instead, looking at Alex with hurt and betrayed eyes.

"Hello Tim," Alex meant to sound calm and friendly, but he knew it probably sounded like a threat. "It's a beautiful day today, how about getting dressed?"

Tim screamed again and threw himself forwards, deliberately tipping himself out of the chair. Alex followed him down to the floor, and still holding Tim's arms, he shook his head in dismay. "I'm not your wife, I don't have to tiptoe around you, and I'm not going to sugarcoat anything either. You disgust me. And I'll tell you something else Tim, it's something very simple. If you don't get your shit together, you are going to lose your wife and child, and the rest of the family too."

Tim didn't give any sign that he'd heard a word that Alex had said, but he kicked up his one good leg, landing his knee in Alex's side.

He released Tim reflexively, and immediately regretted it, as Tim blindly flailed his arms, landing a loose fist against Alex's cheek. As unintentional punches went, it wasn't bad. Alex saw stars for a moment, but he quickly got to his feet and looked down at Tim who was still whining.

"What's your problem?"

"Leave me alone," Tim croaked, sounding thoroughly miserable, but Alex felt in his gut that he was just annoyed that he'd been interrupted in his gaming. Not in any way concerned that he'd been called out as being a bad husband.

"Here's the thing Tim. My sister is suffering, and you're the one causing that. If you don't want to be married, if you don't want to be alive, whatever the problem is, you need to fix it. Grow a pair of balls, and deal with your fucking problems."

Tim just closed his eyes.

"Don't shut down, fucking talk to me," he said angrily.

Tim didn't move.

Angrier now, he slapped Tim, which awoke another round of screaming.

"Alex, what the hell do you think you're doing?!" Christina cried from the doorway, hurrying into the room and crouching beside Tim, putting a hand to his chest.

Tim reacted with violence, screaming out and lashing out at the same time, his flailing fist connecting with Christina's eye socket, knocking her back on her ass.

She held her cheek, looking at Tim with shock.

Alex punched Tim, knowing somewhere in the logical part of his mind that Tim probably wasn't even aware of who he was fighting right now, he was in the throes of a meltdown. He felt guilt as he saw Tim's nose start to bleed, and he knew he'd made a mistake by coming in here.

Remembering what Brad had said once about weight being comforting, he quickly wrapped his body around Tim's, pinning his arms down at his chest and pinning his kicking leg down too, he tried to still Tim, who bucked for a few seconds more, but then began to settle.

Christina was holding her eye, looking warily at them both.

Alex tried to convey a look of apology to her, but he doubted she could see it very well with her swelling eye.

The whining was now descending into weeping, and Tim turned his face into the carpet and began to speak, "go away."

"You can't keep wasting your life in front of a game Tim," Alex said harshly.

"Why not? It's my life."

Why not indeed. "It's your choice Tim, but you're going to lose your wife if you carry on, and your son."

"I don't care. At least the gaming makes me happy."

Christina looked as though she had been struck again.

Alex winced, "Tim, if you choose this, you aren't choosing a life, you're choosing confinement."

"Leave me alone!" he shouted. "I can't do this! I can't be that person anymore!"

Christina lowered her hand and looked at Alex as she said, "Tim, I love you."

Tim was silent.

"Do you love me?" she pressured him to speak.

"Leave me alone," he said quietly. "Both of you."

Alex uncurled his body from Tim's slowly, and got to his feet. He looked down at the pathetic form. "You've still got a chance to turn this around Tim," he said in a soft voice. Then he turned to Christina. "Get your stuff, you're not staying in this room anymore."

"You're not my father," she snapped at him, but still started gathering Alvin's clothes and her own onto the bed, slinging them into a gym bag and stalking from the room.

Alex looked at Tim lying motionless on the floor and felt guilt again. Should he help him up? No, he knew that Tim had received the best after care and physio that money could buy, and he was more than capable of getting himself up when he wanted to.

Grabbing up an armful of the clothing Christina had dropped, he left the stinking room, and closed the door on the invalid following his sister back to the kitchen where he knew she would unleash the full extent of her fury on him.

He was surprised though. She simply

dropped the bags and went to the freezer. Snatching up what looked like a bag of peas, she pressed them to her eye and turned to a startled Jeanie. "I need a different room please."

Jeanie had been spooning the goop into Alvin's greedy mouth, but she had paused as soon as they had entered. After a moment to digest what Christina had said, she nodded in assent, "of course. Whatever you need."

Christina faced Alex then, "I know you were intending to help, but please don't talk to Tim anymore."

"Christina I didn't mean to hurt him."

"I think you did," she said calmly. "I wanted to as well. I've wanted to for a while," she confessed calmly. "But it doesn't solve anything, and it just drives him further within himself."

Alex nodded and averted his eyes to Alvin, he couldn't stand to see the resigned misery in her eyes. She was so accepting of what her life had become that he was genuinely worried that she wouldn't get out of her marriage but continue onward due to a misguided and outdated concept of duty.

SIX

Alex looked down at the boy snuggled against his left side. Lily had fallen asleep a few minutes ago, the limp weight of her was pressed against his right side, and her head had flopped back against the couch as she snored softly. It was way past her bedtime.

Ben smiled up at him, "keep reading," he whispered.

Alex grinned, "I think I should take Lily to bed," he whispered back. "Do you like this book?" he already knew the answer though, the boy was like a sponge when it came to literature.

An enthusiastic nod was his reply, and he peeled himself back from Alex a little, so he could look over at Lily. "She always falls asleep."

"Yeah, she does," Alex looked down at his niece fondly. "Wait here, I'll go put her to bed."

Ben took the book from Alex and looked down to the page he had been reading from.

"Hey, no cheating," he mock scolded in a whisper as he threw back the blanket and got to his feet.

Lily stirred a little as he scooped her up into his muscular arms, but only enough to give him a sleepy smile and curl herself willingly into him.

He sighed, content. At least this part of the day had gone well.

The confrontation with Tim that had expelled Christina from the room she had shared with him, had set a very sour tone to the hours that had followed.

His sister hadn't spoken much but had fixed the frown onto her features. By the time Eric had returned home for lunch, her eye was swollen shut and discolored, and their older brother was immediately concerned.

Alex had allowed Christina to tell the tale, and he was sure that she had deliberately painted him as the villain and Tim the victim, but Eric hadn't questioned any part of it. He had given him a stern look, and that was punishment enough.

Eric had simply agreed that it was best she move herself and Alvin away from the downwardly spiraling Tim and asked if she had needed a doctor.

Christina had declined the doctor, and busied herself with her son, looking thoroughly miserable, and occasionally shooting Alex

58

wounded looks.

The children had come in from play at that point, and very deliberately Alex had given himself over to their demands for play and attention. This he could do without making a mistake. The needs of children were far easier to appease than that of an adult.

Lily's bedroom door was already open, and the lights were low. Stooping down to deposit her, he was surprised when she looped her arms around his neck, holding him down to cuddle her. "Love you," she mumbled sleepily, making his day.

He kissed the top of her head as he carefully disengaged himself from her hold, "love you too, bug."

"Wait I need my gun," she started to sit up but Alex pushed her back down.

"What gun?"

"My monster gun," she sleepily pointed over to where she'd kicked off her shoes earlier.

Alex went and picked up the toy gun, which was a plastic replica revolver and laughed to himself.

She took it with a smile and put it under her pillow where her hand still seemed to grip it.

As he tucked the covers up around her shoulders, she buried her head in the pillow, giving in to sleep without a fight.

He pictured himself then, tucking in his own child, and hearing 'Love you Daddy', and was surprised at how much it pained him to realize it might never happen.

He looked down at Lily for several moments and knew he'd been lying to himself. He had been lying about many things, and Christina had been right. He'd been actively avoiding and rejecting any possibility of a relationship.

Alex thought of Brad then, and the years he'd told himself that he was never going to love anyone but Jeanie. He said now quite plainly that he could see he'd deluded himself to believe that he was in love with Eric's wife, to spare himself the pain and hardship of actually finding it in someone who could reciprocate those feelings.

Had Alex similarly been telling himself that his illness had created an impossible persona to love? Was he that terrified of a relationship?

Lily snored and made him smile. How could he possibly write off the chance at a family of his own? But who would want him, when the dangers were so high?

When he returned to Ben he saw that the boy was reading ahead in The Hobbit, and he snarled at the boy menacingly.

Ben dropped the book guiltily, "I only read a page!"

Alex grinned and flopped down on the couch beside him, "it's not a crime, but I'll have to read from where we left it, or it's not fair to your sister."

Ben wrinkled his nose, "she's not really my sister."

Alex arched an eyebrow, "oh?"

"I mean, I know she kind of is. Eric and Jeanie are like my new Mum and Dad, but it's not the same."

"It's exactly the same. Do you think just anyone can choose to be a parent? They've chosen to love you, and they treat you exactly the same as they treat all their children." Alex didn't use a harsh tone, as he knew the boy wasn't being unkind towards his adoptive parents.

Ben looked sad then, "I know, I guess. I just wish that my Dad had been better."

"That's perfectly natural," Alex knew for a fact that the boy's father was still serving prison time, and that he had willingly signed his son over to Eric and Jeanie's custody, relieved to have the burden removed from him. "But there is a saying, that you can't choose your family. Your Dad was just maybe one of those guys who shouldn't have ever been a Dad. But we're glad that he was, at least, or else you wouldn't be here. And Jeanie and Eric have chosen you to be their son. They wouldn't have done that if they didn't love you."

Ben looked thoughtful at that. "Did you want to be my Dad?"

Alex was surprised, "well I'm not a very good choice for a Dad. I don't know how to do it," he evaded the question. Brad had said before that Ben hero worshipped him, and the thought made Alex squirm a little.

He was flattered, but he wasn't sure that he was ready to take on the sole responsibility for another life. He thought again at the prospect of having his own family and was frightened this time.

Was he schizophrenic? Upstairs staring down at Lily he had almost pined for a child of his own, to turn to him over all others for guidance and reassurance. But now, the idea was overwhelming. A whole life that was shaped and determined by his choices and rules. A life that depended on his ability to not only keep himself alive but them too.

Ben was frowning at him when he realized the boy was silent. "Eric and Jeanie are a good choice, because you've not only got a Dad but a mother too. They're a team. And they have a lovely home. They can give you the best schools and care. All I'd be able to give you is a tiny apartment over a shoe shop and a variety of babysitters. I work a lot."

He thought on that, and nodded, "yeah, I guess."

"And listen, I'm not going anywhere. I'm sticking around. I'll be your uncle for as long as I can."

Just then the front door clicked open and Ben looked panicked.

Alex never listened to the advised bedtimes, and he knew that Jeanie and Eric didn't expect him to either. But Ben didn't know that. "Uh oh," he said dramatically, quickly getting to his feet.

He laughed, "it's okay, it's the weekend."

Indeed, his brother and Jeanie didn't seem to be surprised to see Ben still wide awake. Jeanie just noted Lily's absence and looked to Alex, "she fall asleep?"

He nodded, "I bore her."

Eric laughed and looked down at Ben, "doesn't Alex bore you?"

Ben seemed to realize he wasn't in trouble, and he smiled, "no, I love it when he reads to us."

Eric nodded, "well, do you think you should go to bed now?"

Almost on cue, he stifled a yawn as he protested that he wasn't tired.

"Maybe you should just go and read a book in bed?" Jeanie suggested kindly.

Ben obviously knew that protesting wouldn't get him anywhere and nodded. "Okay. Goodnight Alex," he reached up for a hug, and Alex returned it enthusiastically.

"Goodnight," he scrubbed the boy's hair, and smiled as he went to Eric and Jeanie to hug them goodnight as well.

"Do you want me to come up and tuck you in?" Eric offered.

Ben nodded, shy.

Jeanie kissed the top of his head, "goodnight kid."

Alex watched his brother lead Ben out of the room, and as soon as they were gone, Jeanie flopped onto the couch and kicked off her shoes, "that was a long dinner."

He picked up the blanket and folded it, draping it over the back of the couch, "was the food any good?"

She shrugged, "not after you've had Daisy's cooking. Did they both behave?"

"Of course," he sat down again, smiling.

"Ben seemed to be a little blue."

Jeanie nodded, "I've noticed that too. I think he still doesn't feel that this is permanent. And he might be picking up on Lily's worry about the babies. We've tried reassuring them both, but I think the only way to drive the point home is with our actions not our words."

"Yeah I could see that. He asked if I had wanted to be his Dad."

Jeanie smiled at him, "I don't think he's ever going to forget how you rescued him."

"Brad was there too," he pointed out.

"But you were the one who stood up to his father and made him stop hurting him."

"Do you think that's what it is?"

"Well, if he'd been afraid of his father his whole life, how could he see you as anything other than a hero?"

He felt uncomfortable, and his discomfort intensified when Hunter walked in. He was dressed in formal wear, and Alex knew it was because he had accompanied them to the charity dinner they had attended.

Alex couldn't fault the security measures that Hunter had implemented for his brother and sister-in-law, and he knew through the personal digging he had done on the man that his record was flawless.

But he still disliked him.

Hunter had formerly been a decorated soldier, with a spotless record. When he had been discharged on medical grounds eleven years ago, he had gone into private security, and from the records the police had on him, he knew that he had an excellent relationship with law enforcement to the point where they often recommended his services where they knew they would be lacking.

Still, Alex didn't like him.

The blonde man exuded a confidence and arrogance that instantly rubbed him the wrong way. Perhaps it was because he was so good at what he did, it sometimes came across as careless and cocky. Alex disapproved of his use of less than legal investigative measures, which Hunter confessed he would employ if the situation demanded and as long as he was being paid.

To Alex, the law was black and white. Hunter danced through the grey areas with well navigated ease. And Alex himself had been the subject of such methods, which was what had initiated the dislike.

His own father had employed Hunter to keep track of Alex, when he drifted away from the family unit, and when that discovery had been thrust upon him earlier in the year, he had no choice but to hold a grudge against the man, as his father was no longer with them.

"Nothing to report on the home front, but I'll wait for the mobile unit to contact me in the morning to confirm we weren't followed tonight," Hunter said quietly to Jeanie, ignoring Alex.

She smiled at him, "thank you Hunter, I appreciate you taking the time out of your schedule this evening."

"It was no trouble," he assured her without a smile. Alex guessed he was trying to sound professional, and snidely he thought the only reason the man had put himself in for tonight's guard duty was to get a free dinner.

Christina entered the room then, carrying a baby monitor.

Hunter did a double take when he observed the black eye. "What happened? The team didn't report anything," he sounded genuinely concerned.

Christina smirked, "hey Hunter, I walked into a door," she said sarcastically.

Hunter didn't look amused, "what happened here?" he addressed the question to Jeanie.

"Nothing to worry about, just a little domestic scuffle."

"Mr. Chastain struck you?" Hunter was all business now, but Alex thought he detected a hint of anger.

Christina rolled her good eye, "there was a scuffle, and it was an accident. I'm fine it's just a black eye."

Hunter scowled at her, then at Jeanie, then even Alex received his frown, as if he couldn't believe she was so nonchalant about it and wanted one of them, if not all of them to correct her.

"You should press charges," he said quietly, facing her again.

She laughed as she flopped onto the couch between Jeanie and Alex, "press charges against my husband?"

Hunter's scowl intensified, "yes."

Christina laughed again, and Jeanie touched her hand. Alex couldn't tell if the gesture was meant for comfort or concern, but he felt a tightening in his gut. He didn't want his sister in a situation where this kind of accident could happen and be acceptable.

Yes he held his share of responsibility for the whole thing, but Tim was a loose cannon, and he needed to be diffused.

"Well, maybe Tim should press charges against Alex too, and then I can press charges against Tim, and Alex can press charges against Ben for headbutting him last week," Christina stared up at Hunter with defiance. "Sometimes accidents happen."

"And sometimes husbands hit their wives," Hunter said coldly, and Christina stiffened.

Alex perceived that perhaps this was an area of the law that Hunter didn't find so grey. "The incident was my fault," he spoke up. "I confronted him about his behavior and the situation quickly escalated. Christina entered while Tim was in a frenzy, and in his defense, his fists were flailing around. He didn't deliberately hit her or else I would have dealt with it myself."

Hunter didn't comment but looked at Alex coldly.

Christina quickly interjected though, "oh I think you've done enough."

"I said I was sorry," he said irritably. "You have to get over the attitude. I didn't go into that room with the intention of starting a fight or getting you a black eye."

She narrowed her eye and she was about to retort when Jeanie patted her hand again, "let's not get into another argument please," she said softly. "We aired all of this out earlier on today, and I don't want either of you to keep fanning the flames," she used her maternal kind but scolding tone.

Alex nodded, personally just wanting to forget the whole incident.

Christina's nostrils flared as she took a deep breath and let it out slowly, seeming to relax her body as she exhaled. "You're right," she clasped Jeanie's hand and gave it a squeeze. She extended her other hand toward Alex, and he took it gratefully, hoping it was a sign she was forgiving him.

SEVEN

In his own bed, he always slept naked. At All Saints House it was generally understood that of course you could sleep naked, but the chance of a child running into your room could quickly ruin that experience, and so he never did.

Here though, he awoke naked, and he still had that longing for someone beside him that had struck over the weekend.

His left arm reached out into the empty space in the bed, so cool and unoccupied, and he thought about what Brad had said yesterday.

Eric had decided to invite Brad and Misha and her eccentric parents over for a Barbecue on Sunday.

Vidya had been the quintessential mother hen. Scolding Jeanie to take it easy while fussing over Alvin, Lily and Ben. Misha and Christina had sat and were deep in conversation. Eric was fully engaged with Raiden as they both cooked meat on the large open grill. Alex had felt the need to confess to Brad his change of heart.

They'd walked away from the main body, as Alex didn't really want to engage the entire family in a discussion about his lonely existence, but he'd regained the best friend he'd once had in his brother, and he had simply said, "I want a somebody."

Brad had smiled and given a nod of approval. Since moving back into their childhood home, and finding work at the local hospital, he had gained a new inner calm that Alex hadn't witnessed in him before. When he'd commented on it once, Brad had just shrugged and said, "I've finally stopped overthinking. I'm content."

At Alex's comment though, he didn't just look content, he looked ecstatic. "Awesome news, celibacy doesn't suit you."

He didn't think he was still capable of blushing, but he'd felt his cheeks color at that. "I'm not saying I'm ready to go paint the town red, but Christina and I had a talk the other night, and she pointed out that I'd been repelling people, and that I shouldn't rule it out."

"We've all been telling you that for months now," Brad said with mild exasperation.

"I know, but it's different hearing it from someone so miserable."

Brad had winced then, and looked over at Christina, who looked thoughtful as Misha spoke to her. "Yeah, Eric told me what happened. I had no idea that Tim was so withdrawn."

"None of us did," Alex knew that Christina had tried to coax Tim from the room with the invitation to the Barbecue, but he had just ignored her, and she had left him to his gaming.

Brad was thoughtful for a moment, but then focused on Alex again. "So, you finally woke up?"

Alex nodded, knowing that it was an accurate description for what had happened. "I think so."

"It can be scary, to realize you're capable of lying to yourself so well."

"That's it exactly," Alex was relieved that Brad had understood so completely. "I'm not saying that my reasons were stupid, because they totally weren't. There are major risks to anyone I have a relationship with."

Brad shrugged, "there's always a risk, whether someone has HIV or not."

Alex rolled his eyes. Brad was always one to underplay the importance of his health issues. "Don't imply I'm being unreasonable by saying there is a risk, you always do that."

Brad held up a hand in a pacifying gesture, "I'm not. Honestly bro," he grinned. "I'm truly glad that you're sensible. And I'm ecstatic that you realize now you were hiding behind your illness. Using it as a shield to ward off any human contact that wasn't absolutely necessary."

Hearing the words, Alex knew that was exactly what he had been doing.

"But here is the thing 'Lex, there is always a reason not to do something. You just need to shift your perspectives to see the silver linings and not just the clouds."

That stuck with Alex, and he thought it over now as he rolled into the empty side of the bed and pulled the spare pillow into a hug. There always was a reason not to do something, if you were so inclined to find obstacles.

But the whole thought of 'finding' someone was daunting. He'd always hated the dating scene, and he'd much rather just have an organic interaction with someone and know that it wasn't pre-planned or manipulated.

His 5am alarm went off, and he silenced it. He usually worked out in the mornings before going to work, but today, he wouldn't, as he had agreed to work out late tonight with Charlie.

He wondered if the shy girl would actually be there at the gym at all, as she hadn't had a fun experience the last time, but he hoped she would be. The prospect of having a new friend was pleasing, as that alone would help to ease his loneliness. And he was lonely.

His phone chirped a calendar reminder at him then, and he winced as he read, 'new partner, Joey's 9am'.

Great, a new partner.

Mentally he shook himself, he needed to stop being so negative. Maybe this new one would be a good match. At this point, if the new partner wasn't a homophobe, she was at least ahead of the last one.

He got out of bed and enjoyed a stretch. Spontaneously he dropped to the floor and started doing sit ups. He couldn't have the day without any form of exercise. His body was a machine, and he had to do everything to keep it running.

The fear that came with having HIV was something he was used to these days. After he was diagnosed he had gone through a phase of suffering anxiety attacks almost constantly. He still suffered to this day, though less frequently.

Death was inevitable for everyone after all, but the knowledge that he had a very visible chink in his armor was frightening. Nobody knew how they would meet their end. A quiet little brain tumor, or perhaps a car accident. He had spent so much time pondering his mortality now, but he knew that ultimately, he would probably get an infection due to his compromised immune system. That would be what killed him.

His state of mind had improved after he had made the decision to get in shape and become a cop. He had a purpose and a focus to distract him, and he had pursued that with an intensity that overshadowed any anxiety he felt. Most of the time anyway.

Exercising was a way of not only maintaining the machine, but also it burned off all the excess energy that fueled his overactive imagination and anxiety. He was happiest when he was occupied, and his healthcare routine was the best it could be, barring the cigarettes he still occasionally turned to.

He'd ended up not only doing sit ups, but also pushups, and then he'd rounded out his workout with a brief jog, then a methodical shower. If nothing else it had filled the time before this awkward meeting.

He scanned the busy coffee shop, and he recognized a few faces from his new precinct. A couple even nodded a good morning to him as he entered, and he decided to sit at the counter as he waited. He had no idea what

Kathleen might look like, but there weren't any lone females in the establishment, so he deduced she wasn't here yet.

The young woman who worked the counter placed a coffee cup in front of him and was about to start pouring.

"No thanks," he placed his hand over the cup in the universally acknowledged gesture. "You have apple juice?"

She nodded, "yeah, apple, orange and grapefruit."

"I'll just take the apple thanks." He grabbed a menu and saw the usual fried staples of most breakfasts were available.

As she poured the juice she asked, "know what you want to order, or do you need a minute?"

"I'll have the fruit plate, thanks," he gave her a smile and she bustled away to place his order.

Alex checked his phone while he waited and saw that he had a message from Brad.

MISHA HAS A FRIEND.
WANT A DINNER DATE?

He eye rolled. This was exactly what he didn't want. The thought of a blind date was appalling, and he could think of nothing worse.

He replied with a flat NO, and hoped that Brad wouldn't push his luck. As good as his intentions might be, he didn't want a forced and uncomfortable dinner with a stranger where the ultimate intention was already sabotaged with external pressure.

But then, how was he going to meet anybody if he didn't socialize?

"Steinberg?"

He glanced at the female who had spoken and was momentarily taken aback.

God only knew what her natural hair color actually was, as it was hidden beneath a mix of blue, purple and green patches, and black roots that were so black they had to be from a bottle.

An eyebrow and nose piercing glittered on a face that might have been quite pretty if not for the scowl on it, and the shadows under the eyes evidenced the late nights and early mornings.

He guessed her age to be late twenties or early thirties, and she looked to be as unhappy about the new partner as he was. "Fuller?"

She nodded and sat on the stool beside him, "morning," she said unenthusiastically.

He nodded too, slightly stunned but not sure why.

"I'll tell you straight, I didn't want to be partnered again. I said I wasn't ready. So it's not personal to you," she blurted this out as if it was part of a pre-planned speech that had got jumbled up in her mouth and spat out in chunks.

He didn't know how to respond to that, so he figured he'd let her keep talking until she'd got the whole message out at least.

"Six months I was off. It's way too soon, after Stone and the way he died. The shrink said I could come back to duty, but I wasn't sure. I was going bugshit being away from the job though. Y'know?"

She wasn't even looking at him, so he knew he wasn't required to acknowledge.

Kathleen sighed, "at least you aren't one of those pressed suit jerks," she inclined her head back at the other patrons in the diner.

Alex waited, and finally she faced him.

While she studied him, her frown intensified, "you a meathead?"

He blinked, "what?"

"Do you have a brain or are you all muscle?"

He thought for a moment, "the public is wonderfully tolerant. It forgives everything except genius."

She smiled, and seemed to relax immediately, "Oscar Wilde."

He smiled back. "I didn't want to have a new

partner either. Moving to this town and precinct have been hard and I've had three partners in three months."

She nodded, "I heard you got stuck with Uncle Ben."

He burst out laughing. His first partner had been a colored gentleman that did strongly resemble Uncle Ben. "Yeah, he didn't like me or my lifestyle choices."

She eye rolled, "he doesn't like anyone. He asked me once if I'd ever burned a cross on someone's front lawn."

He laughed again and felt himself opening to the possibility of accepting this person as someone he could actually work with. "And what did you say?"

"I said not yet," she grinned, but then her grin faltered. "Stone was there, he pointed out that just because someone has a tattoo or a piercing doesn't make them a white supremacist."

He guessed that Stone was her former partner. "I'm sorry, I don't know anything about Stone."

She looked down at her hands and shrugged.

The waitress returned with Alex's fruit plate, and she greeted Kathleen with a happy, "hey Kathy, haven't seen you in forever. Want some coffee?"

"Sure Agnes," she gave her a polite smile.

Once she had the hot coffee, she made no move to add sugar or milk, she just stared at it.

Alex started to eat the fruit in front of him, considering how to say what he needed to say. "You should know everything about me up front, as we are being forced together."

"I already know," she faced him again, not smiling. "You're gay." She shrugged, "it's none of my business."

"I'm Bisexual, and I'm HIV positive," he said. He hated the inevitability of the flinch or cringe that came after them, but he'd rather fully disclose straight away.

She didn't cringe. She didn't flinch, or respond in any other way but to blink. "Yeah," was all that she said.

Her lack of response was shocking to him. "Does any of that bother you?"

She looked confused, "bother me?"

"It's why I haven't kept a partner. And as much as they may have been assholes, me being HIV positive is something that could potentially be a health risk to you."

She smirked, "yeah. I had the talk from Markson."

He was interested to know what his new

captain had said, and he cocked an eyebrow in interest.

Kathy just shrugged, "she didn't say anything unkind. She sang your praises actually. Said you were an excellent officer, brilliant record, excellent with the community, bla bla bla."

"I am?" he was surprised.

"She said how you offered your time to that women's charity for self-defense classes, I thought that was nice."

He laughed, "my sister-in-law runs that charity, but yeah, I do a self-defense class every other week."

"It's still a good thing to do," she said approvingly. "Anyway after selling you to me she just tagged on the end, 'he also has HIV'."

Alex laughed, "awesome."

Kathy smiled again, "I'm sure some would have a problem with it, but I don't see how it effects your ability to be a good officer. If a situation came up where you were injured then I'd just put gloves on." She shrugged, "no biggie, we all usually carry them anyway."

Alex sighed with relief, and felt his whole body relax. "You wouldn't believe how many people overreact about this."

"Yeah I would," she finally added sugar to the coffee, but no milk. As she stirred, she added, "I have an allergy to bee stings. Have to carry a pen. If I get stung, you may have to jab me."

"I think I can handle that, where do you carry it?"

"Always in my holster," she pulled back her jacket and showed her holster had been modified to have an additional little slot, where a small epi pen was sitting.

"Good to know."

Agnes returned then, "everything okay?"

Alex nodded, "yes thanks."

"Any food for you Kathy?"

"No thanks. You still having problems with that creepy landlord of yours? Did you buy that lock like I told you to?"

Agnes rolled her eyes, "yeah, but Gerald is angry saying that violates the terms of my lease, unless he has a copy of the key."

Kathy frowned, "you need to get out of there."

"I know, I'm looking for another room somewhere," Agnes shook her head. "There's nowhere that I know of on my salary."

"I'll keep an ear out," she told the waitress.

"Appreciate it."

EIGHT

They sat at the back of the briefing room, as they were the last to arrive, and a few of the officers greeted Kathy happily, welcoming her back.

Alex was a lot happier at the prospect of having a new partner, now that they had met and there didn't seem to be any obvious signs that they would conflict.

Captain Markson waved them in impatiently, as she was mid-sentence. "Half the call-in clerks are off sick with the stomach flu, so I'm going to need manpower in there over the next few days."

A collective groan filled the room, and Markson silenced it with a glare. "Gibson, Carter, Steinberg and Fuller, as you're between cases, I need you to ease the burden."

Alex glanced at Kathy and saw that she didn't seem to be bothered by the assignment. Neither was he. It made a nice change to be indoors at a desk for a few days. They both gave a nod of consent. He saw that Gibson and Carter, who both resembled Patrick Swayze's character in the movie Point Break, were not pleased, but nodded too.

"Report to Matthew Walker downstairs, he's expecting you."

Alex presumed that the other officers had already been given their assignments as everyone rose to their feet at this.

Kathy was patted on the back by a few detectives, and these few also nodded at Alex. He really missed his old team, and tried to recall if he'd ever had this awkward feeling around them when he'd first become a detective.

"Good to see you back Fuller," one man said. Alex thought his name might be Milton. "You got a good partner here," he patted Alex on the back, and he fought the frown. He didn't even know this guy.

Kathy nodded, "yeah, it's good to be back."

When they were alone in the corridor, walking toward the elevators Alex said, "that guy has never even spoken to me."

"Does that mean he didn't know you?"

He laughed, "I guess he thinks he does."

Gibson and Carter met them at the elevator, and they were full of anger about this assignment.

"I swear this is punishment for hanging up on her florist last week," Lukas Carter groaned. His partner, Toby Gibson, was busy frowning at both Alex and Kathy.

85

"Don't know why we get lumped in with the deformity crew," he said under his breath, though clearly deliberately loud enough to be heard.

Alex couldn't help but say, "at least we aren't caught up in nineties nostalgia Point Break."

Gibson sneered, "at least my hair isn't falling out leper."

Alex laughed, "I don't have leprosy and my hair isn't falling out asshole. And I don't damage the ozone layer with my hairspray usage either."

Both looked momentarily confused, and Gibson turned to Carter, "thought he had leprosy?"

"Jesus," Alex muttered under his breath and turned his back on the idiots.

Kathy kept facing them, as if she couldn't believe what she was seeing.

Thankfully the elevator arrived before any more insults could be slung, and they all rode down quietly.

Matthew Walker was waiting for them when the doors opened. Alex had only met the man a few times, he was middle aged and always stressed out, but hugely efficient at managing his team.

The Police Clerks were the first port of call

for many people who needed to make a statement or report a crime. Matthew also had to oversee the evidence logging and filing, and the check in of inmates who stayed in their holding cells.

Matthew frowned when he saw Gibson and Carter, but he made no comment other than a brusque "follow me", before he turned and walked away.

All four detectives followed the man, and he stopped outside the file room. He turned back to them and smiled finally at Gibson and Carter. "Which one of you two actually knows the alphabet all the way to z?"

"Hey," Gibson protested. "We're here to help you out y'know."

"And you will help out by filing all these outstanding files, and so help me God, they had better be done correctly!"

Gibson flushed as if he'd already been caught misfiling. He stepped into the room, and Carter made to follow him, but Walker grinned and shook his head. "I don't think so, I need you to help Sue on the front desk."

Carter couldn't hide his mortification, "are you kidding me?"

Matthew's grin widened, "no, I'm really not. Do I need to call Markson?"

Carter also flushed, "no."

"Sue is waiting for you at the desk," the middle-aged man couldn't hide his glee.

Alex managed to hide his grin until Carter stormed off toward the front desk, muttering under his breath.

"Karma is a bitch," Kathy said quietly with a smile.

"They're both terrible with their reports, that's the only reason they got the shit detail," Walker explained, composing his face into professionalism once more. "You two okay with talking to a million old ladies about their lost jewelry and stolen purses?"

He and Kathy both nodded.

"Good, because I'm only half kidding." He led them into the nest, where a dozen clerks were talking to the public already, and Alex smiled when he saw Carter being talked down by Sue at the front desk.

"You can take this desk," he told Alex as he gestured towards a littered desk. He faced Kathy and gave her a smile, "welcome back dear, you're over here," he led her away, and she gave Alex a 'good luck' smile.

Alex sat at the desk and immediately started tidying all the papers into the correctly corresponding files. He couldn't work in mess.

Walker came back a moment later, nodding in approval at Alex's clean desk ethos. "You know what you're doing?"

"They take a ticket, Sue and Carter will filter them to us and we file their reports appropriately?"

Walker nodded and seemed relieved. "Half an hour for lunch."

Alex nodded, luckily his pockets were loaded as they were everyday with protein bars, and he had his medication with him.

Walker left and Alex continued to tidy. Moments later though, Carter smiled and dropped a clipboard onto the desk, "order up."

Alex didn't even acknowledge him as he continued to tidy, and he could sense the disappointment from Carter that he hadn't responded. Eventually he slunk away, and only then did Alex look at the clipboard, and the scruffy writing that said 'Dorothy Taylor – Lost Cat'.

It was going to be a long day.

After talking to the very frail and elderly Dorothy Taylor about her darling 'Tibbles' who had been missing for nearly a whole day, and then Rose Danon about her neighbor who deliberately kept raising the volume on her television just to annoy her, he knew he needed a cigarette.

When he got to his feet with the intentions of going for one, Sue scowled at him. "Oh no you don't mister," she said fiercely.

Alex couldn't help but respond to her authoritative tone and sat back down. "I'm not allowed to get up and go to the bathroom?"

Her frown deepened, but then it seemed to relax a little when Carter moved away from her, and she realized she wasn't addressing him. "Please don't take long," was all she said by way of permission, and Alex bolted for the doors.

He managed to pee and smoke in under ten minutes, taking no joy in the drags he took, but functionally burned the smoke down to the nub and ran back inside to his desk, and Sue nodded in approval as he resumed his seat, seeing the next case he had in front of him was 'Ryan Miller – sick child'.

Alex collected Ryan from the reception area and knew immediately that this was not a petty complaint. The man was tired, and he had a sleeping infant in his arms as he sat at the desk. "I don't even know where to begin," he said wearily, and he scrubbed his free hand down his stubbled face.

Alex gave him a reassuring smile and put down the clipboard. "Take a minute, would you like a coffee? Or some water?"

Ryan smiled, surprised by the offer. "I'd love a coffee, thanks."

Alex took delight in calling over to Carter to fetch a coffee for Mr. Miller, and Carter obviously wanted to say something snide, but held it in check in front of the civilian, perhaps because he too recognized the exhaustion in the man, and just asked how he took it.

The infant in his arms stirred a little but didn't wake. Ryan took a moment to stroke her wispy hair. "This is Lizzie," Ryan said quietly to Alex. "Thankfully she's not affected, she's too little."

Alex was puzzled, but let the man relax as he got his thoughts together.

"I'll be blunt because I don't know a gentle way to tiptoe around this, but I think my priest has poisoned my children."

Alex blinked. It took a lot to shock him these days, but that was something he'd never heard before. "Okay, I'm going to need you to start at the beginning," he picked up his clipboard and flipped the page over so he could make notes, rather than starting with the name and address.

"My neighbor, Mrs. Tatum, she comes in and helps me with the cleaning and cooking. She's a widow, like me, so it helps her as much as me. The girls love her."

Alex nodded. He still didn't have much of a handle on this guy's story, but he let him talk. A lot of the truth tended to come out once you let someone relax and just say whatever was on their minds.

Carter delivered the man's coffee and shot Alex the stink eye as he slunk off.

Ryan seemed to relax more as he sipped at the brew. "That's good. You wouldn't believe how long it's been since I've had an uninterrupted cup of coffee."

Alex gave him an encouraging look, "how many children do you have?"

Ryan smiled, "three girls. Penny is five, Poppy is four, and Lizzie here just turned one."

Alex gave him a sympathetic smile, "three girls. Quite a handful."

Ryan laughed, "yeah, but they're amazing. My wife, Grace, passed away just a couple of months ago, but she wrangled them all so much better than I can."

"I'm sorry for your loss," Alex said in response. "And in my opinion I don't think you're failing at managing them, women just tend to have a natural ability to herd a flock."

Ryan winced, "yeah, herding a flock. That's

the way Father Francis puts it too. He's always worrying about herding his flock."

Alex scribbled down the name of the priest and then returned his eyes to the worried parent.

Ryan seemed to be about to cry. "Grace died very suddenly. It was a chest infection that turned into pneumonia. She just couldn't fight it. She was perfectly healthy, and within four weeks she was dead. Honestly during that month I don't think I slept more than an hour at a time between work and visits to the hospital and trying to keep things normal for the girls." He looked down at his sleeping baby then, and the infant was drooling on his arm and snoring.

"I took all the help that I could. Mrs. Tatum next door always got on very well with Grace, and she basically knew the girl's schedules and playdates because she used to help out with rides every now and then. She was a lifesaver, and she continues to be."

Lizzie farted, and Ryan laughed. "I'm sorry," he apologized to Alex, who was also laughing. He gestured for Ryan to continue.

"Grace was very religious, and she wanted the girls to be raised in the church too. I didn't object, but I don't believe myself. Mrs. Tatum used to take them all to church on Sunday's, because I worked nights." Ryan paused to sip his coffee and he looked Alex in the eye. "Do you have kids?"

Alex shook his head, "no."

Ryan almost gave him a look of pity, "you wouldn't believe how much your world changes once you've got kids. Aside from the practical changes, it really just makes you see how fragile everything is. And how desperately you want things to be better."

Alex nodded, "of course."

Ryan looked down at his baby and seemed to take comfort from her. "When Grace died, I was in shock. I think I still might be," he joked. "But the church swooped in to help, or at least my house was suddenly full of people who were constantly cooking casseroles and putting my kids to bed and doing my laundry," he laughed. "I was so grateful, to have all that domestic stuff dealt with, and I never had to actually ask for the help. It was the first time I recognized that the church wasn't just a building, but a community."

Ryan seemed embarrassed, "and I saw the value in it, for the girls mainly, but also for me. I'd lost my wife, and that still kills me every single day," he choked up a little. "But I still had a family in the church. And Father Francis was always there to give a word or to help me. When I lost my job because I couldn't work the night shift anymore, Father Francis was there straight away, arranging interviews for me with a local engineering firm, and it was a miracle I actually got the job. It's better money and better hours for me to still spend time with the girls."

Ryan finished his coffee, and smiled at Alex, "I actually started to see a light at the end of the tunnel. But then Penny got sick. And I didn't think much more than the usual childhood bugs that are always going around. She said her stomach hurt, and she was thirsty, and she had a few dry heaves, but no vomiting. I nursed her on the couch, and though she couldn't stand the thought of food, after a few days she seemed to get better. Her color came back and she wanted food again, and she said the pain was gone."

Lizzie chose that moment to wake, and she immediately fussed. Ryan shushed her and switched her into a position against his chest, so her head could rest on his shoulder. He rubbed her back and shook out the arm she'd been laying on.

Alex thought the natural responses of parents

95

was amazing. To ignore their own pains and focus solely on the needs of their young. Ryan had a sweat outline from where she had been asleep against him and obviously a deadened arm from her weight, but he was just shaking it out and still comforting her.

"Would you like me to hold her for a minute?" Alex offered, and wondered where the impulse had come from, and how it might have come across.

Yes he had a niece and nephews and was no stranger to children, but this man didn't know that. To Ryan, Alex was a cop which automatically gave you some trustworthiness by default, but he was clearly tattooed and pierced, and he had no clue that Alex was a good person.

And yet, Ryan just smiled and handed the fussing infant over to Alex, who took her tiny and fragile form in his meaty hands. The baby had bright blue eyes, and they fixated immediately on the stranger.

Alex settled her immediately on his knee, where she could study him, and he smiled at her as she was fascinated by his eyebrow piercing and was reaching out her hands towards it. "Yeah it's shiny isn't it," he leaned forward and let her touch it, not surprised when her spidery fingers turned into talons and grabbed his entire brow into her fist.

"Whoa, easy Lizzie," Ryan was alarmed, but Alex just laughed and eased himself out of her grip.

"It's fine," he told the man, and he handed Lizzie a bright red ruler that was on the desk. "Play with this, you thug," he told her, and she seized the brightly colored object in her hands and put it straight into her mouth.

Ryan smiled, "you're a natural."

"I have a niece and nephews," Alex explained.

Ryan nodded, and just smiled sadly at Lizzie. "I forgot what I was saying."

"You were telling me that Penny had gotten sick, but it was just a bug."

Ryan nodded again, "Father Francis was worried, and came over almost every evening. That wasn't unusual, as he tended to check on us most days since Grace died. It was good because it gave me time to grab a shower or heat the dinner that Mrs. Tatum had left for us. It felt good that he was taking time out of his schedule to remember us."

Ryan took a moment to think, and he glanced down at the desk while he did so. He didn't look up when he spoke again. "Now I look back at it, I think he was giving the girls something to make them sick. Because within days of Penny saying she felt better, she was sick again, and so was Poppy. Same symptoms as before, dry mouth, very sleepy, dry heaving and stomach pains, and Penny's lips were so dry they were cracking and bleeding. This time I called the doctor. And they took both girls to the hospital."

Alex frowned, as he finally saw where the man was going with this.

"The doctor asked me when my daughters had ingested bleach," Ryan finally looked up at Alex. "They accused me of poisoning my girls, and now we're under a social worker, because either I did it on purpose, or they suspect I'm so negligent that they did it by accident while they were unsupervised."

Alex looked down at Lizzie for a moment, as she was using the ruler to hit the desk with a satisfying smack that made her happy. "Are social services taking steps to separate you from them?"

"Thankfully not yet. But we're being watched, and I've banned Father Francis from the house. Coincidentally the girls aren't sick anymore. But honestly I can't see any other way they would have drunk bleach. In the house all the chemicals are in a cupboard they can't reach, and they're never unsupervised."

"And just to play devil's advocate here, is there any way that Mrs. Tatum would leave bleach laying around?"

Ryan shook his head, "the woman is militant when it comes to cleaning and returning things to their proper places. Her faith is no joke, and even she believes that Father Francis did something. Because she believes Penny."

"Did Penny say something to implicate the Father?"

Ryan nodded, but seemed even more upset, "it made little sense, and we've been trying to downplay it, because I don't want either of the girls more traumatized than they have already been. But a few nights after the girls came home from the hospital where they'd been interrogated by the doctors and social services, Father Francis came by. And I didn't want to flat out accuse him, because I had no proof, and after all the help he'd given me, I really didn't want to be hostile. But I had to protect my girls, so I just didn't let him in the house. I blocked the door with my body and just said it was a bad time, I had a lot of work to do, and the girls were already asleep."

Ryan swallowed, "he wanted to just have a

quick chat with me, and to look in on the girls, and of course they heard his voice so they came running up to the door and basically forced it open. Happy to see him. He knew then I had just been trying to keep him out, but he put on a good act for the girls. I kept a close watch on them then, because I didn't want him left alone with them. Mrs. Tatum was in my kitchen then too, she was cleaning the dishes and at that point she didn't believe my suspicions, but thought I was overtired, still grieving my wife," Ryan waved a hand in the air, gesturing that there had been any number of reasons to explain how this tragic accident with bleach may have occurred innocently.

"Penny and Poppy had been playing with their dolls then, and she pulled the priest over, to show him. He is amazingly patient with child ramblings, and he's never bored when he's listening to them," Ryan seemed angry at this. "Penny is prattling on about the new doll's I'd bought them just that day, and Poppy say's thank you to him for the prayer pictures. They worked because she was all better now."

Alex frowned, "Prayer pictures?"

Ryan nodded, "thankfully Mrs. Tatum asked the question, and she worded it more delicately than I could have. She asked him, 'what's a prayer picture Francis?' Poppy answered though, and God love her, she thought she was answering a question in school. She shot her hand straight up, and said, 'The Father has to take a picture, so he can show God, so you get special prayers to make you better'."

Alex didn't think his frown could get any deeper.

Ryan was frowning too, "there was a moment where I swear the Father was blushing at that. Then he just laughed a little and told Mrs. Tatum when a child is sick, it's good for them to know that God is watching over them. It comforts them. But I just asked him then if he'd been taking pictures of my kids, because there was something weird about the whole thing. If you involve your kids in church activities or even something innocent like a birthday party, there's a chance there will be pictures taken, but to know that someone has secretly been taking pictures of your children....that frightens me almost as much as the fact that someone has been poisoning them."

Alex thought immediately of Jeanie's childhood, and the horrific Straker who was still at large. The kind of sick minds who manipulate a child's innocence were a special kind of deviant who deserved the worst the justice system could throw at them.

"Father Francis was definitely uncomfortable to be caught out, but Penny spoke up again. She said 'when we took our medicine we had to rest so it would work, and The Father took our pictures on his phone to make sure that he got the prayers in that day so we got well again. And it was good he gave us that medicine because we sure got sick', she said. And then it dawned on me that he hadn't been there to see them when they were sick, only beforehand. He gave them medicine to make them better before they got sick. And I looked at Mrs. Tatum and knew she realized the same thing I did."

Alex was horrified, "did you notify social services? At that point, did you tell them of your suspicions?"

"Of course I did," Ryan seemed exhausted again. "They've filed my report, but to them it just seems like I'm slinging mud to get attention away from myself. The girls have been interviewed, and thankfully that seems to have given it a little more weight, but now I'm genuinely worried that the priest is a threat. I've stopped them going to church, and even Mrs. Tatum has stopped attending his sermons."

Alex genuinely didn't know how to proceed with this report, as it definitely didn't fall within the realms of a normal dispute. "I would recommend that you file a restraining order against Father Francis, at the very least."

Ryan seemed relieved that Alex hadn't dismissed him, "yes, please, let's do that."

Alex looked down at the form in front of him, then at Lizzie, who was now chewing on the drool covered plastic ruler. "Procedure says that I have to file this report, and the captain will then allocate it to someone to follow up, but I know that can take weeks." He bit his lip, he really shouldn't be saying any of this, but he felt an affinity to this man, who had suffered so much.

"I can't make promises, but I'm going to try and talk to my captain to get this pushed through."

Ryan actually smiled, "thank you, so much."

Alex pushed the clipboard over to him, "fill in all your basic details here, and I'll file this immediately. At the very least if there is an active investigation going on social services should back down."

Lizzie emphasized this news with a solid thump on the desk, and Alex laughed. "Again though, no promises. I'll do everything I can to get this looked into."

NINE

Kathy dropped a footlong sub on his desk and Alex looked up with gratitude, "thanks, I'm starved."

She was already devouring her own and so she nodded with her mouth already full as she took the guest chair.

Alex unwrapped it to see that it was steaming hot and full of cheese, meat, salad and mayo.

After swallowing her mouthful Kathy said, "I wasn't sure what you liked."

"This is great thanks, I was nearly out of protein bars," the time had flown by today, and this was more a snack before going home rather than a lunch break. "How was your day? Anything interesting?"

She rolled her eyes, "an old man hit on me while he was reporting his stolen wallet. And an old lady kept asking me if I was a lesbian. Other than that it was boring. How about you?"

Alex nodded as his mouth was full, but once he could talk, he told her about Ryan Miller, and he asked her if she thought it was worth trying to push through?

She nodded, "I doubt you'll get any joy, but

yeah. Poor guy."

They spent a few contented moments eating in silence, and it was only interrupted when Carter shouted across the room, "Line two Steinberg."

Alex frowned but picked up the phone, confused as he rarely had calls at work, "Alex Steinberg."

There was a moment of silence, then he was surprised to hear Ryan Miller say, "hello Detective."

"Mr. Miller? Is everything okay?"

Kathy looked surprised, as he'd only just finished telling her about him, so she knew who he was.

"Look, I'm having second thoughts about my statement. I think I want to just leave it alone."

Alex frowned, "has something happened?"

Ryan hesitated, "I just think I made a mistake. Accidents happen."

Alex heard a tone that didn't sound mistaken at all, but completely deadpan, as if scripted.

"Are you able to talk freely right now?"

Another hesitation, "of course."

He didn't believe him, and he wondered if the priest was there, or if he was on speakerphone.

"You said there was a back log and there would be delays in filing it, so I'm sure if you just pull my statement it'll be like it never happened."

He could do that, of course. "I'm afraid that isn't how it works Mr. Miller. You're in the system now, and paperwork like this cannot just go missing," he used his most official voice. "If you wish to withdraw your statement you will have to do so in person. And if you wish to recant you may have to seek legal advice," he said this in the hope that whoever else may be listening would know that this wasn't just going to go away.

Ryan Miller exhaled heavily, "I'll come down tomorrow after work, and we'll sort all this out."

"I'll look forward to seeing you then Mr. Miller," he said coldly. He didn't feel cold towards the man at all, but he was sure that there were other ears listening, and he didn't want them to know that Ryan had a sympathetic ear in the police.

The line went dead, and Alex hung up and looked at Kathy, who had followed enough of the conversation to understand what was going on.

"I swear the priest was there," Alex picked up his sandwich.

Kathy shook her head, "fucking religion."

He cocked an eyebrow at her comment, and duly noted her view on the clergy. "He sounded under duress."

"You going to pull his statement?"

He shook his head, "no way."

Kathy nodded, "you do realize that could backfire against you? If it turns out that he was genuinely wishing to retract?"

Alex had a moment of doubt, "do you think I should pull it?"

Kathy winced, "no, I'm just playing devil's advocate here. But it's on you, it's your decision. I didn't meet the guy, and we only met today so I don't know how reliable your gut feelings are."

"Unless Ryan Miller is an Academy Award worthy actor, he was genuinely terrified earlier on today, and that call he just made, was the acting performance. He sounded like a robot, he didn't believe what he was telling me."

Kathy held her hands out as if to say 'well there you go'.

Alex nodded and made the decision firmly in his own mind, he would file the statement as planned. "Any fun plans for tonight?"

"I don't do fun in the conventional sense," she tidied up her sandwich wrapper and wiped her mouth with a napkin.

"You're going to have to explain."

"There's a game I play online, I have a raid scheduled tonight. I'm a healer."

He smiled, but he thought of Tim, addicted to killing imaginary monsters. "Whatever floats your boat."

"It keeps me off the streets," she said. "What about you?"

"I'll probably go home, water my plants, read a book, then go to the gym."

She eye rolled and said, "bleh."

Alex laughed and stretched out his arms, "have to keep this machine well tuned."

Once he was out of the station though, he decided to pay a visit to Ryan Miller. He'd made a mental note of the address he'd been given earlier, and it was near the route he usually took to get home.

The houses were small in this neighborhood, and when he pulled up outside the Miller residence, he saw several children's toys littered the front yard, which was slightly overgrown.

When he exited the vehicle, a middle-aged woman stepped out of the front door, a firm frown fixed on her face, "I think you've taken a wrong turn Mister."

He racked his brain for a moment, then smiled when he placed her name, "you must be

Mrs. Tatum." He gave what he hoped was a friendly demeanor and took a few steps closer.

She was disarmed to have been named by a stranger, but she still held up a hand to stop him coming any closer.

Alex held out both his hands as if he were under arrest, "my name is Alex Steinberg."

She didn't alter her stance at his name, and he didn't want to show his identification just yet. "I was hoping to have a quick word with Ryan, is he about?"

Her frown intensified, but before she could answer, Ryan opened the door behind her, and was instantly shocked to see Alex there. "Oh my God, what are you doing here?"

Ryan made a comedic show of stepping out, sweeping his eyes up and down the street to see if anyone was looking, then gestured for Alex to get inside the house.

He stepped inside, and was quickly ushered to the kitchen by Mrs. Tatum, who was not pleased to have such a tattooed and pierced man in her presence.

The three girls were seated at the small dinner table, Lizzie who he had met earlier was currently pasting herself with some kind of orange mush. The other two, he remembered their names were Poppy and Penny, were curious about the stranger in their kitchen.

Alex smiled at them and said a friendly, "hello."

They didn't answer, but looked at their father, who smiled and said, "this is Alex, say hello."

They both chorused a hello, but Ryan was looking at Alex with confusion.

"I just wanted to see if you were talking under duress earlier," he said plainly.

Ryan rubbed a hand down his face, and honestly looked exhausted, "my boss came to see us."

Mrs. Tatum came forward to the girls and encouraged them to eat their dinner, and offered to brew some tea.

Alex declined, with a thank you, but was still waiting for some kind of explanation from Ryan, who sat down at the table.

Alex hadn't been offered a seat, so he remained standing, but he grasped the back of the only free seat and tried to figure out how a visit from his boss would cause him to recant.

"It has been pointed out to me that I only have the job I do, because kind words were spoken by a certain someone," Ryan said this carefully, as he clearly didn't want the girls to repeat the wrong thing to the wrong person.

Alex was horrified, so this man was now

being blackmailed to keep quiet or he would lose his job.

Alex looked at the girls, and Mrs. Tatum, who was still curious as to his identity, but must have figured out that he wasn't there with nefarious intent. "Is there somewhere we can talk for a moment?"

Ryan shook his head, "there is no point," he said resignedly. "I can't proceed, he's got me by the... throat."

"You are mistaken," Alex spoke equally as carefully. "And how did he know?"

Ryan glanced at Mrs. Tatum, who had the good grace to blush as she said, "he called and asked if you could do an extra shift at work today, I didn't realize he was going to go straight to the Father."

Ryan held up a hand to pacify the older woman, "I'm not blaming you, I didn't realize either."

"This is called coercion, and it is a crime," Alex said softly.

"I also have bills to pay," Ryan said wearily. "And children to feed and clothe."

"Don't let this be about money, what if it happens again?"

Ryan closed his eyes and looked sickened. "What would you do? You don't have a family

to support, you have no idea the pressure…"
he cut himself off as he looked at his daughters,
who weren't eating dinner, and were looking
alarmed at their fathers distress. He
immediately smiled at them and leaned forward,
"girl's I need you to eat your dinner for me,
okay? I'm going to take Alex upstairs for a
moment, but then I'll be back. If you finish
your dinner by the time I'm back, you can have
dessert."

The girls were immediately incentivized by
the bribe, and tucked into their food with
gusto. Ryan got to his feet and led Alex away,
up a narrow set of stairs and into a small
bedroom with a double bed in it. He sat down
and put his head in his hands.

"I'm sorry to have come here and made you
feel worse, of course you have the right to
withdraw the statement. If that's what you truly
want, then I'll see to it, you don't have to come
down to the station again. But I think it's a
mistake," he said this honestly.

Ryan looked up at him, and gave a weak
smile, "Grace always used to say that if you did
the right thing and stayed true to your morals,
things would always work out. She believed
that right up until the end. But I see that I have
less than three hundred in the bank and a stack

of overdue bills on the counter, and I don't see how losing my job will pay those bills Detective."

"He's breaking the law by threatening your job, and if he tried to fire you, you can sue his ass."

Ryan laughed, "I can't afford to do that."

"My brother is a lawyer, he does pro bono work all the time."

"And when I lose my medical insurance and the girls get sick?"

"My other brother is a doctor," Alex realized how ridiculous his counter arguments were, and smiled too. "Please stop worrying and thinking about the worst case scenario's here. One day at a time is what the addicts live by, and it's a good mantra. If you stare at the whole heap of problems, you end up not seeing the wood for the trees."

Ryan looked like he was about to cry, "I'm exhausted."

"I'll go, but please just take some time and think about what's best here. The fact remains that your children were endangered by a man who needs to be investigated. It's always difficult to be the first to speak up, but something needs to be done, and you were that man this morning. Just ask yourself what has changed since then?"

Ryan nodded, "I know."

"Please take my number. Call me in the morning," Alex said. "What time do you start work?"

"9am, but the girls are up from about 6am."

"Call me before work and tell me then what your decision is."

Ryan nodded, "thanks. And I'm sorry, for all this."

Alex shook his head, "don't worry about it."

TEN

His apartment seemed sterile and empty in comparison to the cluttered Miller home. His bookshelves were crammed with his favorite volumes, and his plants were thriving on his window ledges, but other than that, there was no life in the small space.

Ordinarily he enjoyed the minimalistic way he lived, but now he saw it as joyless. He had no photo's or pictures, no memorabilia to mark the place as his.

While he watered his plants and ran a duster over their leaves, he gave himself a good mental shakedown. This was his choice, and his way of life had served him well for years now. He was healthy and organized, and he could put some pictures on the walls if he wanted to. There was nothing to say he was lacking or deficient in any way because he hadn't done so beforehand. He was just now choosing to make a few changes.

After scanning his cupboards and realizing that he still hadn't been to the store, he knew he needed to eat, but he also needed to shop. He hated shopping.

The lure of Eric and Jeanie's fully stocked

kitchen called to him again, and he partly resented it, but also loved that it was a resource he could tap. Maybe he should just move in with them and be done with it. Had he just been stubborn up until this point to have asserted his independence so strictly?

No, he was a grown ass man and he needed his own space.

But he was hungry.

Even as he drove over to All Saint's House, he was berating himself for his laziness, but all he could picture was Daisy's Chicken Pot Pie, or Lasagna that could always be found in the fridge.

Once he arrived at the house, he immediately had regrets though. There were several cars in the driveway, and when he entered the house, he saw Eric talking to two men at his desk in the parlor. He gave Alex a happy smile, but was clearly busy, so Alex just nodded and continued onto the kitchen.

The kitchen was equally occupied. Jeanie was at the kitchen table sat between two women, one of which he recognized as Melissa Ramu, from the law firm she had helped to create with his father and was now run by she and Eric.

He didn't know the other woman, but she was quite plain and mousy, with her brown hair

117

piled into a messy bun. She was looking intently at a document that rested on the table in front of Jeanie, who also smiled as he walked in. "Alex! I wasn't expecting to see you tonight."

"I'm so sorry I didn't realize you would be entertaining," he couldn't help his look of longing at the fridge, and then laughed at himself.

"Don't mind us," Jeanie gestured to the fridge, and Alex took that as leave to help himself. The kitchen was large enough he could eat in the lesser used half of it so he would be out of their way.

While he was considering between Cottage Pie and Casserole, Christina leaned over him to grab a bottle of baby formula out of the door, "hey bro."

She uncapped the bottle and put it on the counter while she took a jug out of the cupboard. She ran the hot tap at the sink and looked at him while she held her fingers under the running water, gauging its temperature. "Wasn't expecting you."

He nodded, "yeah I've crashed everyone's party."

Christina smirked, "it's always like this here. I like it though, it feels alive."

Alex thought of his dead air apartment and nodded; in comparison it did seem nice. "Alvin hungry?"

She nodded, "I'm going to change him to milk soon, the formula isn't satisfying him. He's always hungry, but the nurses are saying to stick with this."

He blinked in ignorance. "I didn't know that was a thing."

"That babies have to change over to milk? Yeah, it's a thing," she smiled and paid attention to filling the jug with hot water and then placing the bottle inside it.

Alex decided on the Cottage Pie, and busied himself with heating it in the microwave. "How's Tim?"

She shrugged, "I haven't gone near that room, so I have no idea. Daisy said earlier she's been sending food up, but it's mostly left uneaten."

"Have you thought about what to do yet?" he asked, concerned once again that the dead tone had returned to his sister's voice.

She faced him, "about what?"

"You were talking about leaving him," he reminded her.

She briefly looked at the floor, "what does that say about me? That I'm weak when it

119

comes to struggle," she laughed without hilarity.

"Christina, nobody is going to see that you're the bad guy here."

She shook her head and turned her attention back to the bottle she was warming, "I'm not ready to make a decision yet."

He nodded, not that she could see it. "Fair enough."

"By the way, Brad is trying to set you up with a friend of Misha's," she said, turning around with a smile on her face again.

"Yeah, I already said no," he eye rolled. "He's just trying to get me to breed, so that he can prove his medical expertise."

Christina wrinkled her nose, "you'd have a hard time breeding with her friend, it's a dude."

Alex hadn't been expecting that, "oh, well I'm still not sure I'm ready. How do you know?"

"Coz we all met him, they dropped by after you'd gone on Sunday, I think they were hoping you'd still be here. Brad had 'forgotten' something, so we all met him and said hi."

"Oh God," Alex groaned, "that poor guy."

"Well, maybe you should take him for a coffee, as an apology for going through that. Not that he seemed to mind."

He sighed, "maybe. I just hate this."

"What? Dating?"

He nodded, "it's so forced and awkward."

"Perhaps you should just view it as meeting new people, and not shopping for a bedfellow."

Before he could respond, Jeanie called him over to the table, "sorry to interrupt your dinner," she smiled. "You should meet Cecily, she'll be taking over a lot of the operations at 'Open Arms' for me while our security situation is what it is, and I'll need to take maternity leave soon."

Alex nodded politely and exchanged a handshake with the woman, "nice to meet you."

"You too, I think we did meet briefly once, when we were younger, but I look quite different now," she smiled as if remembering past times.

"Oh?"

Melissa was putting papers into her briefcase and she smiled at Alex, "Cecily is Maxwell Culver's daughter."

The pieces came together, and Alex was shocked. This woman had spent a large amount of her twenties chasing after Eric. He remembered her being blonde and always perfectly manicured. Not this denim clad woman with messy hair and no make-up.

"Of course you look quite different now

too," Cecily joked.

Alex laughed, "true." He looked over to Jeanie, "so you're stepping down?"

"Just shirking a lot of the duties onto Cecily's willing shoulders," she joked. "I'm so tired these days I can't keep up with the administration let alone the fundraising side of things. And that will only get worse once the twins have arrived," she stroked her belly with a smile.

"Rather you than me," Cecily shook her head and scooped up her papers. "Alex I shouldn't need to bother you much, but as you are here I just wondered if you're still happy with the arrangements for the self-defense classes?"

"Yeah, as far as I know."

"I'll attend the next session, if you don't mind?"

"The more the merrier," he said. "But it gets pretty packed in there, so it gets quite hot."

Cecily cocked an eye, "high demand?"

"Usually."

"Hmm, maybe we'll have to do them more frequently. Get a few more instructors on board?" Cecily directed this question at Jeanie, who held her hands out as if to say it was her decision to make now.

"Okay, well I have to go," Cecily rounded the

table to one arm hug Melissa, and she patted the top of Jeanie's head affectionately. "Thanks for this."

Jeanie nodded and smiled, "someone should be at the front to open the gate for you."

Cecily waved and left the kitchen, and Melissa was similarly arranging to leave. "Try and rest young lady," she said this to Jeanie while stooping to hug her in the chair.

"I have no choice but to rest," Jeanie said wryly. "I'm a whale in the process of beaching."

Melissa patted her briefcase, "well this is something you don't need to worry about now. Focus on your family, okay?"

Jeanie nodded, "thank you Melissa."

Melissa gave her a curt nod, and then gave him a measured look, "I think I like this look on you Alexander."

He laughed, "thanks Mel."

"Take care Tina," she called over to Christina, then left the room as well.

Jeanie sighed and scrubbed her hands down her face, "so tired."

The microwave beeped, and she sniffed the air. "Cottage pie?"

He nodded, "I'm sorry, I'm treating your house like a café."

123

She shrugged, "it's not like we mind Alex, we have the food. And I might join you, I'm starved."

"You want this one? I'll heat another," he offered, pulling the steaming plate from the microwave and placing it in front of Jeanie.

From Christina's pocket, a baby cry could be heard, and she promptly took the bottle and exited the kitchen to feed her son.

Jeanie got herself a fork and smiled at Alex, "how was your day?"

"Yeah, it was busy," he said as he busied himself preparing another portion of food. Just then one of Daisy's assistants came into the kitchen carrying an untouched tray of food, looking distressed.

"Ma'am, uh…" the young lady faced Jeanie as she placed the tray down on the table.

Jeanie winced, "Tim still isn't eating."

"He's gone," she said bluntly.

Jeanie blinked, "what did you say Rachel?"

Rachel wrung her hands together nervously. "He isn't in the room, the computer is shut down, and I can't see any sign of him."

Jeanie looked at Alex with alarm, "Alex could you fetch the security team?"

He nodded, "of course," he was already crossing the room to head to where the security team were situated in the old garage. When he went through the parlor he noticed Eric was stood and shaking hands with whomever he had been doing business, but Alex didn't pause.

After breaching a few doors he entered the old garage, and three men were sat and monitoring the security screens. One seemed to be radioing another pair as they walked the perimeter. "Who is in charge tonight?"

One man stood, and Alex recognized Simons. "Is there a problem Mr. Steinberg?"

"Jeanie would like to speak with you in the kitchen, but I am going to presume she'll ask you to report the location of Mr. Chastain, so if you could have that information to hand it would save some time."

Simon's frowned and immediately turned to another agent, "any logged exits?"

The agent immediately pulled up a screen filled with timed entries, muttering to himself that it had been a busy evening.

Alex knew already how this was going to pan out. Tim had most likely snuck out when another person had left, leaving no trace.

"Have someone check the gate footage, he won't have used his code. Perhaps have someone check the grounds and the house in case he's still here."

Simon's nodded but seemed to ignore Alex as he was already calling up the footage of the gate, which was the only way in or out of the grounds.

Trusting that they knew what they were doing, and would report to Jeanie immediately, he returned to the kitchen where it was clear she had just informed Eric what had happened.

Alex took his food from the microwave, not that he felt like eating anymore.

How could Tim just sneak out? Not that the physical act of sneaking was impossible, though he chose not to move he was still mobile, even without one of his legs. But how could he do this to Christina?

He robotically shoveled hot food into his mouth. Eric sat beside his wife and looked pale, "what the hell can we do, he has a right to come and go, he's not exactly a prisoner here."

Alex nodded, "I've told the team to check the gate footage and do a sweep to check he isn't still on the grounds."

They both nodded.

Jeanie looked to Eric, "what do we say to Christina?"

Eric sighed, "the truth I guess. No point hiding it."

"She's feeding Alvin," Jeanie said.

Eric nodded, "I'll go tell her, you enjoy your second supper," he teased her affectionately.

Jeanie continued to eat, and Alex checked his watch, he still had a couple of hours before his gym appointment. So he continued joylessly conveying the food to his mouth.

"Does Open Arms only help women in bad domestic situations?" he asked, suddenly wondering if the charity would be able to help Ryan Miller at all.

Jeanie shook her head as she ate, "our brief is to open our arms to anyone in need. Hence the name. Why do you ask?"

"I met a man today, I won't go into details, but he may need legal help soon. I don't want to just oblige Eric to represent him pro bono because I've asked him to, but I know his firm does consultations for Open Arms don't they?"

Jeanie nodded, "walk in days are usually quite busy though, I'm sure if you were to arrange an appointment for him it would be better. There's a slightly longer wait but he wouldn't be seen by an intern. You have permission to drop my name if it helps."

"Thanks, I'm not sure it'll be needed yet, I'm just trying to think of ways to help this man."

ELEVEN

Christina looked slightly dazed as the security team reported that Tim had gotten into his adapted car and left behind Cecily Culver. He had been noticed at the time by Johnson, a new member of the team, who did not know that it was significant that this individual was leaving.

As Simon's was delivering this news with a grimace, he didn't need to point out that they weren't there to keep people from leaving.

Eric was the first to speak up. "Could you spare any manpower to check the local area for his vehicle?"

Before Simon's could answer though, Christina cut in. "No," she said firmly.

Alex looked at his sister and saw how tightly she was clenching her jaw. She shook her head at Eric as if to drive her point home. "If he wants to go, then let him."

"Christina, he's not in his right mind," Eric pointed out delicately.

"He's a grown man who has made the choice to leave his family and support system," Christina spat this out with venom. Alex believed that if she hadn't been holding Alvin in her arms, she would have her claws fully extended she was so angry.

Alvin was clutching his now empty bottle to his mouth, sucking at it though it was futile. Alex envied the infant in his ignorance to this situation.

"We could spare someone if it was required," Simon's answered Eric's question. The poor guy was speaking very delicately, most likely because of Christina's response to her straying husband. But Simon's was employed by Eric and Jeanie, not by Christina.

Eric looked at Christina, "are you telling me you aren't the least bit worried?"

"I've been worried since this child was born and he turned into an empty shell. Tim left months ago Eric, his body was just still here."

Jeanie looked sadly down at the table, and Alex felt his grimace as he heard the truth. Tim had been negligent in his duties as husband and father, and that had begun before the loss of his leg.

Christina took the empty bottle from Alvin and shifted him into burping position over her shoulder, "do not waste your security team chasing a ghost Eric."

With that statement she got to her feet, and left the room with her son.

Jeanie waited until she was gone, then she put

a hand on the table. "Do we do as she says?"

Alex looked to Eric, who seemed to be torn. He looked at Jeanie and shrugged, "I honestly don't know. Alex?"

They were asking for his input?

"I think if the manpower can be spared, you should send it. For our own peace of mind we should try," Alex said after a moment to consider.

Eric nodded, and so did Jeanie. Simons took that as a sign he was to proceed, and he gave a nod and left the room.

Alex sighed, "I can't believe he did this to her," he said quietly.

Eric looked as though he was suppressing his own anger. "For years, they seemed to be so happy. I don't understand what went wrong. Or how Tim could flip from being utterly devoted to his wife, to treating her like a stranger almost overnight."

"I'm worried about her," Jeanie sounded tearful, though her eyes were dry.

"We'll keep an eye on her," Eric tried to reassure her. "Maybe you should have a spa day, just the two of you, like you used to do?"

Jeanie smiled, "I'm not sure she'd leave Alvin alone for a day."

"I think it would do her good, to get away."

Eric glanced at Alex, "we could look after the kids quite capably, right Alex?"

"Sure," he nodded, and checked his watch. He got to his feet and looked in the direction his sister had gone, wishing he could do more. "You'll let me know if anything happens?"

Eric nodded and also got to his feet, "will we see you again soon?"

Alex knew he had to do everything he could to help Christina now that Tim had absconded, and he nodded. "Yeah I'll be around."

TWELVE

It was just after ten when he reached the gym, and after a quick glance around he confirmed there was no sign of Charlie waiting outside for him. But as their plans weren't set in stone, he knew she could be inside already, so he went in and changed his clothes.

When he entered the gym proper, he saw that a few middle aged ladies were on the rowing machines, and Charlie was at the furthest treadmill once again, though she wasn't moving.

Alex was pleased that she had come, as he was sure she was reluctant to do so after her last experience. She didn't notice him as he approached, she seemed to be pushing buttons on the treadmills entertainment system.

"Hey," he called as he got closer. He was glad to see that she was wearing a t-shirt today at least, though the grey sweatshirt was on the floor beside her.

She seemed alarmed at first, but then gave him a shy smile, "hello Alex."

He returned the smile, "glad to see you came back."

She shrugged, "I have to do this."

"What are you trying to do?" He was curious. "Run faster, or be healthier?"

"Both," she blushed a little.

"Are you in danger?"

"No, not exactly," she looked down at her feet.

Alex didn't want to push her, "okay. If you want to improve your fitness, first you have to get your heart fit. Have you thought about swimming? It's one of the best cardio options out there."

She shook her head, "I don't know how to swim," she said this still staring at her feet.

"Uh, I could teach you if it is something you want to consider?"

Charlie lifted her gaze, "I couldn't get a bathing suit, but thank you."

"If it's a case of money being the issue, I could help you."

She bit her lip, "maybe at some point, but I don't think I'm ready."

Alex nodded, "okay." He was more than a little concerned by her demeanor, as if she were used to always apologizing. "If you're determined to do the treadmill, I would say you need to warm up, then start out at a walk, and gradually as your blood gets pumping, slowly start to up the pace."

Charlie nodded, "I seem to get out of breath really easily."

"Well, the more you do it, the easier you'll find it. Soon you'll see you can do ten minutes where starting out you couldn't even do five. And you must warm down as well, or you'll just end up with cramps."

"Did you figure all this out the hard way?" she joked.

"Pretty much. I wasn't kidding, I was so skinny," he didn't add that he'd been going through withdrawal at the same time. "But I know for a fact that if you have the determination to reach your goal, you will succeed."

She seemed to study him for a moment, then she smiled, "you're very kind to be helping me this way."

Alex shrugged, "like I said, I know what it's like to want to improve your physical health." He turned to the treadmill and pushed some buttons.

"It's amazing isn't it, you can play songs. I couldn't figure out how to make it work though," Charlie said, turning back to her own machine.

Alex didn't think it was that fascinating, but her own wonder at this mundane fact seemed odd to him. "It just picks up the local radio stations. If you're a premium member I think you can watch tv shows and get Spotify, but you need headphones to hear it I think."

She seemed disappointed, "oh I see. What's Spotify?"

"An app that let's you listen to music," he was baffled that she didn't know this. "A bit like YouTube but not videos. Think you can listen to podcasts as well now."

Another look of confusion, "I'll just confess now I have no idea what half of those words meant," she said with another blush.

He was baffled, "how old are you?"

"Twenty-four," she shook her head in embarrassment. "I've just been raised in a very strict household."

"No TV?"

"No anything," she said this defensively.

Alex winced, "I'll ask again, do you need help? Do you need somewhere to go?"

Charlie seemed to consider it, "I have nowhere to go. And I have no job, no money, nothing. I hadn't got that far into my plan," she halted herself, as if she feared she would be scolded.

"Please ask me for help. I can't force you to do anything, and I never would, but if you are

135

in danger, you don't have to wait for the right time to leave."

Charlie's eyes suddenly filled with tears, "that's just it, I'm not in danger. He provides for me. I have clothes on my back and food to eat, and all I have to do is cook and clean and never complain. If he knew I was here now he'd probably lock me up."

"Charlie, you don't have to live like that," he said gently. "Is he your husband, or boyfriend? Either way you are free to leave."

She shook her head, "it's not like that, he's my father."

Alex was taken aback, and he stared at her for a moment. "You are entitled to live your own life, you're a grown woman."

She blushed again, "not in his eyes."

"Don't you have friends?"

She shook her head, "never."

"What about at school or College?"

"I was home schooled."

He was stunned again, "what about your mother?"

"She died when I was very little," she said, and the tears started to fall. "I'm so sorry," she wiped at her eyes.

Alex shook his head, "why are you apologizing?"

"I must sound silly," she said as she sniffed.

"If I can be blunt, you just sound oppressed," Alex stepped off the treadmill and offered her his hand. "Forget the treadmill, let's go sit down."

She stared at the offered hand for a moment, then met his eyes again, "okay." She picked up her sweatshirt and she clutched it in both hands.

Alex realized she wouldn't take his hand, and he wasn't offended. She was shy, and it was no wonder. He used his hand to gesture to a nearby seat, and without waiting for her, he went to it.

Charlie sat at the other end of it and wiped her face with the sweatshirt.

A comfortable silence fell between them, while Alex tried to wrap his head around a woman being in the predicament she was in.

Charlie interrupted the silence, "what can I do?"

"If you are unhappy and you want to leave, you are entitled to do so," he said simply. He met her eyes, and she seemed reluctant to believe him.

"But where would I go?"

Alex blanked for a second, "I'm sure there are shelters, until we could figure out something else."

"I'd hate to take the space of someone who really needed it," she said immediately.

"I have a place," he offered, and he felt himself blush. "If you won't go to a shelter, you could stay at my place."

She blushed too, "I'd hate to be an inconvenience."

Alex shrugged, "I'm hardly there if I'm being honest. I spend a lot of time either at work, or with my family."

"Your family?"

"Yeah," he smiled. "Two brothers, one sister, and their kids. They have room for me and I stay there quite a lot."

Charlie stared at the wall for a moment, "but if I were to leave, and go with you...What do I do next?"

Alex shrugged, "whatever you like? You could get a job, go back to school, go travelling. The world is your oyster."

She bit her lip, "I have nothing to pay you with, until I can find a job."

"I'm not asking for anything."

Charlie studied him again, "I just don't understand."

"What?"

She hesitated, "what's in it for you?"

He knew that she hadn't meant to hurt his feelings with that, but it still stung. "Believe it or not, there are people in this world who are capable of being selfless. I'm not saying I'm perfect, but this is something I can do, to help another fellow human being."

She was thoughtful again, and Alex really did wonder why he was offering to help her, and thought instantly of his old Captain. He'd taken Alex under his wing with no expectation of a return, and he knew this was his way of paying it forward.

"Once, many years ago, I was in a terrible place. Physically and mentally. And then a man came along, who helped me the way I didn't even really know I needed. It got my life on track, and I know now, that if he hadn't helped me...I'd probably be dead now."

He turned towards Charlie, and held his hands out, "I told you before, that I'm not trying to romance you. That's true, I have no ulterior motives here. You can trust me."

"You're a cop," she said simply.

He nodded, "exactly."

THIRTEEN

After the quick decision that she didn't want to return home to collect anything, they left the gym without the workout. Alex quickly changed in the locker room and met Charlie by the front door, "are you sure you don't want to get anything?"

She paused, "what do you think I should do?" She seemed incapable of deciding for sure. "There are just some clothes."

"I'm sure you'll be more comfortable with some of your own things," he said. "But if you don't want to go back it's understandable, and I'm sure I have clothing you can wear until we can get you some new things."

"When I get a job I'll pay you back, every single penny, I promise," she said immediately.

Alex smiled, "please don't worry about it." How could he explain that he didn't need the money? The fact that his father had been a successful lawyer was one thing, but that his sister-in-law was a millionaire was something else. Money was something that he thankfully hadn't ever had to worry about. But it wasn't a fact he found easy to share, as it tended to cause issues.

At his car, he threw his bag in the trunk, and gestured for her to get in.

She hesitated for a moment, and Alex allowed her the time she needed. It was a big decision, and he didn't want to influence her in any way as she also needed to learn how to think for herself.

Alex started the engine, and that seemed to prompt her to get into the car. "Is it far?" she asked, and he thought he heard a trace of fear.

"No, about five minutes. You don't have anything to be afraid of."

She checked the clock on the dash, "he'll be home again in a couple of hours. He'll probably call the police."

"You aren't breaking any laws. But this is why it's sometimes wise to leave a note or a letter. Save's any potential misunderstanding." Alex didn't put the vehicle into motion, as he'd already proposed this idea to her, but she had said no.

"Maybe I should do that," she winced.

"It would be a good idea I think," he gave her a smile. "You don't have to stay long, and I can come with you if you like."

She looked alarmed, "no, the neighbors would think you'd abducted me!"

He laughed, "do you care? You aren't going

to have to see them again."

"Well," she considered that. "I guess you're right. But I think it's best I do it alone."

"So what am I doing?"

She gave an assertive nod and said, "okay I'll go and leave a note. But please wait in the car?"

Alex nodded, "okay if that's what you want?"

He set the car rolling forward in the direction they had walked before.

"Should I take my birth certificate?"

"Anything you can lay your hands on would be helpful to you at a later date. If you have a passport you should take it as well."

"I don't," she said, and he wasn't surprised. After a minute of driving, she said, "stop here please?"

Alex did as she asked. It was where they'd parted ways when he'd walked her home last week.

She took a deep breath, "wait here please?"

"If you're sure?" Alex got out of the car as she did, intending to smoke a cigarette while she was gone.

Charlie looked at him, confused as to why he'd exited the vehicle with her.

"I'll wait here and smoke a cigarette. Don't take too long or I'll drive around the corner and start honking the horn," he joked.

She looked startled, "I won't be long, I promise."

Alex nodded and watched her jog lightly in the direction she had previously gone. Once she was out of sight he lit a cigarette, and kept a steady eye on the street ahead. There were no teenagers partying tonight at least, and the only sound was the gentle breeze moving through the tree branches.

He was halfway through his smoke when he saw a shadowy figure with a large bag over their shoulder hurrying back towards him, and he came forward to help Charlie. "Got everything you need?" He took the refuse sack from her hands.

She nodded, "I wrote him a note too."

"What did you say?" Alex threw his cigarette down a drain and walked back to the car.

"I've moved out. Please don't come looking for me. I'm a grown woman entitled to live my own life." As Charlie said this, Alex was pleased to see a little smile on her face.

"Good. Now if he calls the police, they'll take one look at that note and tell him there's nothing he can do."

"I got my birth certificate," she said, pleased with herself. "It felt so exciting," she sounded giddy.

Alex stowed her bag in the trunk, and resumed his seat behind the wheel. "Good job."

Once Charlie was seated once more she gave him a real smile, "thank you."

"You're welcome," he said sincerely. "By the way my place is above a shoe store."

"Oh, interesting."

Alex laughed, "well, I only mention it, because we will have to go through it to get to my apartment."

Charlie sighed, "I can't believe I've done this. Run away with a strange man." She laughed again.

"Isn't it great," Alex laughed as well. He executed a U-turn in the road and headed home, already thinking ahead to the fact that he would offer Charlie the bed and he would take the couch. After this first night if she was okay with being alone, he would just move out and let her take over the lease. Eric and Jeanie wouldn't mind if he decided to reside with them, he was sure.

He parked in his usual spot and faced Charlie before exiting the car, "are you okay?"

She smiled and nodded, "yes."

"Okay, well let's get you settled."

After retrieving her bag from the trunk, he led her to the shoe store, where the window display showed silver sequined sandals were on sale.

"Women actually wear those?" Charlie asked with doubt.

Alex unlocked the door with a laugh, "I'm sure some do, but mostly drag queens shop for that kind of shoe." Once he'd unlocked the door he quickly punched in the security code to deactivate the alarm. He stepped inside and held the door open for her.

Charlie was confused, "drag queen?" She stepped inside and looked around. The shop lights were low as it was late at night, but he knew she'd be noticing most of the stock was sequined.

Alex locked the door behind them and reactivated the alarm, ushering her through the store. "Drag queens are gentlemen who adopt female persona's, for the purposes of entertainment, but in some cases for identity."

Once they were in the stairwell to his apartment, Charlie let out a little gasp. "Oh you mean homosexuals?"

Alex laughed at the naivety in her voice. "Well, the majority are, but some straight or transgender people do it too."

145

Alex opened the door to his apartment, and stepped inside to hold the door open for Charlie, who was wide eyed and full of wonder as she looked around. "It's lovely Alex," she smiled.

He was pleased by her approval. To him the space looked sparse, other than the books and plants. There really was nothing here to mark the place as his. "I'm glad you like it," he put her bag on the couch and gestured around. "As you can see there's just a little kitchen," he pointed to his open plan kitchen area, and then gestured through to the little doorway off to the side. "There's the bathroom, no tub I'm afraid, just a shower cubicle."

He went to his bedroom and was glad to see that he had made the bed at least, "you can have the bed, I'll sleep on the couch."

"Oh no Alex, I couldn't take your bed," she objected.

He laughed, "Charlie I'll be up and out to work really early, you won't want me disturbing you." He went to his dresser and removed clothing for the following day. Before he could turn around Charlie barreled into him and hugged him tightly.

Alarmed, as her shyness up until this point had meant she wouldn't even take his hand, he didn't know how to react. "Whoa, you okay?"

Charlie started to weep with huge wracking sobs that shook her body, "thank you…so much."

Alex put an arm around her and did all he could think of to do, patted her hair, which was still piled on top of her head in a red bundle. "Charlie, you're going to be okay."

She stepped away as fast as she had gripped him, and she wiped at her eyes while a heavy blush colored her cheeks. "Is this real?"

Knowing she must be feeling overwhelmed, he gave her the most gentle smile he had in his arsenal. "This is real, and you've taken the first steps at independence."

She laughed, "not really independent when I'm imposing on you."

He shook his head, "I've just expedited a process you had already begun."

She nodded, "I just feel so…" she faltered for a moment.

"Liberated?" Alex offered.

She smiled and nodded, "I've never felt so free."

"Well, welcome to freedom."

FOURTEEN

Alex had a brief moment of confusion when he woke, as he wasn't used to sleeping on his couch, and it was too short for his bulk leaving him with an ache in his hips from curling his legs in.

He rolled over and was surprised to see Charlie sat on the floor in front of his TV, gripping the remote as she watched RuPaul's Drag Race muted.

Alex laughed. He had introduced her to the show last night as a way to distract her from her excitement. He'd believed that she would go to bed at some point, and he must have fallen asleep on the couch.

Charlie looked at him as he'd laughed, and she smiled, "this is amazing."

"I didn't realize you would become addicted," he grimaced as he stretched his limbs.

"I did sleep a little, but I'm used to waking up at 4."

"Good God, why at 4?"

She shrugged and looked a little embarrassed, "laundry had to be done by 8." She paused the TV show and got to her feet.

He saw that she had showered and was

dressed in a simple long sleeved and full length black dress. Shapeless and oversized, it hid any of her shape. Her hair was loose and damp, but it fell to the middle of her back.

"What time is it?" he pulled himself into a sitting position and yawned.

"Nearly six," she smiled. "Should I make you some breakfast?"

Alex laughed, "good luck, I think the cupboards are bare."

Charlie looked a little disappointed, but went to the kitchen cupboards and saw that they were indeed quite bare. She checked the fridge then, and turned her nose up at the expired milk and moldy cheese.

"I'm sorry there isn't any food, but I'll leave you some money today, maybe you could go to the store down the street and get some essentials for yourself." He felt like he needed to emphasize that she wasn't expected to care for him and only herself.

She closed the fridge and clasped her hands awkwardly, "I don't know what to do with myself."

"You don't have to do anything, that's the whole point. You'll probably need a few days just to wrap your head around that fact."

She looked down at the floor and her bare

feet. "I've never not had anything to do."

He winced, "you could read any of the books, or watch TV. When I have some time I'll sit down with you to put together a resumé."

She nodded, "I am grateful to you."

"You keep saying that," he said, not unkindly, getting to his feet. He went to the kitchen where she was and picked up his keys from the counter. After quickly removing his car key, he put them down again, "if you go out during the day you'll just need to lock the apartment door, which is this key. Frankie who runs the shop might ask who you are, just tell him you're staying with me, and I'll talk to him later, to explain the situation."

Charlie nodded, "is Frankie a drag queen?"

Alex laughed, "he might be, I've never asked."

She smiled, "I like drag queens, they're so vulgar."

He laughed again, "true, but you always know where you stand."

"My father always said that homosexuals were perverts," her tone was in no was derogatory, but she was just simply imparting that her father was bigoted.

Alex was angry, "that's a very hateful view."

Charlie nodded in agreement. "Are you-?"

she stopped herself.

Alex raised an eyebrow. "Am I what?"

She blushed, "a drag queen?"

He laughed, "no, but I respect their ability to walk in heels."

"Are you homosexual?"

"Does that matter?"

She shook her head, "no, not to me. I've always thought that my father was very judgmental, when in fact the bible very clearly states that God is our only judge, man is supposed to love as God does. It never felt right that he had so much hatred inside him."

He studied her for a moment, and after he determined that she was just innocently curious, he said, "I'm bisexual. And I know you're just curious, but please be aware that some people aren't comfortable talking about their sexuality so openly."

Charlie considered this, "I'm sorry, I just feel that I have a lot to learn."

"You do, but I'm afraid I need to shower before I go to work." He picked up his phone and saw that the battery was dead, so he plugged it in and then collected his clothing to go and shower. "Do you need the bathroom?" he remembered to ask before he monopolized the only toilet in the house.

"No thank you," she resumed her spot on the floor in front of the TV, and Alex took that to mean that he was free to carry out his ablutions.

FIFTEEN

After leaving Charlie with some cash and a hastily drawn map showing the local grocery store, Alex left to go to work. While he was driving he had a call from an unknown number, which he answered, "Alex Steinberg," with his Bluetooth navigation.

"It's Ryan Miller, I'm sorry is it too early?"

"No not at all, I'm just driving. Are you okay?"

A slight pause, "yeah, I'll go ahead with the statement," the man sounded as though he were grimacing.

"Okay, I'm glad you said that Ryan, you'll feel better once you've got a restraining order in place."

Miller sighed, "I know it's what Grace would tell me to do."

Alex didn't know how to respond to that.

"I don't know what I'm going to say at work, when they ask me though," he added.

"Did your boss leave you with the ultimatum?"

"No, but I'm sure after the way he spoke to me yesterday, he will ask."

Alex winced, "your response is to ask what

your personal life has to do with your ability to do your job. It's none of his business."

Miller laughed without any trace of humor, "yeah I have a feeling that won't fly."

"Honestly, if it gets to the point where he's threatening your job, he is breaking the law. Maybe point that out to him."

"Yeah," he sounded as if he hadn't slept well. "I guess I'll just have to roll with the punches."

"I'll do everything I can to help you, I promise you that much," Alex pledged. "And I want you to call me any time, okay? It isn't my job talking, I want to help you if I can, and I have a lot of people in my circle who can also help."

"If things go as badly as I think they might, I will definitely be in touch," Miller sounded as though he was angry, and Alex didn't blame him. He knew how it felt when life seemed to close in on you.

A child called to Ryan in the background, and he sighed, "I have to go, wish me luck."

"Good luck Ryan." The call ended, and Alex hoped that this guy caught a break soon.

When he pulled up to the station, he quickly established that there was nowhere to park, and he decided to park at Joey's, which was on the same block. He saw Fuller inside as he got out of his car, so he decided to join her.

She was eating toast when he sat down beside her at the counter, and she gave him a nod of acknowledgement.

"Morning," he said. "I couldn't park, so I came here."

Fuller nodded again, "same. Also I thought I'd stuff some carbs as we'll be tied to the desk all day again. I was starving yesterday."

"Good idea," he wondered if he should do the same. "How was your evening?"

She shrugged, "we didn't down as many bosses as we wanted, so it wasn't great."

He remembered she was planning on playing a game, which reminded him of Tim, who had also gone missing last night. He should call Eric. He pulled out his phone and tapped on his contact list, "sorry you just reminded me I needed to call my brother," he explained so he didn't seem rude.

Fuller didn't seem bothered.

The waitress from yesterday came to him while the call rang, and just ask Eric answered, Alex told her, "Apple juice please, and a stack of toast."

"Okay," Eric sounded tired, but amused.

"Sorry, are you at work?"

"I am, and it's fine."

"Any updates on Tim?"

"Yes and no. Simon's found his car headed north on a traffic cam, Lord only knows how they managed that, but then they lost trace of him. We've asked if they can continue the search, but discreetly. Jeanie has considered asking Hunter to execute a separate team to track and trace him, so our security isn't compromised."

"Does he have any other family? Could he be going to them?"

Fuller gave him a curious look, but continued to eat her toast, which looked like it was covered in some kind of currant jam.

"Christina said his parents were dead, and he had no siblings, so we don't think he has any other family. He could just be aimlessly running."

"Not to sound uncaring, but he is entitled to do what he likes."

Eric hesitated, then sighed, "I know. I'm so angry he's done this to Christina."

"I'm angry that he's being selfish in general," Alex gave the waitress a smile as she delivered his toast, and she exchanged a few words with Fuller. "Listen, I hate to impose but I am going to have to move back in with you guys."

"Tired of the shoe store already?" Eric said

with a laugh.

"Not exactly, but someone else is occupying it now," Alex wedged the phone against his shoulder so he could butter some toast. "I'll explain later, I'm running late today."

"Okay, should we expect you for dinner?"

He thought of Charlie, "no, I'll be along after though. How is Christina?"

Eric hesitated, "the same."

Alex could see then that Christina had truly been alone in her marriage for so long now, that the absence of her husband made no difference. "She'll get through this."

"No doubt. But I'm going to have to carry on this chat later, I've got a meeting in ten minutes."

"No problem, see you later." Alex ended the call. Fuller had finished her toast and was sipping coffee, watching him with curiosity. "Sorry about that."

She shrugged, "I love a good family drama. Everything okay?"

Alex shrugged, "it's a long story." He attacked his toast and checked the time, he would need to eat fast.

Fuller smiled, "well it sounds like your life is way more exciting than mine. I'm thinking about getting my first cat, that's how boring I am."

Alex laughed when he realized all that had happened in the space of a week, "my sister is having a few marital problems."

Fuller wrinkled her nose, "that's why marriage is a bad idea. Staying single is the only sure fire way to avoid divorce."

He laughed again.

The waitress returned, "anything else for you?"

He shook his head, "no thank you." He finished his first piece of toast and gulped down his apple juice. When he pulled out his wallet he realized he'd left all his cash with Charlie.

Fuller saw his empty wallet and chuckled, "I got this."

"Sorry, I'll pay you back," he felt a slight flush color his cheeks. "I got a girl out of an abusive home and she's in my place. I left her my cash so she could get food. I didn't plan ahead."

Fuller raised a brow, "you rescued a damsel in distress?"

"Sort of," he picked up his toast off the plate and figured he'd continue to eat as they walked to the station.

His partner put cash on the counter and called, "Agnes, see you tomorrow."

"Thanks Agnes," he called with his mouth

full.

Agnes smiled at them both, "have a good day."

Once they were outside, Fuller pulled on a light jacket as they walked, and she gave him an amused smirk as he continued to eat. "You strike me as a hungry guy."

He nodded, "I work out a lot, and my metabolism burns pretty fast."

She nodded, "looking forward to another day at the desk?"

He shrugged, "it's not the worst."

Within an hour he regretted that statement. The waiting room was filled with angry patrons today, and even the old ladies seemed to be argumentative.

Sue pointed them both to the same desks they had occupied yesterday, and within seconds Carter was at his side. None of the arrogance from yesterday was present, and Alex was glad.

Carter rolled his eyes and handed him the clipboard, "they're rabid today, good luck."

Alex smiled, grateful that the arrogance was gone, "thanks, you too."

Fuller already had an old lady sat beside her, and Alex went and collected the very bruised looking Mr. Owen from the waiting room.

"Glad they gave me a white guy," he muttered when Alex called his name, and he had to bite back his very colorful retort and be professional.

A cookie was shoved at him after he'd filed several reports, and he looked up in surprise. Sue was looking harassed, "want a coffee?"

It was rare that the lady was generous, so he hated to say no, "thank you but no, I'll take a water though."

She gave him a nod and a smile and said, "I appreciate you working so hard, I don't know what's got into them today. And we had another two go sick with the flu."

"It's okay, we're all cops," he said honestly.

"Exactly, we're all on the same team," that earned him another cookie, and he was shocked to see that it was lunchtime already.

"Running to get a sandwich, want the same as yesterday?" Fuller pulled on her jacket and was already heading for the door without stopping at his desk.

"Yes please," he called after her, making a mental note to buy her a few meals once they were released from desk duty. He stood up and stretched, still feeling achy from sleeping on the couch last night. Even his hands seemed to be hurting.

Carter came over with a fresh clipboard and frowned, "you okay man?"

Alex was taken aback by the genuine concern on his features, "just stiff."

"You look kind of pale," he put the clipboard down and seemed to study Alex, which made him feel uncomfortable.

As Alex resumed his seat, he took stock of how his body felt, and he realized that no, he didn't actually feel okay. Panic set in when he realized that the reason he was down here at all was a flu outbreak. "Shit," he groaned and lowered his head to the desk.

In all the madness of the last six months, he hadn't had his flu jab.

A hand that wasn't used to giving comfort clumsily patted his shoulder. "What do you need? Do you need to go home? Sue?" Carter called the motherly woman over.

Alex sat back in his chair, determined to at least finish out the day, "I'll be fine," his voice betrayed him by croaking on the last word. This was kicking in fast!

Sue came over and took one look at Alex, "oh no, not another one. I told Walker we needed to sanitize this whole floor when the first batch went down!" In typical middle aged lady style, she slapped her hand against Alex's forehead, surprising him.

It always surprised him when people were so willing to touch him when they knew about his illness.

"Yep, I can almost feel the fever rising. You need to get home, young man."

He shook his head, "no I'll be fine," again his voice was cracking, and he could feel the raw agony creeping into his throat.

As much as the flu was a pain for everybody, he felt a flutter of genuine fear in his gut. This could be it. He'd been textbook healthy since his attack in avoidance of this exact scenario. HIV didn't kill, but the complications from a simple everyday bug could easily do the job, and he didn't feel like he was ready to die just yet.

Trying to push back the panic, he shook his head again, and saw with dismay that Walker was now looking down at him with wide eyes, "Oh no."

Was he that grotesque? He touched his own forehead, and was surprised that he was hot, and had a sweaty sheen. Dammit. He couldn't even go back to his own apartment and hole up to fight this, he needed to be isolated, and now Charlie was there.

He zoned out for a moment as he tried to

strategize. Should he just hole up in a hotel? He couldn't very well go to All Saints House, he wouldn't want to be around the children or Jeanie like this.

And what about Charlie? He needed to help her get used to being independent. She didn't even have a phone or anybody to call in an emergency.

The self-defense class was tonight too, he'd have to call Jeanie, to let them know he wouldn't be there.

"Alex?"

He looked up at Carter, who was looking down at him with fear, "what?"

"I'll drive you home, give me your keys," he held out a hand.

He shook his head, "no I'm not that bad, I'll be fine." His throat was definitely getting sore.

Sue shook her head, "don't fight young man, you're in no fit state to drive."

Walker pointed a finger at him, "let Carter drive you, I'll let Markson know we're down another body."

Alex wanted to object, but with the rapidity the illness seemed to be hitting him, he didn't know how long until it knocked him off his feet. "I need to call my brother," he croaked, realizing he needed Brad now. He could go

163

there, to the old family home. No children or vulnerable people were there, and Brad was a doctor.

"Alright, give me his number," Carter had already picked up his own phone, and was crouching beside Alex.

He was thrown again by the change in this man today, and he wondered what had caused it. Alex pulled out his phone and was determined to call Brad himself. He wasn't a complete invalid just yet.

Brad answered after three rings, and Alex croaked a greeting, which was almost a whisper that alarmed him. Carter snatched the phone out of his hand and Alex watched as he spoke. "Your brother has caught the flu and it looks like it's hitting him hard. He needs to go home."

"No," Alex tried to protest, but there seemed to suddenly be shards of glass in his throat now.

"And he's in serious denial about it," Carter added.

Alex shook his head, he wasn't in denial about being sick, but he was determined to stay away from the children at All Saints and Charlie at his apartment. He summoned all his strength and reached up for the phone, which Carter surrendered when he realized that's what Alex wanted. "Brad can I hole up at your place?" he forced the words out, though they pained him.

"Shit you sound awful," Brad said instead of answering the question.

Alex closed his eyes in frustration. "Can I? I don't want to give this to Jeanie and the kids."

"Of course. I don't think I've touched your old room though."

"I don't care," his voice failed again, and he opened his eyes as he felt his phone being tugged from his hand. He allowed Carter to take the phone from his hand this time. The body aches were starting, and he had an urge to curl up under a heavy blanket.

Carter put a hand on his shoulder as he spoke into the phone, "Carter here, is there anything we should do for him until you get here? No I definitely wouldn't let him drive, he looks as limp as a noodle."

What on earth could have changed this man's entire demeanor overnight?

Alex was suddenly too tired to ponder it, and he closed his eyes once more.

"Whoa, what the hell happened to him? I wasn't gone that long," he heard Fuller's voice and opened his eyes again, feeling as though he may have actually fallen asleep just then. A

165

heavy coat that smelled vaguely of faded floral perfume was laid over his chest, and he looked around in bewilderment. Carter and Fuller were looking down at him.

Fuller scrunched her nose up, "jeez Steinberg you look awful."

"So everyone keeps telling me," his voice was all but gone, and the stabbing pains in his throat were enough to kill any attempt to try speaking again. What could he do about the self-defense class tonight? "Are you busy tonight?"

She looked confused, "of course not, I have no life, but I don't think you're in a fit state to be making plans."

"I had to teach my class tonight, I need a substitute," he whispered.

Fuller blinked, "your self-defense class?"

He nodded, giving himself a headache, "please?"

After a moment, she nodded, "okay, I'll do my best."

He held out his phone to her, "give me your number I'll send the details."

As she did that he pondered his next problem; Charlie.

He wondered if Christina would look in on her? He'd have to go to his place to pick up some clothes and try to make arrangements for the poor girl he'd 'rescued' but would now essentially be abandoning. He felt awful on top of the flu symptoms. He had encouraged her to leave her terrible situation. He didn't regret that, but in doing so he had made himself responsible for her transition into 'real life'.

He looked up and realized that the crowd around him had now dispersed. Carter and Sue had returned to the desk, and Fuller was perched on the desk, still typing on his phone. "I'm giving you my email as well as my number. Let me know roughly what they're expecting in this class, I've never done anything like it before."

Alex nodded and took the phone back. "Thank you," he tried to say, but nothing came out, and the action sent shards of pain down his throat, into his mouth, and seemed to make a fresh sweat break out on his forehead.

Fuller looked over her shoulder in the direction of the front desk quickly, but then faced Alex again, "Carter seems a bit more human today huh?"

He gave a gentle nod, wanting to elaborate but unable to summon the strength to verbalize.

Fuller suddenly looked sympathetic, "I'm

sorry you've caught this," she leaned down and patted his leg consolingly. It hurt.

With weak fingers, he tapped out an email to Fuller, with the address of Allen House and the time of the class. He knew he was throwing her in the deep end, so he tried to outline the lesson he had planned to give tonight, mainly anti mugging safety precautions, and quick escape techniques.

A strange jolt seemed to happen, where he suddenly realized his phone was slipping out of his fingers, as if he was falling asleep again, and Fuller was no longer in front of him. Gripping his phone, he sent the email he had been in the middle of typing and looked around.

The entire department was continuing as normal. Fuller was back at her desk, and a lady with three children was sitting opposite her.

Jesus, how did he keep slipping into sleep? The coat was warm over his front now, but his rear and head were chilled, making him shudder, but he seemed to be unable to find the strength to move the coat to cover more of him.

With a strange blankness of consciousness, but full alertness of being awake, he deduced he was delirious as a result of the fever, but he could only compare it to the few times in his college days that he had tried marijuana. Time slipped, and random thoughts occurred in a delirium that would make sense to no one but him, and even then he kept being jarred by the occasional realization that he wasn't in full control of his faculties.

Carter is being more human today, wonder what happened?

What the hell can I do about Charlie? I should have left her where she was, she probably wasn't ready to leave.

I wonder where Tim is?

I haven't seen the last two seasons of 24, wonder how it ended?

Keifer Sutherland is totally underrated as an actor.

The Lost Boys was amazing.

'People are Strange, when you're a stranger'.

He heard the song playing in his head.

Flatliners was a great movie too, Julia Roberts was probably the first red head I ever loved.

Sad when she died in Steel Magnolia's, her character was so young.

I'm gonna die young.

The jolt of fear returned, at the prospect of his own demise.

I'm scared of death. I act like I'm not, I act like an adult with a plan for life, and I'm just faking all of it. I'm a scared little kid who has no clue.

"Alex?"

He looked up to see Brad and Carter looking down at him, both with concern.

"I'm a little kid," he croaked, regretting the pain that came with the words and winced.

Brad exchanged a look with Carter who said, "yeah he's been saying weird stuff for the last ten minutes."

Brad turned back to him and gave him an evaluating look, touching his forehead with the back of his cool hand. "Okay, we can fix this, but first we need to get you out of here." He turned back to Carter, "I don't suppose you have a wheelchair here do you?"

Carter nodded, and immediately hurried away. Brad leaned over Alex and shook his head, "you're really hating this aren't you?"

Alex couldn't articulate how badly he hated feeling helpless and weak. All his vulnerabilities were exposed now that he was literally weak. "I'm scared," he tried to say, but a couple of scratchy squeaks was all that came out.

Brad seemed to understand though, as his look softened, and he gave a gentle nod, "I know you are. But this is just a flu bug. Plenty of fluids and rest, and you'll be right as rain. Do you have your meds?"

He shook his head.

"Okay. We'll stop by your place."

"Charlie," he forced out of his mouth, realizing that the name alone would mean nothing to Brad.

Brad frowned, "who is Charlie?"

"Yeah he kept saying that name," Fuller came over and offered her hand to Brad. "I'm Kathleen, I'm Alex's partner."

"I'm Brad, he didn't mention he'd been partnered again."

"It only happened yesterday. But he said something this morning about rescuing a girl from an abusive home, maybe that's Charlie?"

Alex nodded up at them both.

Brad laughed, "you rescued a damsel! Is she stashed at your place?"

Alex nodded, but he hated the laugh Brad gave, like there was anything licentious about his motives. "She needs help," he tried to speak again.

Brad held out a hand in a peaceful gesture, obviously sensing Alex was annoyed by his laughter. "Okay, one thing at a time. You're a terrible patient."

SIXTEEN

Getting into the wheelchair was a humiliating experience. Carter and Brad both took an arm each and hauled him upright, turning him into the chair that Fuller was holding in position.

Alex wanted to cry at everybody's look of pity, so he just lowered his eyes again and clutched his phone tight.

Once at Brad's car, the procedure was reversed, only now he whimpered in pain as he was hauled upright, his whole body wanting to just curl into the fetal position under a heavy blanket.

As he was lowered into the seat, a hand guided his head so he didn't bang it, and he was surprised to see it was Carter. "Is he going to be okay?" Carter asked Brad.

"I don't see why not, depends how much of an asshole patient he's going to be, I might smother him," Brad joked as he closed the car door on him. Alex could hear both of their muffled voices continuing to talk, but he no longer cared. He just wanted to get into bed.

Seconds or minutes later, Brad got into the car and started it. Alex waited for the derisive comments about Charlie or his new partner, but neither came. Brad didn't say anything actually, and he wondered if his brother was angry with him.

"Sorry," he croaked, wincing.

Brad shot him a quick look, "oh you're awake, I thought you were asleep."

Alex just gave a negative grunt.

"Don't worry about it, I was just in the middle of feeding the goats."

Alex frowned, and Brad shot him a grin.

Was this more of the delirium? Did he say goats?

"Vidya and Ray bought some goats. Misha and I were visiting them this morning."

Okay, he wasn't delirious.

"And we were about to leave anyway, I just dropped Misha at her place coz she has a meeting this afternoon, that's why it took me so long to come and get you."

Alex hadn't been aware of any waiting on his part, thanks to his new narcolepsy.

They were outside the shoe store, and Alex wondered how he was going to get out of the car. Brad shook his head, "give me your keys, I'll find your meds."

He realized he'd left his apartment keys with Charlie, "don't have them."

Brad eye rolled, "does Frankie have a key?"

Alex nodded, again feeling mortified that he was so weakened.

"Okay, is this girl going to be there?"

"Charlie," Alex croaked, wishing he could articulate her situation.

Brad seemed to know what he was trying to communicate, "easy, I'll talk to her."

Alex watched his brother exit the car and enter the shoe store, pausing to hold the door for a bag laden man. He closed his eyes against the wave of dizziness that was threatening him, and again he felt the fear rising in him as he thought of his mortality. He tried to logic through it by saying he was in excellent health, HIV aside.

Flu rarely killed people, only the elderly and infirm.

I'm infirm. I'm afraid.

Voices near the car made him open his eyes again, and he saw Brad, Frankie and Charlie stood in a group peering down at him.

When he opened his eyes, Brad bent low and opened his door so he could be a part of their conversation.

"Oh Alex, I'm so sorry you're sick," Charlie said immediately, looking concerned.

Frankie was a greying middle-aged man, who currently looked like a concerned mother, was clucking.

He felt like he owed Charlie an apology, but before he could attempt to speak, Frankie held out a hand, "Alex you need to get to bed, and Brad just told me he's going to nurse you at his house so he can keep an eye on you."

He looked at Charlie, the unspoken concern he hoped was apparent on his face.

Frankie nodded, "I might take this dear thing home with me, if she is agreeable."

Charlie looked surprised, "I don't want to be a bother," she said with a smile.

Frankie ignored her and continued to talk to Alex, "this little darling came to talk to me this morning, and I have to say it's refreshing to see that chivalry is still alive. But she can't possibly stay here alone. I wouldn't feel safe, and she will get along famously with Chantelle."

Charlie was curious, "Chantelle?"

Frankie had an old fat tabby cat, "she could do with some company during the days while I'm at work, I'm sure she gets lonely, poor kitty."

Charlie seemed amused, but looked at Alex, "I'll be fine Alex, please just get well."

Relieved that Frankie was going to step in as guardian of the young woman, Alex looked up at Brad.

"I couldn't find your medication," he explained.

"Kitchen," he managed to croak out.

Brad eye rolled and walked back into the store, leaving Frankie and Charlie peering down at him.

Charlie crouched a little, "is there anything I can do?" she asked with concern.

He gave the smallest head shake and looked up at Frankie. He held up his phone.

"You want me to call you if there are any problems?"

Maybe he did have telepathic powers, he seemed to be pretty good at non verbal communication today. He nodded, longing for the option to climb into bed and sleep. All this adulting was exhausting.

SEVENTEEN

Brad didn't fuss, and Alex was grateful. After helping him up to his old childhood bedroom and dumping him unceremoniously on the bed, he clucked to himself that he would need to get Alex a phone charger, and maybe a change of sheets.

Alex kicked off one of his boots, but struggled to kick off the other, and just fell limply back on the bed that did indeed smell a little bit musty.

"Alex what time do you usually take your meds?" Brad was in doctor mode now, pulling off the boot that had eluded him.

Drowsily, Alex had the presence of mind to open his phone and show Brad the reminder he had set daily for the early evening.

Brad nodded, and set to unbuckling Alex's belt.

Alex was briefly ashamed at this infirmity, but was thankful for the assistance, even his fingers were aching now.

"I'm going to get some paracetamol and fluids. Try to get yourself comfortable and I'll be right back, okay?"

Alex gave a soft grunt to save his throat, and

he started trying to kick his way out of his jeans.

When his legs were bare, he then attempted to unbutton his shirt, but gave up after two buttons and settled for wriggling out of it, but Brad returned while he was stuck in the sleeves.

His brother snorted a laugh and assisted him.

Once he was down to his boxers and t-shirt he allowed Brad to arrange the pillows behind him, so he was propped up.

"Here," Brad was holding out a tall glass of ice water with a straw, and a collection of pills.

Alex took the pills and poured them into his mouth without asking what they were. He didn't care. After a few long pulls on the water, which soothed his throat, he settled against the pillows. "Thanks," he mouthed.

Brad nodded, "I need to go to work soon, but Vidya is going to look in on you with some soup later okay?"

Alex cocked an eyebrow.

"Just be good and allow people to look after you," he said firmly. Then he crouched down beside the bed for a moment and took Alex's phone off the nightstand to plug it into a power chord. "You're powered up, just call me if you need me. And don't be alarmed if Misha comes in either."

He nodded. He didn't care, he just wanted

sleep.

Brad threw the covers over Alex's legs, then gave him an encouraging nod, and left him to rest, and as he began to fall asleep he heard his phone vibrate on the nightstand.

Turning onto his side, he faced the phone and clumsily unlocked it.

A number he didn't recognize had messaged him saying, 'I'm worried about you, let me know if you need anything'.

Without knowing who it was, he just replied 'Kay' and returned the phone to the nightstand.

He didn't know how long he slept for. It was a welcome refuge against the aches and shivers that seemed to alert him occasionally to his infirmity. At one point he woke and was painfully thirsty, so he downed the water that Brad had left, and he wanted more, though he lacked the energy to get it.

Vidya did arrive with Misha, and something that smelled delicious. He opened his eyes to see Misha's long curtain of black hair hanging low as she stooped down over him. "Hello Alex," she said softly as she peeled the covers back from his sweaty body.

He had the presence of mind to be embarrassed at his sweaty body, and the smell that must be coming from him, but she clucked and said "oh you poor thing."

Then Vidya was there. He loved this fussy mother hen, and he had done so since their first meeting when she had both comforted him for not being able to donate blood and scolded him for storming off. Something about her tiny form and the magnitude of her presence was funny, and he released a laugh now, though he couldn't say why.

"Alex we're going to change these sheets," Misha announced. He saw that she had a pile of fresh sheets in her hands.

Vidya was pointing at the armchair near the bed, "sit," she instructed. "You need soup."

Again this struck him as funny. Short people being bossy was always funny.

"He might not be able to sit up," Misha worried.

Oh they wanted him to sit, and go to the chair? That made sense now. Painfully, he rolled to his side, and pushed with his arms to raise himself to a sitting position. The world swirled in front of him, and four female hands reached out to steady him.

Closing his eyes he took a deep breath and croaked a "sorry."

"Silly sorry," Vidya said. "Move your big

bones to that chair Alex," she said with her encouraging tone.

Yes he knew what he needed to do. Feeling steadier, he opened his eyes, and before he could think too much, he pushed himself out of the bed, stumbled a step, then fell into the armchair.

"Are you hot or cold?" Vidya was slapping a hand against his forehead.

"Hot," he croaked. "Thirsty."

Within moments she was holding a tray out to place on his lap. He reached for the tall glass of ice water and swallowed it down, leaving a rattling stack of ice in its wake.

Vidya took the glass from him then pointed to the bowl, "you start eating, I'll get more water."

Alex watched her go, then focused on Misha, who was stripping off the dirty sheets. He felt he owed her an apology too, so he croaked another "sorry."

She glanced over her shoulder as she stripped the pillow and gave him a smile. "Don't be silly Alex, we all get sick."

He knew this, it was a simple fact of humanity. But *he* did not get sick. It had been his mission since that junkie had overdosed him on Heroin, to avoid ever getting sick. Because what was the leading cause of death in the end? Sickness.

Was it all pointless? Had he been in denial this whole time about his mortality? With a sinking feeling, he began to suspect that not only had he been using his HIV as a shield against the world of romance, he'd been using his muscles as a form of denial about his mortality.

Brad was right. We were all *mortal*, on an unknown and ever winding down clock.

The wave of anxiety hit once more, like a blast of heat through his body that wasn't fever, and he was ashamed to feel his eyes filling with tears. "I'm going to die," he said, though he wasn't sure what words made it through his tightening razor lined throat.

Misha was in front of him immediately, cupping his cheek. Her face was full of sympathy, and alarm. "No Alex, you're going to be fine. It's just the flu."

He shook his head, and actually felt the tears falling now. Mortified, he swiped a hand across his eyes to clear them. How could he explain that it wasn't this flu bug he was afraid of? That what was causing the tears to flow right now wasn't a common virus, but the awareness that one day he would die.

One day, he would cease to be. And he had no legacy, no love for him beyond his family. No biological link of life beyond his own. No renown. In a hundred years, who would ever know that Alex Steinberg had ever existed. And what did he care? He wouldn't. He would be dead.

Misha brushed his hair back off his forehead, it was getting long, he had meant to have a haircut a few weeks ago. "Alex, I can't pretend to know how you feel having HIV. I know that it must be like having a constant cloud over your head. But you're healthy, and you're young. You're strong. You will be fine," she said with confidence.

Alex could feel the tears were still flowing, and there was a terrible calm that came with them. "I never thought about death before," he said painfully and with honesty. And it was true. He had been so focused on staying alive and staying healthy, and getting as strong as he could physically. But he had never accepted the fact that in the end, it would all come to the same.

Misha picked up the spoon in the soup, and held it out for him to sip. Maybe to give her something to do to avoid the subject.

As he put his lips to the spoon and sipped,

she gave him a gentle smile. "Mortality is a terrible realization isn't it."

As the soup washed down his throat, warm and soothing and delicious, he knew that she understood, and he gave a small nod.

Misha continued to spoon the soup to his mouth. "I think it's the hardest thing about being an adult. Knowing it's the final chapter."

That was it exactly.

"Not knowing how many pages are left in the book as well, although I'm not sure if it is better or worse to know precisely when the end will come."

"So stupid," he whispered, and he meant himself.

"Alex, you're one of the smartest guys I know. But you feel things to their fullest, like your whole family. I've noticed that you Steinberg's don't do anything by half. Can I speak candidly?"

He nodded again, and sipped the soup.

"The fact that you're so smart probably fuels the level of denial you've had over life, if you don't mind me saying," she continued to smile. "Your focus has been so apparent, that in your quest to stay alive, you've forgotten to live. Because that's all we can do. Make the best of the time that we do have, because God only knows how long we've got. And I know that Brad has told you this a million times."

It was true.

"You haven't done anything wrong either, I think if I'd been stuck with a dirty needle my reaction would have been the same. Get the body to maximum fitness and maintain it. Deny that I'd ever been violated."

Another wave of heat flooded his system when her words brought about another shock. The violation.

"Oh Alex," she lowered the spoon when she saw fresh tears falling. "I'm so sorry," she whispered as she removed the lap tray and held him awkwardly as he wept.

He couldn't even articulate this feeling now. He was reliving the event as if he were watching a movie. The stupid skinny librarian marching up to the junkies as if he had the power. What an idiot. Talking his big words and pointing them away, as if they would listen. This skinny man had no idea he was about to die.

Even though his heart would continue to beat, this man was about to die. This man. This boring man, who had thought he was smart. Thought he knew best. Thought that good would always triumph over bad, because that's what happened in his little story books.

185

Sure there were always casualties, people got hurt all the time, but that was okay, because it was other people. Not people he knew or loved. Certainly never himself, because he was as good as they came. Good and boring.

When the needle had pierced him, he had been shocked, as anyone would have been. But he had thought then, 'I'm going to die.' And as the drug had overridden his senses, part of him hadn't cared, as in that moment he was a part of some unarticulated bigger thing. Cosmic euphoria. He had felt like he had left his body, or that he was only barely clinging onto it as something was pulling at him to leave, to join, to sleep.

Only the fear had kept him clinging to his breath.

The next conscious memory he had was the hospital where they had told him the facts, and those facts had given him that new drive and purpose. The purpose of health and denial. He'd had therapy since, he'd put all this to bed years ago, so why was he so shaken now.

Misha brushed his hair back, and seemed to know where his thoughts were. "Sometimes it can take time to heal, or even accept the things that happen to us," she said softly, and gently released him from her hug, brushing her fingers through his hair again.

He had never accepted the violation that he had suffered. He hadn't mourned for the life he should have lived. The life that had ended when that needle had dosed him with the fatal cocktail.

Therapists had heard him speak the words of acceptance, the logical knowledge of the incident. And he himself had believed it too.

But now, it was almost as if this flu bug had unlocked some secret vault of hurt and feeling that he'd been hiding, along with his vulnerability.

Vidya came in holding a full glass of water, as well as a pitcher. She saw Alex and his tears, and her militant mother look softened.

He was enveloped in feminine touch and he cried unashamedly.

EIGHTEEN

Thirst. And beeping.

His eyes opened and he dimly noticed that it must be dark outside now, and the house seemed quiet, other than his phone rhythmically pulsing on the nightstand. When Alex moved his head toward it, he noted that his pillow was soaked in sweat once more.

Gingerly, he raised himself up on one elbow, and looked down at his phone. It was time to take his medication. He dismissed the reminder, switched on the lamp and then greedily snatched up the glass of water. The ice must have melted a long time ago, but it was still refreshing, and he downed the glass entirely.

Once it was empty, he saw that the pitcher was within reach on the nightstand.

His phone flashed again, this time with a message alert. Picking up the phone, he saw he had a few missed calls. One from Eric, and two from unknown numbers. The same message that had said it was worried about him earlier had messaged again in reply to Alex's 'kay' response. 'I mean it, I know we didn't get off to the best start, and I'm sorry about that.'

Who the hell was this? But now he was stuck in the dilemma of not wanting to ask blatantly 'who are you?' for fear of being rude.

He stuck with playing it safe, and just replied with the truth. 'Slept all day, I smell like Shrek's armpit. I'm sure I'll be fine in a few days.'

And he did stink. Switching on the lamp, he squinted as his eyes adjusted to the glare, then he looked around the room of his childhood, depressed that the young man who had studiously alphabetized his books wouldn't ever be back.

Misha appeared in the doorway again, and smiled when she saw that he was awake. "I was going to wake you for your medication." She was carrying a tray.

Alex pushed himself up weakly, and tried to give her a smile, but he felt like it came across more as a grimace. He tried to say thank you when she laid the tray in his lap, but his throat only allowed a scratchy whistle out.

"Don't try to talk," she shushed him. "Don't even fully wake up. Just take the medicine, and if you like there is some custard."

He sniffed a laugh at that.

Misha sat on the edge of the bed, and poured him a fresh glass of water while he picked up the pills. He recognized his regular medicine, and guessed that the rest of the pills were for his flu symptoms.

Misha explained "Brad told me to give you these now, he won't be home for another couple of hours yet."

After swallowing the pills with yet another full glass of water, he realized he needed to pee. With a nudge he tried to indicate she needed to lift the tray, which she did.

"Where are you going?" she said with alarm when he kicked his legs free of the sheets.

He pointed to his bathroom, and she blushed, but moved away so he could stagger to relieve himself.

When he returned he saw that she had swapped his wet pillows for the unused dry ones, and was standing holding the tray, waiting for him to resume his bed.

"Whenever I was sick as a child, my Dad would feed me custard," Misha said as she replaced the tray in his lap. "It's called Purin," she explained.

Alex envied her multi-cultural upbringing, and the richness of the two cultures that had nurtured her made their restaurant thrive. He gave her a smile which he hoped conveyed his gratitude.

Misha sat in the chair as he took a small nip at

the custard. It was sweet, he could tell that much, but other than that his taste buds were drawing a blank. His nose was starting to block as well as his throat being raw, and he was so tired, though he'd just woken up.

"If you don't like it I can get you some soup," Misha offered as he seemed hesitant to eat.

He shook his head, and took a heartier spoonful of the pudding, giving her a thumbs up.

She smiled, "throat still raw?"

He nodded, and pointed to his nose.

"Sinuses blocking?"

Another nod.

Misha gave a sympathetic nod.

"Mish! Your phone is ringing!" a male voice called.

Alex was startled, she had said Brad was at work for a couple more hours, and the voice was deeper than his brothers. He gave her what he hoped was an enquiring look.

Misha had risen to her feet at the call, "I'll be right back Alex," she said as she left the room without explaining the voice. Not that she owed Alex an explanation.

Probably just a friend.

His own phone rang then, and he saw it was Eric trying to video call. He answered and propped the phone upright on the nightstand so Eric could see him. He waved at the camera and continued to eat the custard. It was good, and the sweetness seemed to restore something within him.

Eric was squinting at the camera, taking in the sight of him. "Brad said you were sick and he left Misha playing nurse."

Alex didn't try to talk, but gave a little nod.

Ben pushed his way into frame, "Alex, you okay?"

Alex frowned and put on a pouty sad face, that made the boy giggle.

"I don't think Alex can talk buddy."

Alex shook his head in confirmation of the fact. He leaned back against the pillows and looked at Eric.

Eric seemed to understand, "I was just calling to check you were okay. And Ben was a little worried, though we all reassured him you just had the flu and that Brad was taking very good care of you."

Alex looked at the boy, who did seem very concerned. He made a show of choking, grabbing at his throat, tongue lolling, then he flopped back, making a parody of a corpse.

Ben laughed, and Alex gave a little smile. "I'll be okay," he whispered to the boy.

Lily burst onto the screen then, "do you got a fever?"

He stifled the laugh at her frantic appearance, but his throat still spasmed in pain. He gave a nod in answer to her question.

"You have to dydrate," she said bossily, and Eric laughed behind her, whispering in her ear. "I mean hydrate. That means drink water," she explained haughtily.

He held up his empty glass and nodded.

"Okay kids, you've all seen he's okay now, and we need to let him rest," Eric said, taking charge before the children monopolized the call and exhausted Alex further. He was grateful, as just trying to smile was a strain. He saw the kids backing out of frame and Eric watched them go with a smile. Alex could tell immediately when they were out of the room as Eric's indulgent smile changed and focused on Alex once more. "You okay?"

Alex nodded, knowing that Eric was enquiring as to his mental health as well as physical, and he wondered if his breakdown in front of Vidya and Misha had somehow been reported back through the grapevine.

Oddly enough, after that breakdown and the sleep he'd had, he felt a strange sense of peace at his situation. A sense of acceptance even.

But he couldn't speak about that now or articulate his new stance, he could barely swallow.

Eric accepted this, "it's cool, just rest little brother. Okay?" he said this gently, and Alex nodded.

After a silent goodbye, he ended the call and saw he'd had another message from the unknown number following his smelly comments.

'Your brother taking good care of you?'

Alex frowned and realized then who the messages must be from. 'Carter?'

Instant reply, 'yeah Steinberg?'

He was stunned for a moment, but needed to ask, 'why the 180?'

'What do you mean?'

'You and Gibson clearly hated me yesterday.'

Quite a long pause before he saw the typing animation, so he ate some more custard while he waited.

'Gibson has issues. I never hated you. I realize as I didn't call him on his shit in front of you it looked like I agreed with his attitude but I don't. I argued with him after work last night.'

Alex was surprised and looked back at yesterdays encounters, and recalled now how

Carter's only comment was that Markson had given them that assignment as he'd hung up on her florist, all the attitude had actually come from Gibson.

'Have I done anything to cause his issues?'

'No, which I pointed out. He's been a dick since Stone died to be honest. He took it personally that the bullet meant for him was what took him out. Been acting like he should have been the one who died. I think seeing Kathy back was what triggered him.'

'I don't know anything about Stone, it sucks being the new kid on the block sometimes, not knowing everybody's back story.'

'Yeah I can imagine. I'd be happy to fill you in sometime ☺'

Alex smiled at the smiley face, and realized he'd made a friend. 'Thanks. Maybe when I stop resembling the swamp monster we...' Alex stopped himself as he realized he'd been in the middle of inviting Carter out for a beer. He dropped his phone and frowned as a new dilemma hit him. Was Carter just being surface friendly? The smiley face emoji told him no, he was genuinely being friendly, but then another horrific though occurred. Was he flirting?

He decided to stick with what he typed but tagged on the end 'could talk.'

195

Carter quickly responded with 'talking would be good, you've been with the department for three months now, and you've barely spoken to anyone.'

Alex couldn't deny it, 'would you believe me if I said I was shy?'

'Actually yes. And I can imagine having the extra pressure of HIV adds to the problems of meeting new people.'

'Nailed it.' Alex smirked.

"Sorry Alex, that was my agent," Misha said as she entered his room.

He looked up to see she looked flustered, and he frowned wanting to ask her if she was okay.

Misha saw the question and shook her head, "don't ask."

That made the frown deepen.

Misha took the tray from his lap, "nothing to worry about, he's just trying to pester me to go on tour."

He felt his eyes widen, that was fantastic news for her career surely.

Misha shook her head again, "I'm not ready," she admitted, reminding him that at one point she had been in a bad marriage, and had struggled to regain her independence. Brad hadn't told him everything, but the few details he'd managed to glean had implied that her ex

196

had mentally manipulated her for years through gaslighting, and she'd prided herself on her own power since she'd divorced him.

Her determined stance now reminded him of Charlie, and he wished he could help once again. He could see how a book tour would be an amazing career milestone for her, but on the very human level, it was a long time to be away from home and security.

Pathetically he reached up and patted her arm, as that was the only comfort he was able to give in his weak state. Misha seemed to understand that this was what he was trying to convey, and she smiled at him.

Looking down at the bowl she said, "good job on the custard," she smiled. "I almost enjoyed getting sick as a kid, just for that."

Alex smirked and nodded.

"I'll get rid of this and bring up some fresh water."

He gave her a thumbs up and watched her go, then unlocked his phone again to see Carter had sent him several messages during his brief visit from Misha.

'Well I'll do now what I should have done back then. Hi I'm Lukas Carter. You can call me Luke or Luka, I'm single, I live with my mother through choice because she's in a wheelchair and I'm a good son.'

'I rarely drink alcohol, but I'm not against meeting for a coffee sometime?'

'Or food?'

'You fall asleep?'

Alex responded, 'here.'

Once he sent that he elaborated with, 'my brothers partner was just mopping my brow.'

Then he reread the messages from Luke before typing again. 'Hello Lukey, I'm Alexander Steinberg, you can call me Alex, or Lex. I am single. I rent an apartment over a shoe store but I actually spend more time at my brother's house. I have two brothers and one sister, and I'm actually a triplet. My parents are dead. I don't drink alcohol, or coffee, but I love food.'

He was smiling down at the phone when he homed in on the words that quickly came back.

'Only my Grandma gets away with calling me Lukey, and that's because I don't punch old ladies.'

Misha entered then carrying a fresh pitcher of water and a fresh glass, "that's a nice smile," she observed.

Alex switched off his phone and tried not to feel like he'd been caught flirting. Had he been flirting?

Misha gave a snort as she placed down his water. "Do you need anything else?"

Alex shook his head and attempted to croak out a "no thanks," but all that came out was a few raspy squeaks.

Misha gestured towards his phone, "you've got my number, call or text me if you need anything yeah? I'm just going to be doing some painting down in the guest room."

Alex must've looked confused, so she clarified, "Brad let me turn it into a little studio for when I stay here. He keeps trying to convince me to move in," she rolled her eyes but he knew she loved his brother.

He pointed to his phone and gave her a thumbs up, meaning yes, he would call if he needed her.

She smiled again, and left with a nod.

His phone buzzed as he was unlocking it, and he saw Luke had replied with several messages again.

'You call me Lukey in public and I'll punch your lights out.'

'I have a younger brother, must be nice to have lots of siblings.'

'What's your favorite food?'

'Xander? You being brow mopped again?'

He got himself comfy against the pillows and

had to question again what was going on here? Was this friendly dude banter or was this flirty banter?

Luke had pointed out he was single, so Alex had reciprocated that detail, but it could mean much more. He was talking more than dudes in his experience tended to. He felt that this was getting to know you talk, not friend talk. Friend talk wouldn't be asking what his favorite food was. That was prospective date talk.

'No more mopping, she was just taking away the tray she brought, and congratulating me for eating custard.'

'Custard huh?'

'My trophy is in the post.'

'Mazel Tov.'

Again Alex found himself smiling.

NINETEEN

When Alex woke up, he found himself immediately reaching for his phone, and it unlocked to the conversation he'd carried on with Luke into the early hours of the morning. He saw now that the time was just after ten and he'd had several messages this morning already, but before he read them he reread the ones from last night.

Alex felt a smile touching his lips again as he read the easy words they'd exchanged.

'I'm gonna have to go and catch some zzzzz's soon, Sue will skin me if I'm late tomorrow.'

'Scared of Sue?'

'Everybody is scared of Sue. Actually, this last couple of days has made me love the old bat.'

'You go get some sleep then princess, or scary Sue will spank you.'

'Easy tiger, we'll resume this banter when you don't resemble a slug.'

'Ugh you're not far off that description, I can't remember ever sweating this much in my life.'

'The joy of a fever, if I were there, I'd mop your brow. Or from what you've described, maybe I'd just mop you.'

At this point Alex must have fallen asleep, because then it was just messages from Lucas.

'Or maybe hose you down prison style.'

'Xander?'

'Okay, I'm guessing you've fallen asleep. Either that or you're mortally offended that I offered to mop you.'

'Don't let the bed bugs bite.'

'Morning.'

'How are you feeling today?'

'Did you die?'

'Lazy is what this is, just pure laziness.'

Alex smiled, 'I'm sick Lukey, not lazy. It's exhausting not going into the light.'

He inventoried how he felt, and the whole body aches were actually a little better. Throat and sinuses though, felt awful, and after drinking some water he determinedly got out of bed and went to the bathroom. As he relieved himself, he saw how pale and sweaty he looked in the mirror, and his t shirt was stained with sweat marks that had dried.

With a groan he knew he had to bathe, so he started a bath running, thinking the steam might also help his sinuses, but mainly thinking that at least he could lay down in a bathtub.

"Bro what the hell do you think you're

doing?" Brad exclaimed when half an hour later he walked in on Alex fresh out of his bath trying to pull the sweaty sheets off his bed and wishing he'd done it before his bath and while he was wearing more than a towel around his waist.

"Clay pigeon shooting," he croaked, pleased that he could articulate some syllables, but regretting it for the pain he experienced.

Brad shooed him away and took over the housekeeping, so Alex slumped down in his chair and leaned towards his drawers, wondering if he had any clothes here. "I packed a bag for you when I picked up your pills," Brad pointed to the floor by the door and Alex saw his bag.

Alex retrieved it and took it back to the bathroom where he dressed himself in shorts and a t-shirt. When he came out again Brad was remaking the bed with fresh sheets. "Thankfully Vidya did a load of laundry when she was here yesterday," Brad said.

Alex sat in the chair and felt like he was ready for a nap already after his exertions of the day, but he hoped at least he would smell better.

On the bedside table his phone buzzed, and Brad peeked at it. "You've got an email from Fuller, do you want to read it now or leave it?"

Alex held out his hand and Brad passed him the phone. Her email was short.

'Class went well. Met Cecily, she wondered about me taking a class regularly as demand is high. Wanted to check I wouldn't be stepping on your toes though? I had fun. Hope you're feeling better, K.'

He was pleased that it had gone well, and he tapped out a reply, 'It's not like you're stealing my baby, we've been needing more volunteers for a long time, so have at it. Still feeling like crap and I can't really talk. Mainly been sleeping. Bored already.'

A beep interrupted his focus, and he saw Brad was pointing a plastic gun at his head and frowning, "still quite high, back to bed with you."

Alex shook his head, "what the fuck is that thing?" he painfully asked with regret, resigning himself to being a mute again.

"It's a thermometer, your fever is still high, but a little better than last night."

He couldn't recall having his temperature taken during the night, or at all yesterday, and Brad's smirk seemed to show that he found his clear memory gaps hilarious.

"Just get back into bed please?" he gestured with the gun, and Alex didn't even want to argue with him.

Brad went to pull the blankets over his legs, but Alex shook his head, he was warm right now, and he needed to cool down.

Once he was propped against the pillows comfortably, Brad started gently probing his neck making him wince. "I'm just checking your glands," he explained. "Throat still sore?"

Alex nodded, and forced out the word, "swollen," on a whisper.

Brad nodded too. "Gonna have to keep an eye on that, but I don't want you to get yourself worked up again, okay?"

So everybody had heard about his meltdown. He closed his eyes and felt ashamed.

"You're doing fine Alex, nothing is alarming here. It's just the flu," Brad used his soothing doctor voice and that made him open his eyes again and give him a withering look meaning to convey that he didn't want to be babied.

Brad laughed. "Think you could handle some food?"

He didn't feel any hunger, but knew he had to keep feeding the machine, so he held up his thumb and forefinger an inch apart.

"Little food not big food?"

Alex nodded.

While Brad left the room clutching an armful

of dirty sheets, Alex checked his phone and saw he'd only had one message while he'd bathed, but he knew Luke was working now, and Sue would likely beat him if she found him texting on her watch.

'Don't go into the light.'

For some reason, Alex felt a wave of confusion hit him. This was definitely not dude banter. And how did he feel about that? Surprisingly, he felt open to it.

He must have been wearing a comical expression on his face when Brad came into the room a few minutes later, as he snorted at him while carrying a tray with a plate of scrambled eggs and a tall glass of apple juice, plus a few pieces of toast. He'd obviously ignored the little food request, but Alex actually did feel a pang of hunger at the sight of the eggs.

"Everything okay?" Brad asked as he waited for Alex to sit up so he could place the tray down on his lap.

Alex held up a hand and tipped it back and forth.

Brad sat in the chair and cocked an eyebrow at him, "yes and no? What's up?"

Alex really wanted to talk to his brother about this, but he physically couldn't. So he did the only thing he could think of, and opened his phone to the chat conversation with Luke and scrolled to the beginning and handed it over to Brad.

His brother took the phone and began to read, so Alex started eating the eggs, and he wished he could taste them fully as they were just the right texture.

He watched Brad's features while he read, and saw a few smiles at what he was reading. After a few minutes, he looked up at Alex with a shrug and a smile, "okay?"

Unfortunately he had to speak, "I don't know how to take it."

Brad frowned down at the phone, and scrolled up through the conversation again, but he quickly said, "he likes you. I don't think this is just friendly interest if that's what you're worried about, but you're right it's quite vague. But us dudes don't share details like this or talk until the early hours of the morning unless we're incentivized." Brad pointed out with an eyebrow wiggle.

Alex nodded in agreement, as that met his own theories.

"You like this guy?"

Alex thought for a moment, then shrugged, "I hadn't…considered him."

"Until he started talking to you?" Brad

guessed.

Alex nodded, and continued to eat and drink, though every swallow was painful.

"Is this the blonde guy I met when I picked you up yesterday?"

Alex nodded again.

Brad's eyes glazed over a little as he went over his memories, "ah yeah, now I think about it he did seem a little flappy like a mother hen. Cute though."

Alex sniffed and tried to stifle a laugh at his very heterosexual brother calling another guy cute.

Brad just shrugged, "I'm secure in my sexuality, and I can objectively say that he was an attractive dude, and I could totally see you two together." Then as if to secure his hetero position he thumped his chest and snorted a spit ball into throat and pretended to spit, making Alex laugh.

He sat back and took a sip of the chilled apple juice, relishing the cool relief in his throat for a moment.

"Did you want advice about this or were you just sharing?"

Alex shook his head, meaning no, he didn't want advice.

Brad nodded, "cool, well as soon as you get

your voice back we can have a proper conversation about boys, maybe do it sleepover style in our pajamas while eating ice cream."

Alex laughed and reached up to his own hair, which was getting a little long and shaggy, and made a motion of twirling it around his fingers, making Brad laugh.

"Exactly!"

TWENTY

Alex spent the rest of the day sleeping, and he briefly recalled a beep waking him up at one point, and he opened one eye to see Vidya aiming the gun at him, but he just rolled over to the cool side of the bed and went back to sleep. He'd thought he was getting better, and though the body aches and shivers had gone that morning, they resumed again and left him huddling under the blankets feeling miserable again.

At least the sweating had eased though, meaning he didn't perpetually feel damp. During a lucid moment he checked his phone as he was drinking and taking more medicine, and he felt disappointment that he hadn't had any more messages from Luke, even though now it was early evening.

Shaking off his teenage girl behavior, he focused on all the other people in his life he should have been checking in with, by first sending a message to Ryan Miller asking if everything was okay, then following that he sent Frankie a message asking if Charlie was okay.

He was in the middle of returning an email to

Cecily who had mirrored Kathy's enthusiasm about her taking on a permanent class position with his endorsement, and he offered to scout out more volunteers once he was back at work when he had a message come through from Ryan, saying nothing more had been said at work, but his workload had suddenly doubled, and he got the impression that he was in trouble.

Alex sent him a link to the website for Open Arms immediately, and explained to him that he needed to book in for a legal consultation and financial aid assistance, and to say in his request that Jeanie Saint John had referred him.

He had intended to try and push through the paperwork for the restraining order had he not been struck with the flu, and he wondered if it was now lost in the mountain of never ending inter departmental paperwork that flowed around that building.

Misha entered just as his early evening medication reminder sounded on his phone, and she was carrying a tray again. "If it helps, you're looking much better today," she commented as she waited for him to sit up before she placed the tray down.

Alex huffed and said, "thanks." More custard, which he was actually grateful for, as it slid nicely down his throat.

She checked his temperature as he took his pills, and she smiled, "temperature is coming down, Brad will be pleased."

Alex nodded, but didn't feel her optimism as he felt a tightening in his chest that could only mean a pending cough or chest infection.

"You must be so bored," Misha looked around at his room, which had no television in it, as he'd always preferred a good book. "Want me to bring in an iPad or anything?"

He shook his head.

She hovered and seemed uncomfortable for a moment, almost agitated.

"What?" he croaked.

She slumped into the chair and dropped her face into her hands. "I'm sorry," he heard her say, then she took a deep breath before lowering her hands and clenching her jaw and repeating "I'm sorry."

"For what?"

She looked down at her hands for a moment, "I'm arguing with myself. It happens quite a lot, my logic half arguing with my scared emotional side. You ever have that happen?"

He nodded and didn't know what had prompted Misha to suddenly open up to him like this. Perhaps it was his own current vulnerability and the breakdown he'd had in her presence had made her feel like they had some mutual ground.

"Can I tell you a secret?"

Another nod, but he tensed himself for whatever he was about to hear.

"I think I'm pregnant," her voice wavered and he saw tears fill her eyes as she looked up at the ceiling.

Alex relaxed but was concerned by her emotional state. "Gratz," he croaked.

She sniffed and looked down at her hands, shaking her head. "I tried for most of my marriage to get pregnant, because I stupidly thought that would fix everything. Then when it got really bad I was so relieved I didn't have a baby, I was grateful every time I got my period. I was pretty much convinced I couldn't have one. Brad convinced me to get checked out when we got together, and it turned out that I have endometriosis."

Misha took a shaky breath, "which meant that my tubes were blocked, and my chances of natural conception were slim to none. The doctor said it wasn't impossible though, and advised a contraceptive, until I was ready. Brad and I discussed it, and we agreed on the shot," she bit her lip at this point though.

Alex waited.

Misha met his eyes, then seemed to realize he was waiting for her, "I'm sorry to do this. I usually talk through big stuff with Brad or my parents, and I can't."

"Misha it's fine," he managed to say.

"What if I'm pregnant though Alex?"

"Are you asking me what Brad will say?"

The tears came again, and she nodded as she sniffed them back.

He thought for a second, and was confident when he said, "he'll be thrilled."

She let out a heavy exhale.

"Look, if you didn't have your bad history with marriage, I'm sure Brad would have proposed to you by now. But he loves you and respects your need for independence. Doesn't mean he's not just biding his time for you to be ready to be his in every way."

Misha looked startled, "really?"

Alex laughed, though he sounded like the cartoon dog Muttley. "Before you, he was alive but not living. Understand?"

She nodded and seemed touched. "I need to see a doctor to confirm, but I'm scared to tell him until I know for sure."

"You know he's a doctor right? He's probably already noticed," Alex took a long

214

drink and started to eat his custard, which eased his throat a little.

Misha considered this, "maybe."

They sat in a companionable silence for a little while, Alex eating, and Misha staring down at her hands, until the doorbell sounded downstairs. She hurried to answer it, and Alex focused on the food, checking his phone quickly and swallowing down the disappointment at no messages along with the custard.

Misha came in then carrying a basket, and a smile on her face. "I think this is for you?" she placed the basket down next to his hip.

He was confused, as at a glance the basket seemed to hold two bottles of wine. But when he studied it further, he saw that the green glass bottles he'd first identified as wine were actually bath salts if the label was to be believed. After pulling a mound of crepe paper aside, he saw a box of paracetamol, throat lozenges, sports drinks, three different spray deodorants, shampoo, shower gel and a loofah.

Misha pointed to the small card attached to the handle of the basket with a small smile, and he tugged it free. Opening the envelope, he felt himself smile when he read 'For Shrek, Rest In Peace but stay away from the light, L.'

Alex grinned.

"Listen, I'm gonna let you rest, I'm really sorry for offloading on you, I'm sure it's the last thing you need while you're sick."

Alex refocused on her, and shook his head, "don't be silly. And trust me, Brad is going to be over the moon as long as you are."

She gave him a tentative smile, "I won't believe it's real until it's been confirmed, but thanks."

He made a locking motion at the side of his mouth, and she nodded, knowing he'd keep this to himself until she was ready to talk about it to Brad.

She placed the basket into the chair beside his bed and gestured to the tray, "you had enough?"

He took another gulp of custard, and nodded, allowing her to remove the tray, "thanks."

After she had gone, he looked down at the card again, and then at the basket. It was sweet and it was funny, and he had no idea how to respond. Was this why Luke hadn't been in touch?

Taking his phone, he knew at the very least he had to say thank you.

'Apparently my stank has reached new levels of gross, as I've just received a hamper of hygiene products.'

He stared down at his phone screen for a ridiculous amount of time waiting to see if Luke would respond. When the typing animation started, he felt giddy with excitement, and knew he hadn't been far off the mark earlier when he'd spoken to Brad, he had it bad like a teenage girl.

'Just doing my part for all of our sakes. How are you feeling?'

'Meh, less gross. Allegedly my temperature is coming down.'

'That's good.'

He felt awkward now and didn't know what to say. He couldn't admit that he'd been pining all day for a message, when he realized that they hadn't even had a face to face conversation in real life.

'Sorry I haven't had much time today. The public were rabid again.'

'That's okay.'

'I enjoy talking to you.'

Alex bit his lip, 'talking, oh how I miss the ability to talk.'

'You'll bounce back from this in no time. Then you can talk the hind legs off a donkey.'

'Pass.'

'Okay, then you can talk my legs off.'

Alex blinked and felt again that he didn't know exactly how to respond to that. It'd been so long since he'd played this game. So he very honestly said, 'um.'

After a very lengthy interlude where he was left on read, he had that panicky feeling that only came with this kind of conversation. So he tapped out, 'don't know where that saying comes from anyway, why would anybody want a donkey's hind legs talked off? And did someone at some point in human history actually have that power?'

He threw his phone down as he realized he was staring at it waiting for a response. He was a grown man for goodness sake, and he would not become obsessed with a man who he had only really met yesterday. He went to the bathroom and relieved himself, and when he checked his appearance in the mirror, he saw that he did look much better than he had earlier, though now his stubble was so long it was almost a beard.

He ran a hand through his hair and saw how thick it was getting, but decided he didn't care. He wasn't greying yet, so fuck it, he would enjoy his jet black hair all the time it stayed that color. Maybe he'd grow it out. He could probably pull off a ponytail.

When he came back to his bed, he lay down across it diagonally, hugging the spare pillow and unlocking his phone.

'I just googled, and apparently to talk the hind leg off a donkey refers to the fact that they don't sit on their hinds, but can collapse after a long time without rest. So I think the implication being if someone talked and talked without stopping, the donkey would eventually collapse.'

Alex took a chance with his reply. 'Well if it's either you or a donkey losing their legs, I'll maim the donkey. But I think you'll find I've never been a huge talker.'

'Me either, in fact this non talking we're doing right now is as communicative as I've gotten with anyone in a very long time.'

'What changed?'

'I guess I really wanted to communicate with you.'

TWENTY-ONE

For the next three days, Alex fought the flu. And he could feel the fight within his body, as every time he began to feel better, a new wave of symptoms seemed to rapidly attack his system again, knocking him back to being bed ridden.

Brad wasn't discouraged by this, but Alex was. He wanted to be done with this. And if he was honest, it was because of Luke. He wanted to be as healthy as he could be to pursue this….whatever it was between them.

They'd continued to talk, and had almost fallen into a routine. While he was at work, Luke would be almost completely silent, and Alex understood why. He said though staff had started to return from the sickness that had swept the department, he'd almost be sorry to see the back of Sue.

In the evening's, he wouldn't jump straight into chat, but usually by eight at the latest he'd be typing away. Alex had learned that Luke made a point of spending time with his mother every day, though she sounded like quite the social butterfly with her bridge and bingo clubs.

Two years ago, she had suffered a stroke.

And since then had had many mobility issues, which is why he hadn't even tried to move out and get his own place.

Alex thought of his own father, and knew immediately that if he hadn't died, he or any one of his siblings would have moved in with him too, so he understood this, and respected it.

He told Luke all about his family, and his fathers passing. And though this message exchange was seeing him through his illness, he wanted to do more.

Not *more* more. He berated himself as he thought over his own frustrations. He wasn't ready for anything too much more, but he just wanted to be able to see Luke. To hear his voice. To know that this little spark of something was actually real and tangible. Face to face he wasn't sure they would have the same chemistry, although how much chemistry they had over emoji's right now was debatable.

Alex had just showered, and was pulling on a fresh T-shirt and sweat pants when Brad entered his room with his stethoscope and a handful of pills.

After telling Brad that the tightness in his chest hadn't gone, though he hadn't had more than a little cough, he'd been having to endure regular checks, which he didn't complain about.

He pulled off his shirt again and gave Brad his back, flinching as the cold metal pressed his flesh.

"In," Brad instructed, and Alex took a deep breath in. "Out," he let the breath out, then repeated this as Brad checked different spots on his lungs, then made him turn around and repeat this on his front as well. When he smiled, Alex relaxed. "All sounds clear, honestly I think it's because you haven't had a cigarette in five days."

Alex blinked when he realized that was true, "wow, I hadn't even really thought about it."

Brad seemed pleased, "a new boyfriend would do that to you."

Alex eye rolled, "please." He pulled on his shirt again.

"Sorry," Brad put the flu pills down. "I think in a few days you might have this licked you know."

Alex groaned, "I've never been more bored." He complained out loud, but he also didn't want to admit that he'd also never been more exhausted, or been away from the gym for so long.

Brad ignored his comment as it wasn't the first time they'd had this exchange. "You think you'll be okay this evening, alone?"

"I think I am an adult, yes." Alex joked, but then saw a strange look on Brad's face. "Everything okay?"

Brad nodded, but was frowning, "yeah I'm meeting Misha for dinner."

Alex had noticed that she hadn't been around for the last couple of days, but her mother Vidya had been doing the lunch time or early evening visits in her place.

"Nice, anywhere fancy?"

Brad shrugged, "just her parents place. At least I think. She's been dodging my calls the last few days." Brad dropped down into the chair and hung his head back as he slumped down.

"What do you mean?" Alex frowned, and though he knew what she had confessed the other day, he didn't think she would be cruel and act like this.

"I mean when I call her she doesn't answer her phone, and when I went to her apartment to surprise her for lunch today she wouldn't let me inside. Stopped me at the door saying that she couldn't come out, because Tony was upset and she needed to be there for her friend."

"Who is Tony?"

"Her gbf, who has been glued to her side for

223

the past week."

"Gbf?"

"Gay best friend. I know the guy, we've hung out before, so I don't know why I'm suddenly getting the cold shoulder."

"Maybe she really has felt like she's needed to be there for her friend," Alex said, as this was a genuine possibility as far as he could see.

Brad winced, "it's just a feeling I've got. Something weird is going on. I feel like she's going to break up with me."

Alex almost laughed, "I doubt that."

"So why is she shutting me out?" Brad was perplexed.

"I'm sure she's not," Alex tried to sound as reassuring as he could.

Brad let out a heavy exhale and met his eyes, "I can't go back to life without her."

Alex shook his head, "you won't, trust me."

Brad nodded, though looked like he didn't fully believe it himself. "You want me to bring up your evening meds or do you think you'll venture down to the kitchen yourself?"

"I'll feed myself, don't worry about me," he said with confidence, as now at least, he could swallow and speak again. A persistent sinus headache seemed to be his newest nemesis, and he could cope with that over a sore throat any day.

Brad got to his feet and pointed at Alex, "okay, I want your homework done before you watch TV, and if you have any boys over you have to leave your bedroom door open."

Alex laughed, and Brad smirked as he walked out. He was sat in his chair with his feet propped up on his bed reading a book a little while later when his phone rang.

Seeing it was an unknown number trying to video call him, he was frowning as he accepted the call, but quickly smiled when he saw Charlie smiling nervously at the screen, "hey Charlie."

"Hello Alex!" she said excitedly. "I have a phone now!"

He laughed, "I can see that." What she didn't know was that Alex had sent extra money with this months rent payment to Frank, for anything Charlie might need, and he'd suggested he take her shopping for a phone.

"How are you feeling? Frankie said you might have your voice back by now."

"Yeah, I'm fighting it. I just struggle with my immune system," he said this honestly.

She surprised him by nodding, "yeah Frankie explained about the HIV."

Alex blinked, "oh."

Charlie just continued to smile.

"Do you have any questions?" he said eventually, knowing how unworldly she was.

She actually laughed at this, "no, it's okay, he's also showed me google."

Alex laughed at this.

"I am going to apply for a drivers permit soon, as soon as I can get a job that is," she explained. "I don't have any qualifications though, so Frankie says I may end up shelf stacking."

"A job is a job," Alex said. "If it pays your bills, that's all people can hope for. And if you want more, or you think you want to go to school, then we can talk about that later. Do you know what kind of things you'd like to do?"

She looked off into the distance for a moment, "I've been thinking about that. And in all honesty the only thing I really want to do is something with kids."

"Teaching?"

She shook her head, "I don't know if I could cope with a whole classroom of them, but maybe childcare or something."

"Maybe you could be a Nanny," he suggested.

She grinned, "Mary Poppins."

"I take it from that comment you've been enjoying the freedom to watch television."

226

"Oh yes!"

Alex laughed again, "so no regrets?"

She shook her head, "not one. Thank you so much Alex."

"You're welcome, and listen, when I'm back to healthy again, we'll work on a resumé and see where you'd like to live permanently. I think Frank's house is a safer option if he's happy with that."

"He loves coming home to a cooked meal and his coffee made for him in the mornings," she laughed.

"I'll just bet he does, I don't know many warm bodies who wouldn't be thrilled with that! But I'm sure the old fart is grateful. Don't spoil him too much or he'll get used to it."

She laughed again, but shook her head a little sadly, "well, I think that now my eyes are a little more open about the ways of the world, I think I can say again a huge thank you for being a good guy Alex."

He was taken aback by her sincerity, "I didn't do anything."

"You did, and I still can't believe I'm finally free. I pinch myself all the time because I feel like this is all some wonderful dream."

"You would have got out, I just expedited

things."

"Yes you did."

Alex was uncomfortable with her praise, so he decided to wrap things up, "look I need to go and fix myself some food. I'm glad you've got a phone now, and you give me a call if you need me for anything."

Charlie nodded, "get well soon Alex."

After ending the call he actually followed through on his words and ventured downstairs to see how well Brad stocked the kitchen, but before he could get there he heard the gate alarm. Frowning he went to the intercom and said, "hello?"

"Steinberg, it's Fuller, open up, I've got food."

Confusion hit him, but he pushed the open button so she could pull into the driveway, and he saw her red mini parking up as he opened the front door. "Fuller," he gave her a nod as she approached, but she just smirked at his frown.

"Back up big boy," she held a box to her chest as she approached, and she nodded behind him, meaning she was coming in whether he liked it or not.

He closed the door once she was inside, and she was walking straight through the living room through to the kitchen as if she'd been here before. "How?" was all he could think to ask.

She snorted a laugh as she put the box on the kitchen counter, "how do I know that you're home alone tonight? How do I know your brothers address? How do I know you're healthy enough to have visitors?"

"Yes," he agreed, to all of it.

She snorted again, "you don't remember much of the day Brad came to pick you up do you?"

He felt his frown deepen as he watched her unload cartons of what smelled like Chinese food onto the counter top. "No I don't."

"Well Carter and I have been in contact with Brad, and he actually came here the other day but a scary Indian lady shooed him off the porch and said you were too ill for visitors."

He laughed at the picture she painted of Vidya chasing off Luke. "Really? He didn't say anything."

She cocked an eyebrow at that, "hmm, we'll talk about that in a minute." She gestured behind her at the cupboards. "Get plates."

Alex did as he was told and fetched plates, then sat down at the counter. She took a seat beside him and started opening boxes.

"So, what are you doing here? You could catch this you're risking your life."

Fuller just shook her head, "I can handle the flu, but Brad mentioned you'd be alone tonight, and I volunteered to feed you and keep you company as others were engaged."

He got the impression she was skirting around the topic of Luke, so he sighed, "just spit it out."

She grinned, "what? That someone likes you?"

He groaned and dropped his head to his plate before any food touched it. "You really came over to talk about boys?"

He heard her laugh so he faced her again, "well I can honestly say that the last few days has been entertaining as far as a guy I've known for a few years coming out the closet to me and requesting a partner change and pining over a guy I've only just met myself."

Alex frowned, "he was in the closet? And what do you mean he's requested a new partner?"

Fuller pointed at his plate, "eat something, and I'll talk about boys, but first I need to talk shop."

TWENTY-TWO

"Can you remember the name of the priest in that restraining order you filed the other day?"

Alex thought back, but shook his head, "Father Francis something Italian sounding."

Fuller seemed satisfied with that, "well what would you say if I told you that today, a Father Francis Cassinelli came in to file a missing person's report for his daughter."

"Cassinelli, that was it! What about his daughter?"

"No no, the first question you need to ask is why he kept asking for a Detective Steinberg."

"Huh?"

Fuller nodded and bit into a spring roll, "weird right. Carter told him straight away you were off sick. When I took him over to my desk and asked for details about his daughter, he couldn't even give me a picture of her, said they didn't believe in cameras in his parish or some shit. Anyway he asked me about you too, and kept looking around as if he could spot you."

Alex shook his head, "I'm so confused right now, I've never met the priest."

"I didn't think so, but then he starts just

opening up files on my desk and looking through them as if he had a right to read private information. So I snatched them back and moved them so he couldn't, and you know what he says then?"

"I can't imagine," Alex really couldn't.

"He says 'sorry a friend of mine came in recently I was just seeing if he was here', like he'd be inside the files."

"Or he was hoping he'd just happen across Ryan Millers file so he could snatch it."

Fuller pointed her chopsticks at him as if to say 'bingo'.

"So what about his daughter?"

She rolled her eyes, "she's of age, took clothing and her birth certificate, and left a note saying she was leaving, he's got nothing."

Alex froze with a forkful of chow mien poised at his mouth, "huh?"

Fuller was surprised at his reaction, "I know, talk about wasting police time."

"Is her name Charlie?"

She was genuinely surprised, "uh, yeah how did you know? Charlotte Cassinelli."

He eye rolled, "she's the girl I helped from the abusive home I told you about."

Fuller gaped at him for a moment, then burst out laughing, "oh my God! That's hilarious!"

He pinched his nose for a moment, "so he came in to report her missing but you think it was just a ruse to see if he could snatch back the restraining order Ryan filed?"

"I think he thought it would be that easy yeah. And obviously he knew your name because Mr. Miller had to own up to what he'd done when he was forced to try and recant over the phone with you."

"So what did you tell him about his daughter?"

"Well obviously I didn't realize that she was the chick you rescued, but I told him that as she had taken clothing and her birth certificate that showed premeditation as well as the note she'd left telling him her intentions meant he had to respect her wishes. He tried to imply that she wasn't mentally fit to live alone or care for herself, but I said without a medical diagnosis to back that up he couldn't make that claim. Then he even tried to bring God into it."

It was Alex's turn to snort, which hurt his sinuses, but it felt good all the same. "How did you respond to that?"

"I asked if I looked like someone who cared for his God."

Alex laughed, "what a fucking mess."

Fuller nodded, "I definitely got creep vibes

from this guy though. He looked like a panty
sniffer, priest collar or not."

Alex cringed and shook his head, "but a child
poisoner?"

She just nodded again, "I've seen some
horrific things in this job, I can believe any
human is capable of anything these days."

Alex had to give her that. They spent a little
while eating and Alex also took his medication
when his reminder went off.

"Brad said to make sure you took that."

"Jesus, it's like he thinks one bout of the flu
has made me forget how to tie my shoes," Alex
grumbled.

"No, he just cares. It's nice," she pushed her
plate away and took a drink.

"Maybe, but I'll be glad once I've kicked this,
I hate being dependent."

"I think we all got that message when you
tried to fly rather than get in that wheelchair the
other day."

Alex laughed, "really?"

"Oh yeah, fever delirium is hilarious when
you're not the one in it. You were saying a lot
of random things, muttering in your sleep
bundled up in Sue's coat."

Alex was embarrassed, "like what?"

"Mainly you kept saying you were scared, and

alone," she said softly with a sympathetic smile.

He groaned again, "great. So I'm a cry baby."

"Not at all, it was quite heartbreaking," she said sincerely. "And it was only me and Carter who heard it, so don't worry."

Carter. He tried to train his face to not react, but she grinned anyway, and Alex actually felt a blush coming on, so he got to his feet to start tidying the food mess up.

"Oh come on, talk!"

"What about?" he said as he scraped food off his plate and rinsed it off in the sink.

Fuller brought her plate over to the sink and stood behind him, "this is exciting stuff Steinberg don't deny me my vicarious romance here!"

"There is no romance!" he insisted, snatching her plate from her hands.

She folded her arms and leaned back into the counter, looking skeptical. "We haven't known each other long, but I'm calling bullshit, or else why are you blushing right now?"

Alex took a deep breath and faced her fully, "okay look, I'll admit I've been struggling with my inner teenage girl this week while I've been fighting this flu, and I don't know where it came from either, so if you call that romance, then fine, have it your way."

"If you make me a coffee I'll tell you what I know," she said in a sing song voice.

He rolled his eyes but didn't want to give in to her demands so easily, "help me clean up and I'll make you a coffee. I'm still an invalid remember?"

She snorted but helped him.

When they were settled in the living room, her nursing her coffee and he with a large glass of water, she burrowed into the couch and looked admiringly around at the walls, "I like this place."

Alex stared at her and didn't speak until she got the message and said what he wanted to hear.

"Okay okay, so I know you've been texting back and forth this week."

"And?"

She sipped her coffee, but it was too hot, so she placed it down on a coaster and smiled at him. "When you got sick, and Brad came in, Carter was panicking. Like he thought you were gonna drop dead or something, and he even started questioning Brad as to whether he knew how to best take care of you or whether you should go to a hospital."

Alex frowned, "really?"

Fuller nodded, "Brad talked him down,

pointed out that he was a doctor, and that relaxed Carter a little, but he still insisted that Brad took his number and he be kept informed about your condition. I got in on that too of course, because you really did look like the picture of death."

"Thanks," he said sarcastically.

She ignored him, "after he helped Brad take you out to the car he really couldn't focus. He kept looking at his phone to see if he'd had an update, and then he started badgering me to see if I'd heard anything. So I got annoyed and said 'Carter when did you get so gay for Steinberg?' and he went all pale and quiet," she cringed. "I do want to state for the record here that I'm not homophobic in any way, but I thought I was just bantering with him, you know? Like we do?"

Alex nodded, he knew the type of banter she meant that came from working in close quarters with anyone.

"So I said sorry to him, and he tried to brush it off. He's never been one of the guys to brag about his partners or anything, but I just always assumed."

Alex knew exactly what she meant, "people do, unless you're wearing the pride flag and ramming it down people's throats, they just think you're straight," he said without malice.

Fuller seemed sad for a moment, "I just don't see why we have to wear our preferences as an identity," she said quietly. "I don't care who you sleep with as long as you're doing whatever you do with other consenting adults."

Alex nodded, "noted."

"Anyway, back to Carter, and after a few awkward moments he just macho'd it out and said he was worried because he knew you'd had a hard time fitting into the team and now you were sick."

"He sent me a message and I didn't know who it was at first," Alex confessed.

"Yeah I gave him your number and told him to just reach out."

"Well the idiot didn't identify himself at first, so I was being very vague until he mentioned that he hoped Brad was taking good care of me, so I figured it had to be you or him, but I had your number saved, not his."

She eye rolled, "men are so dumb sometimes."

He nodded, "we are."

"The next day he's looking like crap, but he's grinning at me like he's got some super secret he can't wait to share with me. And he tells me you've both been chatting most of the night, but he was worried that you were just being friendly."

Alex laughed, "I was worried about that too, I mean I still am to a certain extent."

Fuller slapped herself in the forehead, "I say again, men are so dumb."

Alex didn't argue with her, "so are you saying that he's interested in me, in more than a friendship capacity?"

"Duh, yes I think he wants to hold hands and talk about paint swatches."

"Do you think all gay guys like interior design?"

"Don't you?"

He hesitated, "that's beside the point."

"Yes Alex, he is very interested in you, hence he tried to visit you."

He laughed, "what happened? Vidya didn't say anything."

"He said he came over and asked to be buzzed in but this woman tried to tell him you were too sick, but when he said Brad had given him the green light to visit, she let him into the driveway, but she wouldn't let him in the door. Just stomped her foot and said you were too sick and outside germs would jeopardize your health too much."

"That's my brothers girlfriends mother, she's

239

sort of adopted us."

Fuller tried her coffee again, and cupped it in her hands when it seemed to be a better temperature. "Either way it's been like Degrassi High this week. But it's been nice to see Carter perk up a little."

"And what about Gibson?"

"Apparently he's got a drinking problem and it's been escalating. He was drunk when he was being rude to us, and Carter went to Markson about getting him some help. He's been suspended with pay on the understanding that he get treatment."

Alex winced. Cops quite commonly struggled with drink, as he'd witnessed for himself over his years in service. It went back to the fact that in the job, you did see humanity at it's worst. If you couldn't process that without it tainting your own core, you turned to substance abuse, or at least that seemed to be the pattern he'd observed.

They were sharing another comfortable silence when Fuller smiled at him, "anyway, he'd be here tonight, but his mother has a bridge game, and he wouldn't have been able to get over until late, so I said I'd come."

Alex shook his head, "I didn't need a babysitter, I'm on the mend now."

"Well I will admit, I wanted to gossip," she said with a wink.

Alex laughed, "so, if he had come here tonight?"

"I have no doubt you'd be giving him all your germs by now," she laughed too.

Alex blanched at that, "no, no no no, I'm not that kind of girl."

"Sure."

"I don't even know if I can."

Fuller frowned, "forgive me here Snow White, but I presumed you weren't a virgin?"

He felt a blush again coloring his cheeks, "I'm not, but it's been a long time."

"How long are we talking?"

"Since I was attacked and diagnosed with HIV," he explained.

"I say again, how long?"

He mentally calculated, "almost seven years."

Her eyes went wide, "oh."

Yep, he was definitely blushing, "for a long time I was scared to be with anyone. I hid from my own family for years because I didn't want to admit what had been done to me, and what I'd become. And I convinced myself that nobody would want me, because I was dirty," he admitted to her, and he was equally grateful for and angered by her look of sympathy.

241

She hesitated before saying, "that's kinda dumb."

He laughed, "maybe."

"And someone wants you all right. I'm sure he'll be down with taking it slow though, he's been super psyched just with your messages."

"But there's something I've been worried about though, and it's retarded, but we've been exchanging messages because I lost my voice. We've never actually had a face to face or even voice to voice conversation. What if there's no spark in person?"

She thought on that.

"I hadn't looked at him as anything other than another cop, and I thought he was a bit of a peacock with that hair of his if I'm honest, but then when we're talking, I've had to reassess how I view him, and I feel like I need a better look because although I can acknowledge that I like the way he looks, I feel like we need a new first meeting. That make sense?"

She gave a slow nod, "it does in a way. But that's what first dates are for right? And when you guys are at work you are just cops, coz Markson will ship one or both of you to other precincts if you parade your smooches in front of everyone."

"There would be no parading, trust me."

TWENTY-THREE

Brad had called not long after Kathy left at around 10pm, saying he wouldn't be back tonight, but to lock up and to hydrate and not die until he'd returned in the morning. When Alex had asked if Misha had broken up with him, he laughed and said, "no, she was just pmsing. It's all good."

Alex wondered then if Misha had confessed the truth, but they'd decided to not tell people yet, or if she still didn't know and therefore hadn't told Brad anything? Either way he had to play along, and he just assured his brother that he would be fine.

After locking up, and returning to his room, he checked his messages and hadn't heard anything from Luke since earlier in the day. So feeling brave, he decided to reach out.

'Fuller surprised me with Chinese food, she just left.'

'I can't do this anymore.' Luke fired back almost instantly.

Alex frowned. 'What do you mean?'

No reply, so rather than give in to the hysterical panic he was trying not to feel, Alex went to brush his teeth. Placing his phone on

243

the side and eyeing it, he went through the motions.

He tried to ignore the sinking feeling that was intensifying in his stomach. The twisting knot that was sure that Luke was done with messages, and Fuller was wrong, he wasn't interested that way. It was just a friendship, but unfortunately now Alex had pinned certain emotions and longings on the other party. The one who couldn't do this anymore.

After brushing his teeth as slowly as he could, and his phone had still not illuminated with a reply, he picked up the floss, and meticulously did the deed.

Still nothing.

So he studied his stubble. He really was more into beard territory now than stubble, and he made the solid decision to grow it out and go with it. Why not? Picking up a comb he rarely used, he went through his hair too, then followed with his fingers, picturing it longer. No, maybe he couldn't pull off the ponytail. He squinted his eyes at his reflection and wondered if he should shave the sides.

Holding his hands to the sides of his hair to hide the hair from his eyes, he was trying to picture how that would look when he heard the gate alarm from downstairs, and his heart leapt in his chest.

His phone was still blank, and he blinked at it for a second before hurrying down the stairs to the intercom where he breathlessly said, "hello?"

"Open the gate," a male voice sounded strained.

He pushed the button and dazedly crossed to the front door. As he opened it he saw a car pull in haphazardly, the driver's door opened, and a man stepped out.

Alex took it all in. The golden blonde hair flowing back from his handsome face that seemed strained right now as the strong legs carried his muscular form over to where he stood numb in the doorway.

They were matched in height, so seeing the grey eyes sweep his face and focus on his lips gave him only a moment to prepare for what happened.

Hard strong hands cupped his head in a possessive grip, and he was being kissed for the first time by Lukas Carter.

That first moment where their lips met seemed to awaken something within Alex, and he parted his lips with a groan, which in turn seemed to spur on Luke.

As he felt the first sweep of his tongue inside

his mouth, he felt his own arms wrapping around Luke, holding him as an equal captive in this kiss, and they both stepped into each other, in that primal need to just be as close as they could be.

As he felt himself relaxing into Luke, unfortunately other parts of him were most definitely not relaxed, and he tried to move his hips back to relieve some pressure, but Luke let go of his head to grab his hips, holding him still.

Their kiss ended, and he opened his eyes to stare into the stormy grey ones now looking at him as if he was going to be devoured whole. Luke pressed his own hips forward, and Alex felt his erection against his thigh. And though he spoke no words, he knew the message being sent by Luke. 'Don't you move, I feel you. And now you feel me too. This is what you do to me.'

He didn't know how long they stood there, just holding each other and sharing breath, but Luke finally closed his eyes and leaned his forehead against Alex's. "I needed to tell you that."

Alex cupped Luke's face and pulled him back enough so that he could look into his eyes. "I don't think there is a way to say that via text, you're right."

Luke squeezed his hip, then eased back a little once he saw that his message had been received. But then for good measure he said, "I want you," quite plainly.

Alex nodded, "got it," he replied as he genuinely didn't know what else to say. But he had to say something.

Luke smiled, but his eyes still looked hazy with lust, "and when the time is right, I'll have every inch of you Xander."

He felt his jaw drop at that. He was usually the aggressor in his former relationships, but then perhaps that was why they hadn't worked. "Is that right?"

Luke nodded confidently, "oh yeah. And I don't want you stressing out about the how or when, honestly I don't care. But I had to come here because I couldn't stand another minute of doubt between us. Consider this me staking my claim."

Alex raised an eyebrow, "oh?" He grinned, "gonna get your branding irons?"

Luke also raised an eyebrow, "maybe."

Not wanting to remain passive in this exchange, he reached within him and found his former sexual confidence, and grasped hold of Luke's shirt, yanking him closer so they were within kissing distance. "Try it Lukey. I may be yours but *you* are *mine*! And I'll let you play out your little delusion that you're top here, I hope it makes you even harder for me," he growled out these last few words and then initiated his own kiss. Showing exactly who was boss right now.

Which Luke allowed, for all of about thirty seconds, then he growled back within the kiss and pushed Alex back against the doorframe, once again becoming the aggressor.

At the same time, they laughed as the kiss diffused and became playful, affectionate, and soft.

Both smiling and delivering little pecking nipping bites and kisses at each others lips, and Alex couldn't recall a first kiss that had been so much fun.

For long moments, they just looked into each others eyes, and he felt the perfect moment of understanding when they both realized they had to say goodnight. This passion couldn't be allowed to burn right now, despite the intensity with which it sparked between them.

"Go to bed Alex," Luke said softly.

He nodded, and nipped out one more quick peck at Luke's nose. "Drive home safe Luke."

Luke gave him the cocky sexy grin once

more, and pushed himself away from the door.

TWENTY-FOUR

Life was good, and he woke feeling as though his kiss with Luke had actually cured his flu. He showered and he was fully dressed and eating a plate of scrambled eggs and toast when Brad came in grinning.

Alex returned the grin and was happy for a moment that Brad seemed to know why he himself was happy, then he remembered Misha's little secret, and wondered if it wasn't so secret anymore.

Brad just snagged a piece of toast from Alex's plate and took in his fully dressed and wearing shoes state. "Feeling better I see?"

"Yeah, much better."

"How is your chest feeling?"

Like it can't contain my bursting heart, he though ridiculously. "The tightness has gone."

"Good, I told you you'd lick it soon."

"You called it," Alex grinned.

Brad grinned back, "okay, Misha told me you already knew, so I guess you know that she's told me and you're ecstatic to be an uncle again?"

Alex laughed, "of course I am!" He really wanted to talk to Brad about what had happened last night, but now wasn't the time. "Congratulations!" He stood and pulled his brother into a hug and tried to convey all his love and hope into the squeeze. "May your spawn take after it's mother."

Brad laughed and slapped Alex on the back, and he felt a shake that at first he though was laughter from his brother, but when he pulled back he saw that it was, but it was twinned with a sob, "I never thought I'd ever be this happy."

"Aw," he pulled Brad back into the hug and rubbed his back. "It's okay princess, you're gonna be fine."

Brad snorted a laugh and pushed him away. "Dickhead, good to see you're back."

Alex nodded, "do you think you could drive me to go and get my car?"

"Yeah, I just need to go and change my clothes quick. Finish your eggs."

He did just that. While he was eating though he got a message from Luke. 'Captain just came down and asked us if we knew how you were doing or if you'd said when you'd be back. I told her I'd heard you were improving and vaguely said soon.'

He frowned, 'think I'm in trouble for something?'

'Who knows, she probably just heard you

were sick and she was the one who sent you down to the germ pit and is worried she's going to get sued by you.'

'Not a bad idea. I'm actually feeling pretty great so far today.'

'You're welcome.'

'Big head. Brad's actually going to bring me to Joey's to get my car back. Think you'll get a lunch break today?'

'Are you kidding me? Sue doesn't believe in taking breaks. I don't think the vampire even sleeps.'

'It's the weekend! Don't you get any time off for good behavior?'

'As much as I'd like to say yes, you know it's not going to happen. Dinner might be an option though, and I have a day off tomorrow.'

"By the way Ray and Vidya invited the whole family over for dinner tonight. Eric's already said yes for that lot," Brad said as he entered the room again, pulling on a zippered hoody over his jeans and t-shirt.

Alex's face must've fallen as he took that statement in, and looked down at Luke's last comment. "Um…"

Brad burst out laughing, "you can bring a plus one if you like."

Alex winced, "it's a bit much to pile onto a

first date."

"They won't be offended if you don't come Alex," he said with a wider grin. "First date huh?"

A blush flushed his cheeks and he couldn't help the smile that accompanied it. "I'll let you know if I'm coming later, okay?"

Brad shrugged, "whatever Casanova."

He dumped his plate in the sink and sent Luke a message, 'Brad just dropped a dinner bombshell on me, I'm saving you from meeting my entire family, so I'll have to take a raincheck.'

"My car is parked at Joey's down the block from the station, so you can just drop me there," he told Brad as he checked he had all his belongings before stepping outside so Brad could set the alarm.

"It's been sat there a week, so how about I see if it starts before I drop you anywhere, you may need a jump." Brad started the car.

Alex groaned when he realized that was true. "By the way does anyone else know about the baby bomb?" he asked as they started the drive.

"No not yet, just you, me, Misha and her parents. Oh and gbf Tony. Her doctor as well I guess."

Alex laughed, "how did her folks react?"

253

"Well she told them same time as she told me, so I kind of got shoved aside while Vidya was hysterically crying and Ray just looked like he was torn between crying as well or punching me out, or shaking my hand."

"Happy tears I take it?"

"Shit yeah, this is the best news. At least now she'll have to seriously consider moving in with me."

Alex burst out laughing, "yep that's one way to get a girl to move in with you. Shove your DNA up there far enough she'll have to!"

Brad grinned, "so many dirty jokes, but that's the mother of my child you're talking about now."

"Of course, because I have no idea how babies are made. You shook hands really fast didn't you."

Brad sobered suddenly, "shit, now I'm wishing Dad was here to make fun of me too."

Alex winced, "he'd be balling his eyes out right now, you know he loved a happy ending."

They both pondered their father in silence while Brad drove them the rest of the way to Joey's. "Where is your car?" Brad pulled into the packed car park.

Alex scanned the lot and had a sinking feeling when he realized his car was missing. "Shit,

I've either been towed or it's been stolen."

Brad winced, "shit."

Alex got out the car and quickly jogged around the lot, confirming his car was gone. "Dammit!"

"Call the police?" Brad joked.

For the first time in several days he wanted a cigarette, but he actively stopped himself from thinking that it was an option now. "No I'll just walk to the precinct and get to the bottom of this. I needed to talk to my Captain about coming back to work anyway."

Brad winced, "sorry bro. Want me to come?"

"No I got this, what time is dinner?"

"Seven thirty?" Brad returned the question as if he wasn't sure.

Alex nodded back to his car, "maybe see you later then. And congratulations again."

Brad grinned, "call me if you need another ride."

Alex waved him off and went into the diner and up to the counter. Agnes recognized him straight away, "hey," she said brightly.

"Hey, sorry to bother you but I parked my car here the other day, but I got taken sick so it's been about a week and now the car is gone. Do you know if there's any chance it got towed?"

She winced, "maybe. Want me to call Terry out? He usually keeps a list of cars he gets towed."

Alex nodded and tapped the counter while she went in the back to get the manager, who came out after only a couple of minutes holding a tablet in his hands. "What was the registration?"

Alex told him, and Terry scrolled and scrolled and scrolled. "Nope wasn't towed by me buddy."

He pinched his nose when he thought of the stress of having to file it as stolen, but for the insurance he would have to go through it. "Thanks for checking."

Terry limped away to his office again, and Agnes looked sorry.

Alex shook his head, and reminded himself that life was good, "two meatball subs to go please Agnes."

Fifteen minutes later, he was laying a sub sandwich down in front of a smiling Lukas Carter and saying, "I'd like to report my car stolen officer."

Luke cocked his head to the side, "those words don't go with the act of laying a sub down in front of me."

Alex smirked, "but unfortunately they are

true."

"Oh shit really?" Luke did a quick look over at Sue who was on a call, then scooped the sub off the counter before she could confiscate it.

Fuller came over then, and Alex offered her the other sandwich, "hey, here you go, I owe you a few meals."

She laughed, "your car really got stolen?"

"It wasn't towed, and it's not at Joey's, so yeah."

Luke winced, "on the plus side you don't look like a sweaty slug anymore."

Alex laughed, "always the silver lining."

Fuller gestured to her desk, "come on back I'll get it logged for you quick."

"Thanks," he said with genuine gratitude. Waiting with the public would've taken a while, and he was going to have to go car shopping now today.

"Thank you for the foot long," Luke said with a deadpan expression that Alex struggled to return without cracking a smile.

"Enjoy."

Fuller basically let him fill out the paperwork by himself and just signed off on it once he'd finished, allowing her to start to eat. Her only comment was, "you going to see the captain?"

Alex nodded, "I was, do you have any idea

why I'm on her radar?"

"No, but it might have just been to see how you are."

He nodded again, "maybe." While he had a moment he checked his phone, and saw a message from Luke had arrived a few minutes ago. 'I'm not scared of meeting your family by the way.'

Alex considered the options and snuck a quick glance over at him. Luke was talking to a man who was holding an ice pack to his eye. Could he handle them all?

'Have you not been paying attention when I've said my family is big and loud?'

Luke changed his stance, but didn't miss a beat as he continued to listen to the man and make notes on the clipboard, while pulling his phone from his rear pocket with the other hand and unlock it beneath the counter. A single glance down and then he tapped the screen then locked it again and continued to make notes and returned his phone to his pocket.

Alex watched the words appear on his screen, 'chicken?'

With a smirk he shook his head, and typed back his decision. 'If you can handle children asking you if you're my boyfriend, and fully grown adults asking you the same, plus potentially getting puked on by a baby, then be at the Jade Palace by 7:30pm. I'd pick you up but my car was stolen.'

Switching his phone off he looked at Fuller, "wish me luck, I'm going to go and see the Captain, but I'm intending to be back on Monday."

She nodded, "okay. Let me know what she wanted."

"Enjoy your sub," he told her as he got to his feet, and made a point of not looking at Luke as he headed through the office and up to the Captains office.

When he saw her door was closed and her blinds were drawn he hesitated for a moment before knocking.

"Come in," he heard after a minute, so he opened the door and was surprised to see the Captain at her desk, but another man was in the office with her and they seemed to be scanning over several files together. "Oh Steinberg, your timing couldn't be more perfect," Markson said with a smile. "Please come in."

Alex was confused, but he did as he was asked. Once the door was closed behind him he shook his head, "I'm sorry to interrupt, I just wanted to let you know I was intending to come back to work on Monday, and the guys

259

downstairs said you'd been asking after me."

She leaned back in her chair and smiled, "yes I'm sorry to hear you were hit by the flu wave."

"Thankfully I think I'm over it," he said all this politely, but knew full well by her tone she was just ticking off the pleasantries before she got to her point.

Markson gestured to the empty chair beside the man who was studying him quite openly, and Alex sat down, meeting the strangers gaze. "Alex, this is Holden Marlow, he works with the Child Protection Unit."

TWENTY-FIVE

Alex's confusion must have been apparent, as Markson held up her hand. "Just bear with me, I believe you'll be able to assist an ongoing investigation."

Holden Marlow gave a nod to Alex, "have you ever heard of The Clave?"

"No, I don't think so."

"I'll boil it down to say that it is a known international Pedophile ring."

That had been the last thing that Alex had been expecting to hear.

"It's been operating under different names for the last twenty years or possibly more, but the major players have always been the same, and the network is vast," Markson explained. "And as you can imagine, tracking and tracing a lot of these individuals is quite difficult due to the power that a lot of the big dogs wield."

"Big dogs?"

"Some powerful men are involved, and they have some powerful protection."

"Okay," Alex couldn't understand what could possibly involve him.

"I understand that recently you've become acquainted with Father Francis Cassinelli?"

Holden asked.

Alex shook his head, "I've never met the man, but yes I filed a restraining order against him on behalf of Ryan Miller."

Markson held it up, "I am afraid we need to freeze this."

"What? That fucker poisoned those girls! Miller could lose his children over this, and his job," Alex was furious.

Holden held up his hand, "we've been watching the priest for too long to jeopardize the investigation now."

"Are you going to arrest him? Because I'm sorry, that is the only alternative to the restraining order."

"A very large and coordinated seizure is in the planning stage and will be executed very soon, we just need a little more time."

His frown just kept deepening, "how much time? If it's anything more than a few days it's too long."

"The task force is covering several countries at once, you must understand that this is a drop in the ocean."

He wanted to slap the guy but held himself in check in front of his Captain. "I take it you didn't bring me in here to piss me off?"

"Fuller met the Priest and he wished to file a

missing persons report for his daughter, and I
do believe that you know where that daughter is
now."

"Oh I see," Alex said, though he didn't, not
fully. "She's safe and I didn't do anything
wrong in getting her out of there. And at the
time I had no idea she was Cassinelli's
daughter."

"We would like to bring her in for
questioning," Holden said.

"I'm sure you would, but I'm sure she hasn't
got a clue what her father was up to."

Markson interrupted again, "Steinberg, she is
a person of interest. Be reasonable."

"She was home schooled and bullied her
whole life what do you hope to learn from
her?"

"If she can even give us the location of his
home computer it will have helped us," Holden
pointed out.

Alex was loathed to admit he was right. "I'll
need to stay with her during the talk," he
demanded.

Markson nodded immediately, "done."

Alex exhaled, and stared up at the ceiling,
"and what about Mr. Miller?"

Markson looked at Marlow, "he needs to
recant. We need for the good father to believe

that the heat is off."

He was appalled, "are you kidding me? That man came to us and believed that he was doing the right thing, and I convinced him to keep strong and have faith that we would do our duty."

"We have to look at the bigger picture here," Holden insisted.

Alex stared between them both, and after a beat he shook his head, "I'm sending him and his children on vacation."

Markson blinked, "excuse me?"

"You're going to ask me to stand by and let that man leave himself defenseless to a poisoning priest, who has twice dosed his eldest daughter with bleach, and you're expecting me to take no action at all. Correct?"

Markson winced, "it isn't as if we're leaving him defenseless, the man is being very discreetly watched."

"Does that help him when it happens again and social services take that as strike three against an innocent widowed father?" Alex shot back at her angrily. "I'm not kidding I'm sending him to Disneyland until you lock that fucker away!"

Holden patted the air in an attempt to calm Alex down. "Just wait a minute - "

"Am I breaking the law by gifting the poor man a vacation?"

Markson smirked, "no Steinberg."

He wanted to growl. No, worse, he wanted a cigarette. He got to his feet and clasped his hands behind his head and looked down, trying to reign in his temper, "I hate this. I cannot stand the grey areas that always become so convenient for the service of the greater good, it's always the little people that suffer."

Markson nodded, "it's true, and it sucks to be the person that makes those decisions, but it has to be done so we can get all those deviants locked up, not just one or two." She gestured at the pile of files stacked up between her and Holden, and he saw at least a dozen names. "That's just in this town under this precinct."

Alex looked, and the name he saw at the top of the pile made him groan. William Straker. "Captain I need to recuse myself immediately."

She frowned, "explain."

He pointed at the incriminating name on the file, "William Straker was sent down years ago by my sister-in-law, and he's currently at large and stalking her."

Markson looked at Holden, and they both exchanged a panicky look.

"I've done nothing on this task force, I'll

arrange a different escort for Charlie and her chat, and I'll get a third party to send Miller on vacation, but I shouldn't be involved any further." Alex was so frustrated, but thought he may finally have a use for Hunter to act as an intermediary.

Markson looked as though she may vomit, but gestured for him to leave, "glad you're feeling better, see you Monday morning."

Once outside the office he leaned against the wall for a moment to catch his breath, then made his way back downstairs, where he saw Fuller had two young girls sat at her desk and Luke was filing.

He waited as he needed to speak to Kathy.

Sue spotted him and smiled, "so glad you're back in the land of the living," she patted his arm as she walked past him, and he returned her smile.

Luke glanced up then, and smiled, but continued his work.

Alex took the time to study him, and he got the sense that Luke knew he was being checked out, as the smile remained on his lips.

But staring was creepy, so he stopped himself and pulled out his phone while he alternated his glance between Kathy and Luke, and he called Eric.

"Hey, Brad said you were healthy again. That's great news."

"Yeah I feel much better," Alex agreed. "Listen though, I need to talk to you and Jeanie and Hunter. Is he around today? I also need a ride, my car was stolen."

"Where are you?"

"I'm at work right now, but I really need to get to All Saints as soon as possible."

The girls left Kathy's desk and he hurried over to sit down before she could get her next case file. He held up a finger saying he needed a minute.

Eric must have guessed that he didn't want to discuss his business over the phone, "I'll send Ernie over to collect you, and have Hunter and Jeanie ready for you."

"Thanks bro, I'll wait out front for Ernie." He hung up and looked at Kathy, "sorry, I need to inconvenience you."

She didn't look surprised, "go on."

"Charlie is going to need escorting and accompanying in for an interview with the Captain. You'll need to talk to her about that, but I need to prepare Charlie. I've had to recuse myself," he admitted, though he still felt angry about it.

Kathy blinked but didn't question it. "Right,

send me the details."

"Thank you, I don't know them yet," he realized he'd have to break the news to Charlie that she would have to talk to the police and potentially learn what a sleaze her father was.

Kathy patted his arm, "chill. It'll be fine."

Alex winced, "I know, I just haven't had a cigarette in days and I want one so badly."

She laughed, "you're definitely better if you can think about doing that. But I'll look after Charlie, you can trust me."

Alex nodded, "thanks," he tapped on the desk and got to his feet. "I'll be in touch."

When he turned he almost bumped straight into Luke, who smirked as if he hadn't placed his body there for that purpose.

Alex smirked right back and whispered, "sorry Lukey."

Luke looked as though he wanted to burst out laughing, but just shook his head as if to say 'oh you've done it now'. What he actually said was, "see you later alligator."

TWENTY-SIX

On the ride over to All Saints House, Alex called Charlie, who was thrilled to be receiving a call.

"Listen Charlie, I need for you to stay calm but I'm about to tell you some news okay?"

"I'm calm," she assured him.

"Okay, well your Dad came to the police station to file you as a missing person, that's the first thing I need to tell you."

She was quiet for a moment. "Didn't he see the note I left for him?"

"Yes he did, and the police told him that he couldn't do a thing, so that's good. Okay?"

Charlie sounded relieved when she said, "okay."

"However, the police would like for you to come in and talk to them."

She didn't respond.

"Charlie?"

"Am I in trouble?"

"No, not at all, don't think it for a second. They just need to talk to you about your Dad. And unfortunately I am not able to come with you, so I've asked my partner to come and get you and she'll stay with you during the whole thing, okay?"

"Why can't you?"

"Because I've had to recuse myself due to a conflict of interest in the case."

"What case?"

He winced, "against your father. Because before I helped you leave him, I took a report and filed a restraining order against your father. Only I didn't know it was your father at the time."

"Someone filed a restraining order against my Dad?"

"Charlie I'm not allowed to talk about that with you, I'm sure you understand why."

She was silent for a moment. "I understand," she sounded a little stunned.

"Okay good, now I'm really sorry this has happened, but I promise my partner will take good care of you. Her name is Kathy, and she has multicolored hair."

Charlie laughed, "really?"

"Really."

"Okay, so when is this happening?"

"Can I give your number to her so she can call you to arrange it?"

"Yes, that's fine."

"Good, I'll do that now. And Charlie, if you feel uncomfortable or don't want to talk about

270

things they ask you, make sure you tell them."

"I will," she sounded scared now though, and he berated himself for saying too much.

"Don't worry," he said confidently. "Talk to you soon, okay?"

"Okay Alex, bye," she said brightly.

Alex hated that she was going to learn her father was a pervert, but he knew Markson was right, she had to be interviewed.

Hunter was waiting outside All Saints House when Ernie dropped him off, and Alex thanked him as he got out the car.

"You needed to see me?" Hunter said straight away, the scowl ever present on his face.

"I do, but with Jeanie and Eric."

Hunter nodded, and indicated that Alex should follow him into the house and he led him into the office that Eric had set up off the parlor. Jeanie was already on the couch there, but she got to her feet when he entered, and hugged him, her large belly making it awkward for both of them.

"So glad you're feeling better," she patted his cheek, and scrubbed at his beard, laughing at it.

"Thanks."

Eric encouraged her to sit down on the couch again, and he took a seat beside her. Hunter perched on the desk edge, and Alex pulled one of the chairs from it and sat. "Sorry about this, but I need your help."

Eric frowned, "it's fine, but which one of us do you mean?"

"All of you actually, but I need to explain a few things first," he said honestly, and he began his tale. Starting first with meeting Charlie at the gym, then taking Ryan Miller's report, then helping Charlie leave her home. He ended with what he'd just learned from his Captain. Hunter had begun to pace the office and was looking thoughtful when Alex announced that Straker was on the list of local's about to be taken down.

Jeanie looked concerned more than stressed out, so Alex grimaced before he said what he needed to. "Jeanie, you know I'd never ask you for anything for myself, but I feel in my gut that Ryan Miller and his daughters are not safe in that situation if they force him to withdraw his application for a restraining order."

She shook her head, "I agree with you, it's terrible that they even want him to take that risk, but what can I do?"

"You have money, and I hate asking, but I hate the thought that the law has failed him. Would you be willing to help him financially? He's the man I was talking to you about before, who might need help through Open Arms. I told my Captain I was going to send him on a vacation to get him out of the way."

She laughed, "of course I'm willing to help, but won't you get into trouble?"

Alex shrugged, "if it's acceptable to be selective over not prosecuting child poisoners until the appropriate time, then I think it's acceptable for an anonymous person to gift a vacation to the victim. Not me of course, but giving a gift isn't against the law."

Eric smiled, "you said something about his job being at risk?"

"His boss came to visit him the same day he filed, and pointed out that it was only on Father Francis's recommendations that he'd been given the job in the first place. That's what pisses me off even more, I convinced him to do the right thing and have faith in the system, and now he's going to know it was for nothing."

Alex looked at Hunter, who had been silent through all this. "Would you be willing to speak to him?"

Hunter smiled, "I'm a very good whore, I do whatever I'm paid to do."

Alex laughed, "I mean it. If I go anywhere near him right now I could jeopardize the entire operation just on a technicality because of my association with Straker."

Eric nodded, "I agree you can't go near him."

Alex nodded at Hunter again, "however I do believe you can convince him that taking a sudden and extended vacation right now is the best thing to do. And if someone else is paying the bills, he can't complain."

"What if he says he can't leave his job?" Hunter asked immediately.

Alex winced, "I know, and I can't tell him to quit, but I just think as far as the bigger picture goes, his children's safety is more important."

Jeanie got to her feet, "just give me a moment," she said as she left the room.

Hunter waited until she was gone before he said, "did they give you any indication how long before the mass seizure was happening?"

Alex shook his head, "no, and I wish I'd found out all the details before I saw Straker's file." He ran a hand through his hair and exhaled. "I'm so frustrated," he admitted.

Hunter nodded, "that's the law."

Jeanie returned holding a brown envelope which she handed to Hunter, "that's for Mr. Miller. Alex you said he had outstanding hospital bills from his wife and no savings?"

Alex nodded, "yeah the poor guy was hanging on by a thread."

She nodded, and spoke to Hunter, "tell him that an anonymous party is donating this money to him on the understanding that he pay his debts and takes his girls to see Mickey Mouse."

Hunter hefted the envelope but didn't open it, "seems like a more than generous amount."

She shrugged, "I'm a generous lady, and I hate hearing this shit. If having money thrown at it will help then I can do that much."

Hunter hefted the envelope again, "you're sure? This is a lot of cash."

Jeanie sighed, "he needs to make a lot of quick plans right? A cheque or a bank transfer will take time. Could you escort him to a bank?"

Hunter nodded, "of course."

Alex loved seeing this side of his sister-in-law. She had been poor for most of her life, until inheriting a large fortune from her grandfather, and with her charity work she had made it her mission to help people with her money rather than just sit on it.

"Hunter, while you are talking with Mr. Miller please assure him that after settling his debts and when his vacation does finish, he will not be unemployed," Eric said.

Hunter raised his eyebrows, "oh?"

Eric shrugged, "Open Arms always needs more hands on deck."

Jeanie nodded, "that's true, we do have a lot of volunteers, but I think we actually need more men available, I've been seeing more and more Dad's suffering these days."

Alex was relieved, "thank you guys, this is everything I could have asked for."

"I'm glad you came to us with this," Eric said.

"Yes, now what about Charlie?" Jeanie said.

Alex blinked, "well, she's safe at the moment, living with Frankie."

"But I'm guessing she'll need a job soon at the very least," Jeanie said.

Alex nodded, "yeah, but like I've said she's been very sheltered. I don't think for a second she's unintelligent but I don't know how well she's able to cope with anything public facing."

Jeanie shook her head, "how is she with children?"

Alex blinked, "she said she'd love to work with children."

Jeanie grinned, "well this will work out nicely for all of us then won't it."

TWENTY-SEVEN

Like a nervous girl, he paced outside the front of The Jade Palace and waited for Luke. He'd tagged along with Eric, Jeanie, Christina and the kids in their mini-van, and they were all inside the restaurant already.

Whenever Vidya and Ray invited them to dine with them, they would reserve an entire banquet table for them, and just let them have at all the food. This had happened a few times now since they'd been accepted into the family, and they always had a great time.

Tonight he suspected they had all been gathered so that Brad and Misha could announce their happy news, and Alex didn't blame them for the setting as it was a place for great memories.

He hadn't told anyone that he was bringing a guest, at least until he hovered at the doorway and didn't follow them inside. When Eric had looked back at him curiously he'd just said, "waiting for a friend."

Eric had grinned and followed his family.

He checked his phone again, and just saw the message that Luke had sent twenty minutes ago saying he was just setting off.

277

He'd called Kathy and given her Charlie's number and explained what needed to happen, and how she had no clue what her father might have done, beyond being a terrible father. She'd told him she had already gone to Markson and got the lowdown on what needed to happen, and not to worry she would take care of Charlie.

He pocketed his phone and scanned the lot again, just in time to see Luke's car parking up, and he couldn't believe he felt butterflies when he saw how good the man looked walking towards him. Black jeans, grey t-shirt, and a beaten leather jacket made him look just the right amount of bad boy.

"Hey there Steinberg," he stopped in front of him grinning.

Alex felt himself returning the grin, "hey, you look good."

Luke made as if to flick his hair over his shoulder, and Alex was curious about something. He reached over and ran his hand through the blonde locks. They were soft, and the action made Luke's eyes soften. "It's naturally curly, I don't style it or use hairspray."

Alex nodded, "my apologies." He held his hand at the nape of his neck and he held him in place so he could step forward and kiss him.

Luke returned the kiss, but they were both holding back, as once again this wasn't the time for passion.

Luke sighed, "okay, I'm ready. My safe word is pineapple."

Alex laughed but grimaced, "by the way you're a surprise guest."

Luke eye rolled, "is there going to be enough seats?"

Alex laughed, "trust me, there will be more than enough seats and food."

Luke linked his arm through Alex's, "okay, so am I just your work colleague or am I your new boyfriend?"

"I don't tend to kiss my colleagues," Alex turned them to enter the restaurant, and they strode in slowly. "Last chance to run," he warned.

"I got this," Luke said confidently.

Alex admired his lack of fear. "Okay, it's officially too late to back out," he said this as they entered, and stopped at the hostess desk, where the girl smiled in recognition of Alex and waved him past the group already waiting.

"You come here a lot huh?"

"Well the lady who chased you off my brothers porch the other day owns the restaurant with her husband," Alex laughed.

Luke laughed too, "great."

Alex saw Eric first, as he was stood and pointing to Lily, obviously trying to get her to sit still next to Ben, who was being well behaved for a moment. Christina was standing Alvin on the table where he was stomping his pudgy legs in excitement

As they got closer, Jeanie was the first one to crack a smile at them both, but then everyone else seemed to turn their heads and stare at the same time, and all the adults had the same smile, even Christina, who looked extremely tired.

Alex unlinked his arm from Luke's and put that arm around him to clap him on the back. He took a deep breath, "everyone, this is Luke Carter."

Eric came forward first, "hi, nice to meet you, I'm Eric."

"Nice to meet you too," Luke still sounded confident, but Alex was pleased to see he wasn't as poised as he'd been faking, as a flush colored his cheeks.

Jeanie got to her feet then and pointed at both Lily and Ben in a 'stay' gesture. "Hello Luke, I'm Jeanie, I'm Eric's wife, but I'm a hugger so get down here."

Luke laughed but stooped to hug her, which

he did gracefully considering the obstacle of her belly. She then gestured to Lily and Ben, "these are our children, Lily and Ben, who will probably talk your ears off tonight."

Luke acknowledged them both, "do you want handshakes or hugs?" he asked them.

Ben was closer and he stood up and offered his hand, "do you like books?"

Luke shook the little hand, "I do."

"What's your favorite?"

"Oh boy," Luke winced. Alex thought Ben's opinion would greatly be influenced by the next words out of Luke's mouth. "The Count of Monte Cristo."

Ben frowned, "I haven't read that one."

"Well, when you have, we'll talk about it, okay?"

Ben nodded, "okay."

Lily shoved by Ben, and Jeanie coughed, "nicely young lady," under her breath.

Alex had to suppress his grin when Lily put her hands on her hips, "are you a cop?"

Luke pulled his jacket aside and showed her his badge, "yup."

She squinted for a moment, and finally offered her hand to him, "okay."

"Okay?" Luke asked, shaking her dainty hand.

Lily nodded, "okay, you can be his

boyfriend."

Alex burst out laughing at the audacity of his niece.

"Well thank you Lily." Luke resumed his full height and met Alex's eyes, "I have your niece's blessing."

"Yeah but you haven't met the Don of the family yet," Alex gestured over to Alvin, who was still stomping, but when Alex stepped into his line of sight, the stomping intensified and he spluttered happily spraying Christina with his drool.

"Thanks kid," she muttered with a smile, but she got to her feet, still supporting Alvin with him gripping both her hands as he wobbled. "Hi Luke, I'm Christina, and this is Alvin."

"I'll shake your hand when you have one free," Luke smiled at her, but earned points when he grabbed a napkin and wiped the drool off her face.

She laughed, "thank you, nobody warns you how moist parenting is."

Luke laughed too, but used the same napkin to wipe a string of drool from Alvin's chin. "Well this big guy clearly thinks you're doing a great job, I don't think I've seen a happier baby."

Eric interrupted then, "I'm fetching drinks,

what do you guys want?"

"Coke, thanks," Luke said straight away.

"Ginger beer," Alex said, and he decided to give Christina a break by taking over on Alvin watch. As soon as the baby latched onto his own fingers, Christina gripped his arms, "thanks bro, I've been dying for a bathroom break."

"No worries, maybe bring back a T-bone for this guy to chew on," he joked.

She snorted, "you're not wrong," she patted Luke's chest, "really nice to meet you."

Luke watched her walk away, and seemed to realize he'd passed the first phase of greetings, and let out a relieved exhale, which Jeanie laughed at, "you're doing great. Take a seat Luke."

He removed his jacket, and without consultation, he took over holding Alvin's hands so Alex could remove his own jacket, which struck him as thoughtful. "Thanks," he said as he took back his nephew, and Luke surprised him by pecking his cheek and saying, "you're welcome," then held out Christina's chair for him so he could sit.

Lily giggled at this.

Luke looked at her seriously then, "pay attention young lady, a gentleman should always do this for you on a date. If he doesn't even pull out your chair for you, he's a stinker."

Lily laughed, but Jeanie nodded in good humor, "very true."

Luke sat beside Alex, and Alvin decided he was done with stomping, and dropped into sitting, yanking his hands back from Alex and trying to shove them both into his mouth making garbled noises while he gummed them.

"Oh that's so much drool," Alex cooed, and Jeanie threw a cloth across the table.

"He's teething," she said with a wince.

Without missing a beat, Luke took the cloth and tried to catch the worst of the spray. Alex held Alvin around the middle, and smiled at Luke, "didn't I tell you this would be a glamorous evening."

Luke smirked, "well I'm enjoying myself, and sometimes, things need drool, right Alvin?" he asked the baby, who was still trying to console himself with his fists.

Alex took a look around and realized then that there was no security team, and he shot his eyes to Jeanie. "Where's the security?"

Jeanie snorted, "they got here first, swept the place and stuffed their faces. They're at the entrance. Didn't you see them when you came in?"

Alex peered around Luke and was relieved to see a couple of familiar faces near the entrance, and another by the wall keeping an eye on them. "Thank God," he sighed.

Luke looked as well, "private security huh, I figured someone famous was here."

Jeanie grinned, "nope, just us."

Eric came back carrying a tray of drinks, along with Ray who was also carrying an ice bucket. Ray smiled at Alex, and took in Luke's presence with a nod.

"Well hello, I am Raiden Tanaka, but you can call me Ray."

Luke had been unprepared for this, but he held out his hand as he got to his feet again, "hello, I'm Luke."

Ray put down the ice bucket on the table and shook the offered hand, "I believe you've met my wife."

Luke was confused for a moment, until Alex said, "Vidya is the lady who refused to let you see me."

Luke laughed, "oh, then yes I've met your lovely wife." He sat back down when he saw Ray laughing.

"Yes, my wife is the stuff of nightmares, I know she can be terrifying."

Alex agreed, "first time I met her she told me

off and hugged me within the same minute," he explained to Luke.

Ray held his hands out for Alvin though, "oh my poor baba, come to Ray, I have something for you."

Alex loved witnessing both Ray and Vidya and how they embraced them all and their children as if they were blood. He reached into the ice bucket and pulled out what looked like a glass pacifier, but seemed to be more pliable. Cradling Alvin's chunky form in one arm, he offered the cool object to the fussing infant, and once he managed to work it through his fists and applied the cool to his gums, Alvin was on board, and was finally quiet.

"That's my good little baba," Ray cooed, and walked around the table rocking him gently.

"Did I just witness magic?" Luke asked on a whisper.

Alex laughed, "yup."

Christina was coming back with a plate of jelly blocks in various flavors, but she saw that Ray had it handled, so she put the jelly down as a back up plan and just gave Ray a kiss on his cheek.

"Here you go," Eric said, placing their drinks down.

"Thank you," Luke said promptly.

He met Eric's eyes and nodded his thanks. "Where are Brad and Misha?"

"On their way," Ray said softly, "and Viddy will join us shortly too," he cooed this down to Alvin, who was gripping the pacifier and seemed to be wanting to ram it deeper into his mouth.

Ben and Lily were starting to get restless, and he could see Jeanie's mouth tightening as she kept asking Lily in particular to keep from fidgeting.

Leaning into Luke he whispered, "you wanna earn some brownie points?"

"Tell me everything you know," Luke whispered back.

Alex held back his laugh, "go to the hostess station and ask for the crayons and paper menu's they have stashed there, and challenge the kids to a drawing competition. Best dog, best horse, that kind of thing."

Luke nodded and immediately got to his feet and strode away. Alex unashamedly watched.

"Oh I like him," Christina said, also checking out his rear.

Jeanie laughed too, and Alex blushed, but gave his sister a quick hug. "Thank you," he said into her ear.

She seemed confused, "for what?"

"Waking me up. You were right."

She seemed sad for a moment, but then scrubbed his beard the same way Jeanie had. "I like the beard. Suits you."

"And I'm glad your eye is healed, it didn't suit you," he joked, but perhaps that was still a sore subject, as her smile dropped a little. "I'm sorry," he quickly said, but she shook her head, brushing it off.

Then he felt like shit.

Luke came back and very loudly announced, "I'm gonna draw, and I bet nobody can draw better than me."

Lily and Ben immediately took the bait and came to sit opposite them.

Jeanie mouthed a 'thank you' in their direction and got to her feet to stretch her legs. She arched her back and grimaced, and Alex worriedly looked at Eric, who was also studying her, but his face was full of sympathy as he patted her belly and murmured something.

She patted his hand and smiled, murmuring something back. He knew this pregnancy had been hard on her, and the fact that she was carrying twins had to be twice as uncomfortable in his mind. Once again he was glad he was male.

Alex got his own paper menu and took an

orange crayon, "what are we drawing?"

"Pussy cats," Luke challenged, using his own purple crayon to deliberately draw the scariest looking cat he'd ever seen.

Lily laughed at the way Luke was deliberately poking his tongue out and screwing his face up in mock concentration, and even Ben was starting to lose his guarded look.

"But I can't draw cats," Alex whined and drew a stick figure cat with huge pointed ears which earned him a laugh from the kids.

TWENTY-EIGHT

As soon as Brad and Misha arrived, Misha was overjoyed to meet Luke, and she shook his hand and hugged him before hugging Alex too whispering a little too loud, "I'm so happy!"

Alex blushed at this, but knew as well that her happiness stemmed from the little miracle he was sure she was about to announce.

Brad was cool in his introduction to Luke, as technically they'd already met. He just shook Luke's hand and gave him a nod, "nice to see you again. Good Cow," he gestured at the drawing Luke was working on, and he had the good grace to laugh.

Vidya had obviously been waiting for her daughter to arrive before she left her beloved kitchen, but she cooed over Alvin with sympathetic clucks as she saw his reddened cheeks.

Alex waved her over, "Vidya, please come and meet Luke."

She couldn't stop her blush as she nodded to Luke, "hello again young man."

"Hello, ma'am," Luke said politely, though he was smiling. He obviously wasn't holding a grudge.

Vidya looked between them both, and surprised Alex by cupping both their faces and studying them together. Luke allowed himself to be studied, and they as a couple to be studied together.

Finally she smiled brighter and patted them both, "yes, I think you fit quite nicely together. Though Alex you need a shave. Call me Vidya Lukey."

Alex laughed, "Vidya I love you!"

Lukey blushed, but due to his no battering of old ladies policy could do nothing.

"Okay," Brad called out over everyone, and Alex saw that Misha grinned and hurried back to his side.

Already Jeanic had her hands to her mouth, suspecting something.

Christina's eyes widened.

Ray and Vidya took a seat which left Brad and Misha looking at each other, grinning like fools.

"We have an announcement to make," Brad said down at Misha who was already blushing. She faced them all and blurted out, "we're having a baby!"

Jeanie burst into tears, and Christina didn't look far off it herself. Eric got to his feet straight away, and Alex laughed as Lily and Ben wrinkled their noses at the news, obviously not seeing the great news of a baby, but they joined the crowd of hugs being given to the happy couple. Luke wasn't shy either, giving his sincere congratulations, and Alex repeated his earlier sentiments that he hoped the child would take after Misha. He hugged Ray and Vidya too, as this would be their first grandchild.

Just as everyone was resuming their seats though, Alex saw Misha nod to her father, who passed her something behind his back.

"We also have something else to announce," she said loudly, this time grinning alone as Brad was looking down at her curiously.

It quicky became apparent what she intended though, as she got down on one knee in front of Brad, and opened a small box. "Brad Steinberg, will you marry me?"

Now, even Vidya was gasping in surprise, along with Christina and Jeanie, and Eric all were poised waiting to see what Brad's stunned response would be.

And he was stunned. For several beats the room seemed to be silent before he said, "does this mean you'll finally move in with me? Yes!"

Misha laughed as she allowed herself to be pulled onto her feet where she was swiftly kissed in a way that wasn't strictly appropriate for children to witness. Not that they wanted to witness it, as again there was much nose wrinkling.

Alex leaned down to Lily, "you should be happy, this means you'll get to be a bridesmaid," he pointed out.

She perked up a little at that, "I'm happy, I'm just hungry," she pointed out, and he realized that life for a child really was that simple.

Luke stooped down too, "bet I could sneak you that plate of Jelly while nobody is looking," he offered with a wicked smile.

Ben's ears practically pricked up at that too. "I'm starving too."

Luke nodded, "leave it to me," he whispered with a wink, and Alex watched as he leaned over, picked up the plate, and placed it in front of the kids. And genuinely all the other adults were so occupied with congratulating the happy couple that they didn't blink at the two hogs that were currently scarfing down the sweets.

Alex met his eyes then, "smooth."

Luke snorted, "I'm starving too. Any more announcements coming?" he whispered.

"You think I'm in control of any of this?" Alex said. "I warned you, big and loud and busy."

Luke nodded, "you did warn me."

"Second date, we'll do something quieter."

"Don't count on it, second date you're meeting my mother, consider that the ultimate payback."

Alex grinned, "your mother huh?"

"Oh yeah she's already planning the menu, and compiling her questions."

He snorted, "old ladies love me."

"Old ladies love me too," Luke returned the smirk. "I got so many cookies from Sue this week I swear she's ready to adopt me."

Eric was thankfully the parent that learned of the Jelly that had been inhaled in record time, and rather than make a big deal about it, he quickly glanced around to check Jeanie hadn't noticed, and threatened both Ben and Lily that if they didn't eat some real food too, they would suffer their mother's wrath.

"Does that mean we can eat now?" Lily whined.

"Yes, both of you come with me," Eric shot a quick eye roll at Alex and he just laughed. Once Eric was out of earshot he told Luke, "Eric used to be the one sneaking us sweet stuff before our dinner, then threatening us to make sure we ate the real food too or Dad would hear about it."

Luke smiled too, "the way I see it, the role of Aunt or Uncle is to introduce a child to corruption."

"You're not wrong," he slung his arm around Luke again. "Ready to hit the buffet?"

"If I don't eat soon I'm going to swoon, but not in the damsel kind of way."

So they heaped their plates, and it was lovely that now all the happy announcements were out of the way, not to mention awkward introductions, everyone seemed to relax, and Alex was relieved that the evening had panned out this way, and was grateful that Luke had been brave enough to endure it.

He reached down and put his hand to Luke's leg and squeezed gently. "Thanks for coming," he said softly.

Luke met his eyes and switched his fork to his other hand so he could place his over Alex's, "thanks for inviting me. I'm having a great time."

They held their gaze for several moments, but true to the spirit of their company, Lily piped up with, "are you guys gonna kiss?"

Luke didn't miss a beat though, and just cocked an eyebrow at her and said, "what's that about Jelly?" in a really loud voice, making her shoot a panicked look at her mother, but Ben and Alex laughed, as did Eric.

Luke gave Lily a wink and said quietly, "don't worry, no smooches. You've already endured a lot of boring grown up stuff tonight. Actually I think you've both done really well," he said this like it was a big deal, but Luke obviously saw the strategic value in getting the children onside.

"That's true," Alex agreed.

Lily nodded and looked over at Brad and Misha, "I just don't get it."

"What don't you get?" Luke asked.

"Why grown ups love babies so much," she sounded as though she was on the verge of being upset, and Alex knew that this was all about the siblings she was soon to have in her life.

Luke looked stumped for a moment, and Alex saved him from having to answer, by squeezing his leg. "When you are a grown up, you will understand better. But having a baby means that you have someone to love who will always remember you and carry on your love to their own children. It's the way life works. And the more children you have, the more love there is."

Lily frowned, "I think it's a load of crap," she said with a blunt brutality he'd never heard from her before, and Alex was shocked, but schooled his features to remain bland.

Eric was there in a flash, and he'd scooped up his daughter and taken her seat, then held her in his lap. "Lily," he said in a soft chastising tone. "If your mother and I hadn't had that love and wanted a family, you wouldn't be here now. And we've talked about this already, haven't we?"

Lily crumpled under her father's scrutiny, and her lip started to tremble. "But nobody wants me around anymore," her eyes filled with tears and her little lips trembled.

"Now that there is the load of crap," Luke pointed out.

"Yeah," Ben said in agreement. "I always want you around."

"And me," Alex said.

"I think you're just a little scared that babies are loud and stinky and take up a lot of time, and you're worried nobody will play with you anymore or read with you or want to do anything with you," Christina said in a soft voice.

Lily shot her a look of pure shock that a grown up had accurately said what she was thinking.

Christina was eating while Ray was still

holding a now sleeping Alvin, and she smirked at Lily.

"It's okay to be scared that things are changing," Ben said wisely, and took her hand to hold.

Lily looked at her adopted brother, and Alex nodded at him, "very wise words there Ben."

Luke nodded, "I was an only child, and I was so bored and lonely growing up. My Dad was in the army, and we moved around a lot, so all I really had was my Mom, and we'd read books together all the time, and play games or watch movies. Every time we moved house I made new friends, and every single time I hoped we would stay, so I wouldn't go back to being alone with just my Mom as my friend again. But then I got a little brother, and you know what?"

"What?"

"He was stinky, and noisy, and my Mom was so tired taking care of us, and I got mad about it. She didn't read books with me or play with me anymore. I even wished he'd never been born at one point, which was a bad thought Lily, don't be like me," he chastised mildly, but pointed his fork at her. "But you know what happened?"

Lily shook her head, her eyes wide.

"I realized, that my Mom needed my help. If I helped her with looking after my stinky baby brother, then she wouldn't be so tired, and she would be able to spend time with me again. If I wasn't so mad, I'd be happier, and so would she. And so I asked my Mom what I could do to help her look after Matty."

Alex realized the whole table was now listening to Luke, who had his eyes fixed on Lily.

"And that made my Mom so happy, just me being kind instead of angry. And so she gave me a list of jobs to do. I would sweep the floors for her when I finished school, and I would do all my homework, and fix my own cereal. But to help my brother, I would look after him so she could go and shower, and help to feed him so she could do the dishes. We did everything together again, it was just different. But with my help, we could read together again, and watch a movie when Matty went to sleep."

Lily blinked at him, "so you say that I shouldn't be sad or scared I should be happy."

"Only you are in charge of how you feel and act Lily," Luke said. "But, everyone understands you are scared. This is new for you. However, I didn't get to tell you the best part about my stinky baby brother."

"What?"

"He didn't stay a baby for long, and he ended up being my best friend. He'd come to me for advice, and I ended up reading to him and watching movies with him. He's still my best friend now."

Lily wrinkled her nose, but surprised everyone by looking around her father to Brad and Misha, who had also been listening to Luke's tale. "Can you make your baby be a girl at least?"

TWENTY-NINE

Eric and Jeanie offered him a ride back to their place, but he declined.

Brad and Misha also offered him a ride back to their house, but for many reasons, mainly being the new engagement giggles they had which promised the kind of night they were about to have together, Alex declined again.

Luke stood beside him outside the restaurant and he watched Brad give him a wink, then took his new fiancée to his car.

"So," Luke said, finally turning to Alex, who returned the smile.

"Yeah," was all he said.

"You're without a car," Luke pointed out.

Alex nodded, "it's true."

"Hmm," Luke took hold of the lapels of Alex's jacket. "I could be a gentleman and offer to drive you home."

Alex laughed, "yes, I don't think I have the capacity to order an uber."

Luke looked down at his feet for a moment and seemed to be considering something. "Will you trust me?"

Alex sensed the implied depth to that question, and he knew that although he was nervous, he knew he had to take a leap of faith. "There's a lot we should talk about."

Luke nodded, "talking is fine, I've got a whole day off tomorrow that I will dedicate to the talking. If that's what you want?"

"What I want is more than anything to not have to have the talks at all, but I have to be responsible with the risks involved," he said soberly, and with genuine regret.

Luke eye rolled, but not in anger. "Okay, I'll specify here. Will you trust me, and the fact that I am a grown man, who is fully aware of what he is entering into? I know, and I have researched, and I have considered and weighed and hesitated, and tip toed, and I get your position. I fully get it," he said this with a little shove to the midsection for emphasis.

Alex looked down to where Luke was gripping his jacket, and he felt something akin to defeat. "I'm so tired of being scared," he admitted. "And I'm tired of being alone, tired of having to think of all the risks and dangers and of being responsible."

Luke lifted his chin, "I know. All those things, and more. I can see it. You're an open book to me Xander. But I need you to trust me, and I'm not going to do anything to hurt you."

He didn't even need to think about, "yes, I trust you."

"Good," Luke kissed his lips quickly, then clasped his hands, "come on."

Alex allowed himself to be led to the car, was in the passenger seat, and was being driven before it fully sunk in what he'd done.

He'd given up control.

As if sensing the potential for panic, Luke reached over and patted his thigh, and Alex exhaled. "I'm so glad you came tonight, you were amazing, especially with Lily."

Luke snorted a laugh, "that girl has balls of steel, she is going to be a real nut buster when she grows up!"

"Yeah I hope so, she's been having a tough time adjusting to the thought of two babies coming."

"Oh man, twins? Really? Poor Jeanie she's so tiny, and you Steinberg's are all huge."

"Yeah, I could make a dirty joke there," Alex laughed.

Luke groaned, and muttered, "give me strength."

"No? Okay. Moving on then, I think everyone scored you highly, and I can even go so far as to say that if my Dad were alive, I think he would have too."

303

Luke smiled, but there was no arrogance in it, just happiness. "Thanks, and I'll admit now it's over, I was a tiny bit nervous."

Alex laughed, "yeah, I know." He saw with interest that he was nowhere near his apartment, not that he thought Carter knew where it was. "Where are we going?"

Luke grinned, "I'm taking you home."

He sighed, "okay. I'm guessing you mean *your* home?"

"Oh yeah," Luke nodded.

Alex absolutely loved the satisfied look on Luke's face. "Can I borrow your toothbrush?"

"I think it can be arranged."

"What will your mother say?"

"Well, she'll say a lot, if we let her. But tonight, she'll say nothing, as I'm hoping she'll be tucked up in bed and we'll be able to just tiptoe in and get upstairs without interruption."

Alex burst out laughing, "your speeches about being a grown man are looking a little flimsy right now, you're about to sneak a boy into your room."

Luke saw the humor in it, but just smiled, "yeah I am."

A short while later, Luke pulled up in front of a modest town house that had a porch light on, but none others seemed to be lit, and he allowed Luke to lead him up the ramp and to a front door, which he unlocked with care.

Ushered inside, he watched Luke lock the door behind himself, and switch off the porch light. It was dark, and Alex kept rooted to the spot as Luke reached out in the dark and hit a light switched.

The entryway they were stood inside was illuminated with light spilling from an upper floor, and Luke gestured that Alex should go up the staircase before him.

Trying to keep his steps light he walked as directed, hoping that he wouldn't trigger a creaky step or stumble. Once at the top of the stairs he saw an open landing, and a few doorways, but another set of stairs, which Luke gestured to.

Alex ascended again, and though there was darkness, a hand at his back guided him forward a few steps, then a door was opened for him and a well-practiced hand found the light switch, and he was stood inside a very large open plan apartment.

He had pictured a bedroom in his mothers house, not a living space and bedroom and bathroom.

A large television was on one wall, and it was able to be viewed from the bed, but at the foot of the bed was a large couch where a few items of clothing were draped.

Luke hurried to clear off the clothing, and he stuffed the items into a laundry hamper outside the bathroom door. "Sorry, I hadn't planned this," Luke said as he hurried back and gestured to the couch, inviting him to sit, and Alex heard a hint of nervousness.

"Neither had I," he said honestly, and he took off his jacket, dropping it on the arm of the couch.

They both stood though, and Alex almost laughed at the absurdity of the moment. "Take off your jacket Lukas," he instructed with a grin.

The smirk appeared, but he complied, "think you're in charge again?"

"You don't want to talk tonight, so I'll offer a suggestion of what's going to happen instead. Ready?" Alex kicked off his shoes.

Luke tilted his chin up, listening.

"I'm going to go into that bathroom, and I'm going to pee, use your toothbrush and wash my face. And while I'm in there you are going to strip and sit on the bed with your back to the headboard, and wait for me to come out."

Luke seemed surprised, "oh really? Then what?"

306

Alex smiled, "then I am going strip too, and I'm going to stand right here and watch while you show me how you jerk off. I might just join you. But then we're going to sleep, because it's been a long fucking day. And if you're a really good boy and cum when I tell you to, I'll let you be the little spoon."

THIRTY

Heat at his back told him that somehow during the night, he'd become the little spoon, and he smiled into the pillow and shifted his weight.

"No don't wake up," Luke groaned in an almost whisper behind him, and an arm snaked around his middle holding him still.

Alex huffed a laugh, "don't tell me what to do."

He felt a kiss press into his shoulder, and he held the arm that was holding him.

Luke yawned and stretched his back, but didn't break his hold, just tightened it when he was done with the stretch. "Morning," he said still sounding sleepy.

As much as he loved being spooned, he needed to see Luke's face, so he turned, causing more grumbling.

The blonde hair was adorably mussed, and his jaw was now peppered with stubble. His eyes were shut, but he seemed to be trying to open the one that wasn't mashed into the pillow.

Alex grinned, "aw you're cute in the mornings Lukey."

Another groan, and the hand that had been

around his middle now slid up and over his chest, touched his beard, then clamped over his mouth.

"You keep working that pretty mouth and I'll have to find ways to silence it," Luke said softly, finally opening his eye.

Alex pulled the hand from his mouth and kissed it, "yeah yeah, you big bad alpha male you." He stroked Luke's hair back from his face and scooted his body closer.

"I never pegged you as a morning person," Luke grumbled.

"I'm not particularly, I'm just happy this morning."

"Yeah seeing me naked will do that for you," Luke said with bravado, and he finally smiled too. He stretched again, and this time he rolled onto his back and reached both his arms up while arching his back up off the bed.

Alex enjoyed seeing the stretch of his torso, and especially as the bedsheets slipped down to his waist. "What time is it?" Luke asked as he slumped after his stretch.

"No idea," Alex realized he'd left his phone in his jacket, so he got out of bed and stepped to the couch to retrieve it. "Ten thirty," he looked back to Luke, who was smiling up at the sight of Alex's naked form.

"Want a rerun of last night?" Luke wiggled his eyebrows.

Alex laughed and came back to the bed, placing his phone on the nightstand and sitting up against the pillows. "Maybe," he didn't try to cover himself, and loved that Luke wasn't shy about scooching straight to him for a cuddle. He lifted his arm and Luke rested his head against his chest.

"I'm sensing serious thoughts," Luke said.

"No," Alex said honestly as he started to stroke the soft hair beneath his palm. "Quite the opposite actually."

"Good," Luke stroked his chest. "No serious yet. I need coffee before I get serious."

Alex laughed again, "well, one thing you need to know about me, is that I need to eat, a lot, and often. So if you like, I'll go and fetch you coffee as I'll have to get some food in me soon."

Luke didn't stop stroking, "I'll make you food, and I'll get my own damn coffee when I'm ready thank you. But right now, I want to snuggle."

"You're quite vehement about your morning snuggles," Alex observed.

Luke sighed, "it's the first snuggle," he said simply, making Alex want to simper at the romantic comment.

He closed his eyes and relaxed into what was indeed their first morning snuggle.

His phone started to ring, and they both groaned, but he didn't break their cuddle, just picked up his phone and saw Hunter's name on the screen. "Sorry I need to take this," he apologized as he took the call. "Hunter?"

"Miller and his daughters, and their neighbor are on a plane now, I thought you'd want to know."

He did want to know, "did he fight you on it?"

"Surprisingly not, you were right, he was hanging on by a thread. He was grateful for the help, and he did ask if you were the one who had sent the money, but I told him for legal reasons, your involvement was severed. I told him about the forced recant and he was worried, but when I told him it was temporary and in the service of ending the situation, he accepted that it had to happen."

Alex felt terrible, but most of all he just felt relief.

"I took him to the bank while the neighbor stayed with the children, and I assisted him with all the calls he made to the debtors. And he quit his job, I didn't even have to encourage him to do that so I think they'd been making his job difficult for him since he refused to recant sooner."

Luke could obviously hear what was being said as he sat up with a frown.

Alex gave him a reassuring smile and pinched his cheek as Hunter continued his tale.

"I stayed with him and took him to the airport, where we played at the arcade there with the kids for a couple of hours until his flight departed, and I instructed him not to contact you at all, but as soon as it was safe to return, someone would contact him."

"Thank you, you did everything I asked."

"Of course," Hunter acknowledged. "I told you I was a good whore."

Alex laughed, and Luke shot him a puzzled look, "well you earned your money whore."

Hunter hung up, and Alex dropped his phone in his lap, exhaling the tension he hadn't realized he'd been holding.

"Everything okay?" Luke asked.

Alex nodded, "there's a situation, or several situations that have become interconnected and some of it involved my family, and some of it involved work. And the reason that Markson was looking for me yesterday was because the two have become one, and I've had to recuse myself, but in amongst all that, was a poor innocent guy who I could no longer help, but I arranged for someone else to help him instead."

Luke took all that in, "I take it that was the whore?"

Alex laughed, "he's a private investigator and security consultant, he referred to himself as a whore first."

Luke sighed, "okay," then scrubbed a hand down his face. "I guess snuggles are over."

"I'm willing to try it again another morning, but yeah, I think so."

Luke looked over his body, and Alex felt himself responding as he hardened, defying his last statement that snuggles were over. "Just a little snuggle?" Luke suggested, fixing his eyes on his hardening cock.

He shook his head laughing, "I wish I could stay in this bed with you," he got to his knees and pulled Luke into his arms.

They held each other, and he loved this learning of new bodies that came with a new relationship. And it had been so long since he'd experienced it, he wanted to savor this all the more. So seizing the moment, he kissed Luke and pinned his arms down to his sides with his embrace. "Tell me you have condoms."

Luke nodded, "in the drawer."

With that assurance he recommenced the kiss and was bold enough to grab Luke's ass as he felt a hand reach between their bodies to cup them both together, and he'd never felt anything finer, but he needed control.

He released Luke and nodded, "I need a condom."

Luke leaned away, and Alex ran a hand down the lean muscle of his partners flank and watched as he retrieved two condoms and shoved one into his hand, tearing open his own.

He was thrilled however, when Luke grinned and grabbed Alex's cock and very slowly slid it on him. He grinned back and kissed the man who was the embodiment of every hope Alex held for his own future happiness. And it was something he hadn't considered for so long.

Happiness. Companionship. Partnership.

Not only did he want it, he needed it, and he was going to fucking take it.

Unrolling his own condom slowly along Luke's own shaft, deliberately prolonging the act and teasing until he made the man gasp, he pushed him back on the bed and straddled his hips.

"What's your plan big boy?" Luke's hands were running up his legs, stopping to grip his waist then slide around to cup his ass.

Alex reached down to grab Luke's dick and his own in his hand and he stroked as he gyrated his hips, moving them both into the stroke of his grip. "I don't have a plan," he said breathlessly.

Luke sat up so they were face to face again, and he surprised Alex by gripping the back of his head forcefully and going in for a kiss.

But as Alex opened his mouth to accept it, Luke paused to gyrate up against Alex, matching his rhythm.

He could feel they were both enjoying this, but once again he needed control, so he pushed Lukas back once more, but this time followed him down. "Stop trying to top," he growled.

Luke groaned, "I'm not used to switching," he said, but physically he gave over control by laying back and submitting.

"Get used to it."

THIRTY-ONE

Tillie Carter was a vibrant woman, who dominated her little modified kitchen, even though she was in a wheelchair.

It was lunch time, and now Alex was being barraged with talk as she cooked them bacon and eggs and pancakes.

She had been surprised, but not displeased when they had both entered the room after they'd showered together. Even though Alex was wearing yesterday's clothes, he felt fresh and renewed in a way that was more spiritual than physical, and he knew it was thanks to his new boyfriend.

Tillie had been on the phone to one of her friends and sipping a coffee when Luke had entered with Alex at his heels, and he'd watched as he leaned down to kiss his mother's cheek, which made her smile, but then her eyes widened when she took in Alex, and she quickly ended her call so she could start fussing.

"Oh my, aren't you a handsome one. Call me Tillie, I think your name is Alexander?" she wheeled herself away from the table and stopped where he stood in the doorway to offer her hand.

Alex shook her hand and allowed her to cover it with her other hand. "I think my name is Alexander too," he said with a smile. "It's very nice to meet you Tillie."

She grinned, "I'm sorry I didn't realize we had company," she said this over her shoulder aimed at her son's back.

Luke was busy pouring himself a coffee, but he shot back, "it wasn't the kind of company that you needed to know about," he said this kindly.

Tillie blushed a little but shook her head at her son's candor.

"I apologize, I hope my being here doesn't inconvenience you in any way," he said with the hope he could put her at ease.

She patted his hand then released him, "don't be silly, it's lovely to finally meet you. Luke has been acting like a lovesick girl this last few weeks, so I'm glad things are progressing."

Alex looked at Luke, "few weeks?"

Luke was coming back to the table, "yes I had a crush on you as soon as you joined the precinct. Happy?"

He blushed, "aw, just when I think you can't get any cuter."

Luke rolled his eyes, "beverage of choice?"

"Any kind of fruit juice or water please?"

"Luke told me you were unwell, are you feeling better now?"

"Yes thank you, it was just a nasty flu."

"But your brother was taking care of you," Tillie said this as fact, not a question, so Alex just looked at Luke again. "I'm guessing you tell your mother everything?"

"When it comes to talking about boys, my mother is my go to, yeah," Luke joked.

Tillie laughed, "please don't be embarrassed, I'm so happy that you two seem to be getting along. Now Alex come and sit down, you both must be starving as you slept the day away."

And she then began ordering her son to make toast while she began loading different pans onto her lowered stove top, talking nonstop and predictably asking Alex questions about his family and interests but refusing his assistance with the cooking or serving.

When they were all sat with plates of food in front of them, Tillie sat between them and asked, "so what are your plans for the day? Or should I say afternoon?"

Before Alex could speak, Luke announced soberly, "we have to talk."

Tillie looked between them. "Talk?"

Alex laughed, "because I'm a cautious guy who likes to lay things out in the open, I insisted we needed to talk, and he promised that would happen today, as opposed to last night."

Tillie nodded, "I see." She fixed her gaze on her son, "talking is important."

"And so is getting laid," was Luke's answer.

Tillie swatted her son around the back of the head, as Alex choked on his mouthful of pancake. Luke just laughed at them both, "what?!"

"I did not raise you to be so crude," Tillie scolded, but she was smiling as she said this.

Alex managed to catch his breath, and he met Luke's eye as he said, "you raised me to be honest, which I just was."

Tillie fumed, clearly embarrassed. "Good luck Alexander," she said under her breath.

He found himself laughing again, "call me Alex, and don't worry, I think I've got a good handle on Lukey."

She laughed as well, "I'm pleased. And I'm glad to hear that you like to be open and honest. I think that's very important in a good relationship."

Luke said nothing as he ate his bacon, but he did shoot Alex a wink. "Well mother dearest, I thought that I would take Alex to the lake for a nice walk so we could feed the ducks while we talk. How does that sound?"

Tillie smiled, "that sounds lovely. Oh it's a shame we're eating now you could have taken a picnic."

"We'll do a picnic another time," Luke said resignedly. "I just couldn't wake him any earlier he's so lazy."

Alex just smiled at him, "I'm sure your own mother knows better than anyone when you're full of crap."

They both laughed at that. "True Alex, I tend to just tune it out for the most part. He blusters because of the lack of male influence he had growing up," she divulged, making Luke shake his head with another eye roll at his mother. She flipped him the bird without even looking at him or seeing the eye roll.

Alex loved their relationship, "or you raised him to be so confident in your love and support of him that he feels free to be the sarcastic prick he is."

Luke was surprised, "wow swearing in front of my mother on first meeting." He whistled, impressed.

Tillie was just smiling at Alex, "I like you."

"These pancakes are delicious, I like you too," he said honestly.

Twenty minutes later, after Alex had insisted

on doing the dishes in the low sink, they were in Lukas's car and driving with a bag of bread for the ducks.

"I think she likes you," Luke said.

Alex sighed, "yeah I like her too."

"Matty moved away for work a few years ago, so he doesn't get home very often."

"You worry about her," Alex observed.

"Of course I do," Luke shook his head. "But, I know full well this whole talking thing isn't so we can talk about my mother."

"You make it sound like I'm unreasonable for wanting to talk through HIV with someone who has 'staked a claim' to me."

Luke sighed, "no, it's not unreasonable Alex. I guess I'm being difficult because I really struggle with serious talks."

"Does this mean you have a struggle with commitment also?"

"Shit no, I just can't reign in the sarcasm for long. You're mine, I'm yours. And we're exclusive, monogamous, officially a couple," Luke shrugged. "Bedfellows."

"That is a word that doesn't get used often enough, so I congratulate you for that. And thank you for the clarity, I'm happy that we are declared as a monogamous pair of bedfellows."

Luke grinned.

"Don't you have questions? Don't you care? Don't you want to know the risks you are taking every time you tease me and get me hard?"

Luke sighed again. "I wasn't kidding yesterday when I said I'd done research."

He parked the car and got out. Alex grabbed the bread and followed him.

Luke took his hand and they walked away from the cars and started on the trail that circled the lake. There were people, but as it wasn't the height of summer, it wasn't overly crowded, and Alex felt like it was a great place to talk openly.

"The first time I saw you, I could tell you were angry, and it's kind of why I didn't approach you sooner. And I saw Markson keep pairing you with the worst people, and you just got angrier and angrier." Luke laughed at this and nudged his arm into his side. "Should I have asked you out then?"

Alex shook his head, "yeah looking back I don't think I made a great impression on anyone."

Luke sighed, "when I heard Fuller was coming back, I was worried about who they were going to partner her with, so I spoke to Markson who told me about her plans to partner you both. And then I got the lowdown on you."

"What was her lowdown exactly?"

"That she felt you hadn't been given the best opportunity to show your capabilities yet, but that you seemed to be struggling to fit in with the team as well, possibly due to your health concerns."

"How polite of her," Alex said dryly.

"I have to admit, hearing the term HIV positive was a shock for me, but I knew it was something I didn't know nearly enough about. So I chose to educate myself. And it put me at ease, because I knew there was a chance for us. I just had to wait for you to thaw out and stop being a scowl monster."

"From my side of things, since I joined the team, everyone I met hated gays or thought I had leprosy," Alex defended himself.

"Yeah, and I'm just bullshitting, I was scared of rejection and using your angst as an excuse to not expose myself."

They came to a picnic table near the lakeside and decided to sit on it and open the bag of bread.

"So you googled HIV and you're cool with it," Alex still sounded skeptical.

"I went to a HIV counsellor and got advice

323

on how to live with someone who has HIV and how best to reassure them that I am serious and I take seriously the health implications."

Alex blinked, "you went to counselling?"

Luke looked embarrassed, "I've never been what you'd call promiscuous, and for all my bravado with you, I'm quite shy as far as relationships go. I haven't had many, and I really didn't want to screw this up with you."

"That's…maybe the most touching thing I've ever heard."

"Well, I like you moron."

He laughed, "I think I'm getting it."

"And yes, I care about how you were infected, yes I care about your health. But I want you to tell me about all that because you want to, not because we're following your prescribed responsibility checklist."

Alex thought on that, "well, I felt that I had an obligation to declare all the facts up front. Full disclosure, I guess it's the cop in me."

Luke laughed, "and I appreciate that sentiment. And if you feel like you need to do all your talking now, then go ahead babe, I'm listening."

THIRTY-TWO

Alex talked, and when they ran out of bread to feed the ducks with, they continued to walk around the lake, and Luke said very little.

"Hold up, you were a sexy librarian?" was one of his comments.

"I didn't say sexy, I just said librarian."

"Sexy librarian is maybe my all time favorite fantasy," Luke ignored him, so Alex chose to ignore him in return, and continue his tale.

They were almost half way around the lake when he had finished telling him about the attack, his withdrawal, the rehabilitation and how he'd decided to become a cop. "And looking back now I know I didn't tell my family because of the classic shame and denial, but at the time I thought I was doing the right thing by keeping my diseased butt away from them."

"Dumb," was all Luke said, but he said it kindly.

Alex nodded, "yeah, but then six months ago, my Dad had a stroke. Both me and Brad had separated ourselves from the family for years, and even though his reasons were different, that event brought us both back into the fold."

"Did you get to say goodbye?" Luke asked in

moment of sincerity.

Alex nodded, "yeah, and then I found out my Dad had a whole dossier on my activities over the years, including my medical diagnosis and the fact that I was a cop. He'd been keeping tabs on me."

Luke grinned, "I think I would've liked your Dad, he sounds like a sneaky bastard."

Alex grinned as well, "oh yeah he was a master at it."

They entered into a park area that had banks of swings and slides and a few children were playing, and in the distance he could see some families had set up a volleyball net.

"So anyway, that was why I moved back to town. I realized my own stupidity, but I also hated how much I'd missed Lily growing up, and after what happened to Tim at Dad's funeral, I really didn't want to turn my back on Christina and Alvin, or just leave everything to Eric with his babies on the way too."

Luke smirked, "you do have a lot of breeders in your family."

Alex shrugged, "yeah, and if you're serious about being with me you'll have to learn to love kids."

"I like kids just fine, I just don't want to poop out any of my own," Luke said simply.

"You do know how babies are made, right?"

Luke gave him a sidelong glance, "you know I'm kidding."

Alex elbowed him as they continued to casually stroll. "To me, being an uncle is the closest thing to being a parent I'll ever be."

"Do you want children?"

Alex thought about this once again. "I like the idea that a part of me would live on when I was gone. But I never factor in children when I think about my future. If someone asked me what my happily ever after looked like, I'd say it was a comfortable home and someone who set my world on fire. And I still feel that now." He shook his head frustrated by his own conflicted feelings.

"When Brad finally found out that my viral load was negligible, he went into overdrive pointing out that it was safe to put my sperm in a female," he said this with a laugh, but little humor. "None of my family understand that being bisexual doesn't mean I'm just playing with dicks as a side hobby until I found a girl."

"Do you really think that's what they are thinking?"

He thought of how welcoming they had all been to Luke last night. "Not after how they were all fawning over you last night, but up until then yeah I thought that."

"Just an observation here, but I think you think too much."

Alex laughed, "yeah you're probably right."

Luke stepped in front of him, stopping him from walking. "Have you got more talking you want to do?"

"Bored already?"

"No, the guy at my six is taking pictures of the little kids and I want you to go and talk to the parents while I keep an eye on the dude who is sure to split when he realizes he's been rumbled and I want to detain him."

Alex let his eye focus on the man who at first glance was dressed like a groundskeeper with a large sun hat, but he was just standing by a bush a tracking the children on the slides with his phone. He saw a group of picnicking mothers sat on blankets adjacent to the play area.

He gave Luke a nod and strode over to the group of mothers who were all drinking from plastic cups, laughing and obviously enjoying themselves. The first lady to spot him was a plump brunette, who flustered and nudged her companions to pay attention to him approaching them.

He put the friendliest smile on his face that

he could muster. He stepped closer than he potentially should have when greeting strangers, but he hunkered down so he was at their level, still smiling. "Please keep smiling ladies, I am with the police and I need you to stay calm and listen to what I need to say?"

The brunette was still smiling, but her eyes were widening, "are we in danger?" she asked, almost as if she thought this was some kind of joke.

"No danger, but I need to ask you all if those are your children?"

"Yes," another woman squeaked, starting to panic. "What's wrong?"

"Please, I need you to stay calm. My partner is about to detain a man that we believe has been filming your children, but I need you to not alarm him by altering your behavior."

"So what do you want us to do?" the brunette asked.

Alex saw in his periphery that Lukas had approached the man and was holding his hand out asking for the phone. "I need you to stay calm right now, and soon I'll need contact information if you wish to press charges against the man, which I would advise you all do. And if we manage to detain the man quietly enough I suggest your children remain ignorant. No need to ruin their fun, right?"

The group of mothers all agreed, but their smiles were more grimaces at this point.

The man suddenly made to run, and stupidly was running near the group of now pissed off parents, one of which threw their empty bottle of prosecco at him which fell short.

Alex ran after him, and tackled him down after only a few short strides, and the man had the audacity to throw his elbow back, catching Alex in the lip.

Lukas was there in an instant, securing the man with cuff's he'd pulled from his jacket. "Congratulations you just added assaulting a police officer to your list of offences," he said calmly to the idiot on the ground.

His eyes fell on Alex, who was panting and laying on his back where he had fallen, and he was holding his lip, which was bleeding.

The panic he felt at seeing his own blood was one he logically knew he needed to contain. He needed containment. Control. Think Alex, he chastised himself.

Luke reached for him, but Alex barked out, "no."

Luke winced, then reached into his jacket again and pulled out his phone, dialed and put it to his ear. While he listened he reached into another pocket in his jacket and pulled out a pair of gloves and slowly pulled them on. "Lukas Carter, badge number 86573, send a squad car to the picnic play area northside of Samson Lake park. Currently have a suspect in custody. Child endangerment."

Alex ridiculously felt like crying when Lukas ended the call and then held out a tissue toward Alex with his gloved hands.

"I'm sorry," he said miserably as he took the tissue and placed it to his lip.

Luke shook his head, rejecting the apology, and focused on the detained man. "Come on pal, it's time to mirandize. On your feet. You have the right to remain silent, anything you say can and will be used against you in a court of law. You have a right to an attorney. If you cannot afford an attorney one will be provided for you. Do you understand the rights I have just explained to you?"

The man glared at Lukas.

"I'll take that as a yes. Let's take a walk over there buddy, away from these good folk."

Alex took a deep breath, and pulled himself together, realizing he needed to get contact information. Getting to his feet, he did a quick jab at his lip with his tongue, and though it felt swollen, the bleeding seemed to have stopped at least.

"Oh! Are you alright?" The group of mothers all seemed agitated now after witnessing the tackle.

"I'm fine, thank you ladies. Could I please take your details?"

One of the women reached into a tote bag and pulled out a pen and paper. The paper was a contact sheet for their group she explained, and after crossing off a few names, she said that was all of them. "That's very helpful, thank you," he smiled.

"Do you want a band aid?" another mother offered, holding up a first aid kit.

The offer sobered him again, "no thank you, but I appreciate your assistance. Someone will be in touch. Enjoy the rest of your day."

He went in the direction that Lukas had taken the man and saw that he'd actually marched him out to the car park at this side of the lake where he was stood with him off the main walkway, obviously trying to keep him away from the main drag of foot traffic.

Alex handed the sheet of paper over to Luke, who looked down at it then nodded, but averted his eyes to scan for the squad car they were waiting for.

He was in trouble.

THIRTY-THREE

The squad car arrived, and Lukas gave his report to the officers and gave them the contact sheet which was essentially their witness list. He retrieved his handcuffs and assisted them putting the man in their own cuffs and securing him in the car.

Alex watched all this, and waited.

Luke watched the car go, and once it was out of sight, he came over to the bench and sat beside Alex. He was still wearing the gloves, and he still refused to look at him.

Alex couldn't take it any longer though, "Luke, I'm sorry."

"Me too," he said regretfully.

"It's the first time I'd seen my own blood in a while, it always freaks me out," he tried to explain, but it felt like a limp excuse.

"Of course," Luke nodded, still staring ahead.

"What is this?" Alex asked. "You're angry with me?"

Luke groaned and dropped his head to the back of the bench. After a beat he said, "no, I'm not angry. I'm hurt. That you wouldn't let me help you when you were hurt. But I know this relationship is all new and it's going to take a while for you and me to adjust to how to cope with stuff like this. Logically I know that. But it still hurt."

Alex put a hand on Luke's thigh, which made him finally look at him. "I'm sorry, it was a reflexive move. Not personal at all. And if you still want to, you can tend to my wound."

Luke snorted but sat up straight again, "it was hardly a wound, I've had bigger paper cuts."

"But I really feel like it might need kissing better," Alex said with a deadpan tone and face.

Luke took his chin and studied it, "wow now you mention it I think you're right. This is more than the average boo boo."

Alex nodded, "I felt that it was."

Laughing, Luke leaned in and gave him a gentle kiss. "I'm sorry too," he said in a whisper.

He was about to lean into another kiss, when his phone began to ring in his pocket, and he saw his battery was almost dead, "Fuller? My battery is about to die, what's up?"

"The interview is scheduled for the morning with Charlie, Markson asked that I give you the day off."

He rolled his eyes, "I'll be glad when this bullshit is done with. Did Charlie seem okay?"

"Yeah, she loves to talk-"

His phone battery cut off then, and he groaned. "Fuck."

Luke checked his own phone, "we should go in and write this up. So much for a fucking day off," he sighed.

Alex nodded, "okay, I think I've got a charger in my desk. Let's go."

On the ride over he realized he'd have to go to the pharmacy before he went home tonight, and he wondered if Luke would give him a ride.

They didn't speak when they went to their desks. They seemed to both have an understanding that they just needed to file the incident and get out again as soon as possible. Unfortunately though, Captain Markson was on the floor as they strolled in and were heading to their desks.

"Steinberg? Carter? Neither of you are meant to be here today." She was staring at the cut on Alex's lip.

"Ma'am there was an incident, we're just here to fill out an incident report," Lukas told her.

She folded her arms, "explain."

Luke sighed, "we were at the lake and witnessed a man filming the children. I detained him. He's downstairs now being processed and we supplied a list of witnesses."

Through all this though, Markson was staring

stonily at Alex, and he was about to ask what he'd done wrong when she frostily said, "my office now, both of you."

Luke frowned at Alex, but he just shrugged and followed his captain.

When Luke closed the door behind them she looked at them both, seeming to be waiting for something.

After a long silence, Markson focused on Luke. "Please tell me the name of the detainee?"

Luke frowned, "Pepper Morris."

Markson immediately pinched the bridge of her nose, and Alex had a horrible feeling he knew what this was going to be about.

"And what were you doing at the Lake?"

"Taking a walk," Alex supplied without breaking his scowl at her.

"You expect me to believe that you just happened to be in vicinity of one of the names you saw on my desk just yesterday Steinberg?" she said this accusingly.

Alex's frown deepened, "I did not see that name. You know the only name I saw and I fully disclosed its significance to me. And yes, I was taking a walk." He spoke very clearly before his anger could betray him.

Beside him he could feel Luke's confusion,

"Ma'am?"

She turned her eyes on him, "and you Carter? What were you doing at the Lake?"

"Like he said we were taking a walk. It's a public place, people walk there. What the hell is going on?"

She closed her eyes and pinched the bridge of her nose once more, exhaling heavily. "Don't file the reports."

"Are you fucking kidding me?" Alex couldn't hold back his fury.

She fixed her furious gaze on him, "we are days away from bringing down an international child pornography ring, and you are threatening the entire operation!"

"We were taking a walk," Alex repeated with calm anger. "And if you accuse me once more I will be filing a grievance," he threatened.

She blinked and looked between them both.

Luke was the one who broke the silence first, "I don't fully understand what's going on here, but I have to say Ma'am, that I was the one who saw Morris, and detained him. Steinberg was injured as Morris tried to escape. If there is an issue here, it was my fault."

"Do not file," Markson repeated without acknowledging what Luke had said. "Did Fuller speak to you Steinberg?"

"My phone died," he said coldly.

"I asked her to relay that I needed you out of the building tomorrow, but after today I really feel that it's in our mutual interest if you take the week off."

"Are you suspending me? For taking a walk?"

"You are endangering the integrity of this investigation, it is best that you are temporarily...not here."

He shook his head, "I can't believe this, are you forcing Carter on vacation as well?"

"Carter was not aware of the investigation, and you were."

"I was taking a walk, I did not deliberately detain one of your precious pedo's!"

She looked even more angry with that comment, "you think I enjoy coasting along and waiting? I don't! But this has to be handled delicately. And you have unknowingly made yourself a problem."

He seethed but had to bite back his retort before he did something that would land him in a disciplinary hearing.

"Carter, I need you to forget this incident," she finally looked at Luke.

Alex couldn't stop glaring daggers at Markson, so he didn't see the anger for himself, but he heard it in his tone when he said, "why wouldn't I detain a threat to children?"

"There is a larger operation ongoing right now, and as I said, it's a matter of days for it to be wrapped up."

"So lose his paperwork for a couple of days until it's done. Don't put him back on street!"

Markson took a deep breath, "I have my orders, and you have yours. Or do you need a vacation too?"

Luke stiffened beside him, "no Ma'am," he said quietly.

Alex finally looked at him and was amazed he'd buckled.

Luke's frown said he wasn't happy about it, but he had given his answer.

"Call me when I'm actually allowed to do my job," Alex said angrily and stormed out of the office.

He was down the stairs before Luke caught up to him, "wait, Alex!"

Alex stopped, but he was still wearing his anger on his face, he could feel it.

"What the hell is going on?"

"The situation that's merged with other situations I mentioned earlier," he bit out.

Luke flinched, "okay now you're pissed at me?"

Was he? He closed his eyes and took a deep breath. "I'm not," he said. "She put you in a difficult position. There's a lot you don't know."

"So look at me," he demanded.

Alex looked and immediately felt his anger turn to sadness when he saw to worry in the stormy grey eyes. "I am really struggling to not want a cigarette right now," he admitted.

"Alex what is going on?"

"Could you drive me to a pharmacy please?" he ignored the question.

Luke stared at him, "I need to know that we're okay?"

"We are I just really need to get out of this building right now," he said, which was true.

THIRTY-FOUR

Luke drove him to the pharmacy and went with him to collect his medication. Alex couldn't seem to uncoil the knot of rage that was holding him bound, so when they were sat back in Luke's car and he was being asked where he'd like to have dinner, he couldn't comment.

"Fucking talk Alex, you said you wanted to talk today, this is the opposite of talking."

"I don't know where to fucking start okay!"

Luke sighed, "okay, well I've already figured out that there's an embargo on arresting and capturing local pedophile's because of the international operation she mentioned. Why are you a part of that?"

"I'm not," he breathed. "Years ago, Jeanie as a child had her foster father sent down for taking kiddie pictures. He got out last year and killed his wife and found Jeanie and has made threats against her, hence all the private security, they have. That's one situation."

Luke nodded, "okay."

"Last week I took a statement from a man named Ryan Miller who believed his priest was poisoning his children. He filed the request for a restraining order against that priest, and by the time he got home his boss was there reminding him that the priest was the one to get him his job, and did he really want to go ahead with the restraining order?"

Luke balked, "that's coercion."

"I convinced Miller to proceed with it. But Markson pulled the paperwork because of this international operation bullshit, so I sent the man and his kids on vacation."

Luke smiled, "of course you did. So that is another situation."

"And the girl I helped escape her oppressive home last week also coincidentally turns out to be the daughter of the priest, who now is a person of interest, but I'm not allowed to escort her for the interview anymore because of my involvement with Miller already, and the stalker my sister-in-law has means I have to recuse from anything to do with that operation or I jeopardize the whole thing."

"And today we nabbed another local pedophile, making Markson think you are meddling or deliberately being difficult when you're not." Luke sighed and wiped a hand down his face. "What a fucking mess."

"I don't know how to handle this," he admitted with a humorless laugh.

Luke put a hand on his leg and squeezed, "listen, you don't need to handle this right now, just put it out of your head. Okay? Don't let this ruin our time?"

Alex growled and closed his eyes but covered the hand on his leg. He screwed up his face as he tried to erase the last two hours that had in fact ruined their time. He took a few deep breaths and focused on his stomach. "I'm feeling pasta, I want death by carbs."

When he opened his eyes and looked at Luke he saw a smile. "Home cooked or restaurant?"

He smiled too, "are you offering to cook for me?"

"Yes," he said. "I can handle a pan of boiling water quite efficiently."

"Okay, but I will need to borrow a phone charger. And I will need to go home after."

Luke started the car, "not that I'm trying to abduct you but why do you need to go home?"

"Because I've worn these clothes for two days already."

Luke considered that, then started to drive, "we could pick up clothes, or I could come back to your place?"

"Not sick of me yet?"

"I have a feeling that tomorrow, when I have to go to work, this little bubble we're in will be

well and truly dissolved, so I want to prolong
the inevitable return to reality."

THIRTY-FIVE

It was ten thirty when he pulled into All Saints House in his new car, a second hand Jeep that he could luckily afford to buy outright without tapping his savings. As his registration wasn't listed for the security team, he wasn't surprised when they were all waiting to inspect the vehicle when he pulled up and they confirmed it was him.

"Am I good to go in?" Alex asked while they were checking the interior of the Jeep.

Simon's waved him inside the house, and Alex headed straight to Eric's office and flopped down on his brother's couch.

Eric was on a phone call, but gave him a nod in greeting, and Alex laid an arm across his eyes to rest them while he waited.

"Hey," Eric said when he hung up.

"Morning," Alex looked over at Eric, but continued to recline on the couch. "This is comfortable," he observed.

Eric laughed, "you're here to lounge on my couch?"

"Yeah, kinda tired."

Eric raised a brow, "any reason you aren't at work on a Monday morning?"

"Yeah I'm suspended. Or should I say I'm on a non-voluntary vacation."

"Really?" Eric frowned.

Alex rolled his eyes. "I had a busy day yesterday."

"If you can give me an hour to tie this up, you can tell me all about it."

Alex nodded, "kids at school?"

"Can't you tell, the house is nice and quiet," Eric joked.

Alex stretched, "I'm gonna chill in the garden."

"I think Jeanie is out there if you want emotional company," he joked.

He laughed and went through to the garden, mentally acknowledging that this is when he would normally light a cigarette, but as he'd made it through a week without one, he figured he was officially quitting.

"Hey," Jeanie called happily. She was reclining on a shaded lounger by the pool, wearing shorts and a tank top.

"Morning," he took the lounger beside hers and sighed as he lay back. He was wearing black jeans and a long sleeved t shirt, so he felt overdressed, but it felt so good to be relaxing.

"So I have to say for the record, I really like Luke," she turned to him as much as her belly would allow comfortably.

He couldn't help the grin that split his face, "yeah, I do too." He met her eyes and confessed, "I've got that giddy, like him too much feeling."

Jeanie clapped her hands together, "he's gorgeous."

"Yeah."

"And he did great meeting everyone."

"Yeah."

"Survived the kids."

"Yeah."

"Good in bed?"

Alex laughed, "you really want to know those details?"

Jeanie shrugged, "I want to know that you're happy, and yes if you tell me he's got a tiny wiener after ticking all those other boxes, that's just going to be disappointing."

"All my boxes are well ticked."

"Excellent," she grinned, then grimaced and rubbed her belly. "Easy boys," she said.

"When's your due date?"

"Technically in five weeks, but I don't think I'm going to last another one."

Alex was alarmed, "really?"

She laughed, "it's fine you don't need to look so panicked. The babies are both a really good size, and I could safely deliver. It's quite common for multiple births to not go full term."

Alex winced, "that's terrifying."

She laughed, "which is why God didn't give you a vagina."

"Clearly."

"What happened to your lip?"

He frowned, "I'll tell you and Eric over lunch."

"Hmm, okay. Wasn't Luke was it? Or some kind of weird sex injury?"

He laughed, "no and no."

They shared a comfortable silence for a while, both laying back and just enjoying the peace.

Until Alvin could be heard bellowing as Christina lugged him out to the pool. "He's driving me nuts today, so you're all going to suffer," his sister grumbled as she stomped over.

Alex took in how tired she looked, and felt immediate guilt for living in a lovesick bubble while she was struggling with a teething infant. "Come here big boy," he held out his hands for his nephew, and Christina dumped him down on the lounger with Alex.

"Thanks," she flopped down on another lounger. "He's not sleeping well, fucking teeth."

Alex winced as he watched Alvin fisting his mouth again.

Jeanie adjusted her position again, and Alex really didn't know how women dealt with all this crap. "You sure you're okay?" he asked Jeanie.

Both ladies just gave him a withering look and she said, "this is pregnancy Alex. It's not glamorous, or comfortable, and the glowing thing is just a myth."

Christina nodded, "I think I was comfortable for a total of two weeks for mine. Some part of you is constantly getting kicked, or stretched or pulled or is aching. It sucks. But at least I never have to do it again," she said with a bitter edge to her sarcasm.

Alex shared a look with Jeanie, and neither commented.

Alvin chose that moment to slap him with a drool covered fist, getting his attention. "Okay okay, I'm sorry," he apologized to his nephew and sat up straighter, allowing him to stand and stomp, which was his new favorite thing to do.

"So how's things going with Luke?" Christina asked.

"Good."

Jeanie piped up with, "they're doing it."

349

Christina laughed, while Alex objected. "I didn't tell you we'd done it."

"You said he ticked all the boxes," Jeanie pointed out.

"Yeah he does," he grinned, making Christina laugh again.

"I miss that," she said sadly, though still smiling. "The happy beginning part of a relationship."

"Oh honey," Jeanie sighed. "I'm sure he'll come back."

Christina flinched, "who?"

Jeanie frowned, "Tim."

Christina shook her head, "I'm done with him."

Alex noticed then that she no longer wore her wedding ring and wondered when she had removed it.

Jeanie looked upset but gave a nod of understanding.

"I'm already thinking I need some new dick in my life," his sister said bluntly.

"Really?" Alex was surprised, he thought she would be more upset about her marriage. But then he remembered her reaction when Tim had left without a word, and how flatly she'd refused to let the security team follow him.

"Yeah," Christina got up and went to the

pool to sit on the side and dunk her feet in. "The thing about being abandoned is it's just made me super horny."

"I'm not sure if that's a healthy reaction or not," Alex said honestly. And also, he didn't strictly enjoy hearing that his sister wanted dick.

She seemed to sense this as she just shot him a look, "I'm not dead, and I miss sex. I'm not interested in a relationship or finding a new daddy for my baby, I just want a good fuck."

"I got the message," Alex shook his head and focused on Alvin who was getting bored. "I'm gonna take Big Kahuna here for a walk around the flower garden so you girls can talk about dicks."

Baby on his hip, he left his sister and sister-in-law to stroll around the garden, hoping the bright colors would distract Alvin. He even took a couple of selfies with him while he took a break from chewing his fist to crushing daisies within his iron grasp, and the camera actually captured the hint of the new tooth poking at the gum.

Feeling playful, he sent the best picture to Luke, who quickly responded with, 'cheating on me already I see.'

'Na, he's just using me. Needs someone to literally wipe his ass for him.'

Alex was just sitting on the grass with Alvin laying on his back between his knees, and letting him rip the grass up with his outraged fists when Eric stepped out and spotted him with Alvin, and smirked.

"I'm worried about Christina," Alex said as he got to his feet, then scooped up Alvin and threw him up high for a bounce, making him laugh.

"I know what you mean, she's so detached right now," Eric held out his hands for Alvin, and Alex handed him over gratefully, the kid was heavy.

"Detached but wants to go out and get laid," Alex amended.

Eric frowned, "figures."

"Really?" Alex was confused.

"Of course. She wants validation right now, in it's most basic form."

From that point of view it made sense. "I guess."

Eric took over bouncy steps to jiggle Alvin, which made their nephew giggle as they went over to the ladies, but as they neared Eric stopped focusing on the bouncing and took larger strides when he saw Jeanie bent over, and Christina rubbing her back.

"Jeanie?" Eric handed Alvin back to Alex and

rushed to his wife's side.

"I'm fine, but I think it's started," she smiled up at Eric.

"You're sure?" he cupped a hand under her stomach and another to her lower back.

"I'm just timing the cramps now," she said calmly.

Alex shot a panicked look at Christina, "okay, so we need to get you to the hospital right?"

Christina rolled her eyes and reached out for Alvin, "it'll be hours yet, if she goes to the hospital right now they'll just send her home."

It was clear he really didn't have a clue what was involved in a normal labor.

"Let's go in and have lunch," Jeanie said as she looked at her watch.

"You're sure?" Eric asked.

"Yes, I'm hungry."

After a relaxed lunch of sandwiches, during which Alex filled them in on the circumstances of his forced vacation time, Jeanie started packing a bag for her hospital visit, and Eric was making frantic phone calls to his work notifying them of his pending absence.

"What are you pacing for?" Jeanie laughed at Alex who was indeed pacing their large living room.

"I'm nervous," he admitted.

She laughed, "nothing is happening yet." She patted his arm reassuringly.

"Is there anything I can do?"

"Mind sticking around for Lily and Ben this evening?"

"Of course," he felt better immediately, knowing he had a role to play in this now.

"Bed by 9 at the latest, it's a school night, but I've already arranged for Rosa to come and oversee the morning, so don't worry about that," she said. "At least two vegetables in their dinner, or no dessert. And I don't think they have homework due, but check for me please?"

"Two vegetables and bed by 9 and check homework, I can do that."

She smiled and checked her watch again.

"Were you just contracting that whole time you were talking to me?"

Jeanie laughed again, "you really have no idea do you," she patted his cheek patronizingly.

Alex shook his head, "clearly not."

She sat down and checked through the side pocket of her bag when Eric came in, "all set, I'm just going to go and change," he too seemed to be more on Alex's level of panic than Jeanie's.

She laughed, "take your time."

She got to her feet again and Alex hovered

over her as she continued to pack things like her kindle and phone charger.

"Alex, I'm not going to suddenly collapse or explode," she snapped when she bumped into him for the third time.

"Okay, I'm sorry," he backed up but still hovered. In part to distract himself but also so Luke wouldn't be expecting him for dinner as they had planned, he sent an update to him. 'Jeanie is going into labor, so I'm on kid patrol this evening I'm afraid.'

'I'd help you babysit, but I'm not free until after 8. Have to taxi the old lady to Bingo.'

'You want to babysit with me?'

'Sure.'

"Jeanie?"

"I told you I'm fine," she snapped again.

Alex looked up from his phone and saw she was holding her belly and rocking her hips from side to side slowly. Her face was red and she was staring at her watch intently and taking measured breaths. From two minutes ago this was suddenly a very different picture.

It was very obvious now that she was definitely in labor, and he decided to hold his question about Luke coming over, he didn't want to irritate her any more.

He was glad when Eric returned and was

carrying his own bag, and Hunter came into the room as well. Alex watched as the man took in the sight of Jeanie and frowned. "Are you," he started to ask her, then looked to Eric instead, "is she?"

"My ears work fine Hunter, yes I'm in labor!" She snapped at the man.

Hunter actually wilted a little under her fury, which was hilarious to witness the little pixie attacking the armed man.

"I'll call in the back up and get the car ready," Hunter said and left the room.

Jeanie actually growled at his retreating back, and Eric shot a warning look to Alex as if to say, 'save yourself'. "Sweetheart," he said softly.

"What?" she asked on a heavy exhale.

"I'm going to guess that it's getting stronger, so we should probably go to the hospital sooner rather than later."

Whatever she was about to say was lost in a look of shock as her waters broke, and her argument faded as she nodded up at Eric, "okay."

Christina came in then, "I called your doctor she's going to meet you at the hospital."

Eric nodded his thanks to her.

"I'll go get Daisy," she wrinkled her nose at

the mess on the carpet.

Jeanie chose that moment to crumple, and she burst into tears, and clutched at Eric's front, "I can't do this!"

Eric gave her his best smile and said soothingly, "yes you can, you're amazing. And I'm going to be right there with you."

Her blue eyes were wide and filled with tears, "I love you."

Eric laughed, "I love you too, now let's go get you into some dry clothes, and we'll go get our son's.

Once they had left the room, Alex looked at the puddle and grimaced, "definitely glad I'm not a woman."

Christina snorted as she came back into the room, "the joys of childbirth aren't beautiful?"

The joy of childbirth had been what killed their mother, and had nearly killed Christina just six months ago. "I don't think anything will ever convince me."

Daisy came in then carrying a bucket and an armful of towels. She smiled at Alex, and set to work.

"Do you mind if Luke comes over this evening?"

Christina raised her brows, "it isn't my house I don't care. As long as you don't think you'll get any time to get freaky, coz I doubt the Muppet's will settle easily tonight, with their parents missing."

Alex nodded, "I wasn't intending to freak it on every surface, he just offered to come over," he shrugged.

"I get it, and it's cool. Spend time with your hot new boyfriend," she rolled her eyes. "He got any straight single friends?"

Alex shook his head, "how would I know that? I don't even know when his birthday is yet."

THIRTY-SIX

Maxwell Alexander Saint John was born at 9:37pm, and his brother Arthur Bradley Saint John was born just four minutes later.

Mother and babies were doing well, though Jeanie was quite naturally exhausted. Eric had sent him all this information in a text message. Alex relayed this news to Lily, as she was still out of bed and refusing to settle.

"Do we still have to go to school tomorrow?" Lily was bouncing on her bed.

"Yes you do," Alex was exhausted by her energy. "So you really need to get into bed now, and get some sleep or you'll be a space case tomorrow."

Lily grumbled, but very dramatically flopped herself down on her bed.

Luke was in the doorway trying not to laugh as Alex was trying to be the literal bad cop.

"But I'm not tired," she whined.

"Lily," Alex warned. "Now is a very important time for you to show you can be the grown up girl I know you're capable of being," he used a mild scolding tone, hoping he could appeal to her deeper need to be treated like a grown up.

She sobered at that.

"And how about this for a deal," he tucked her in and crouched down. "You go close your eyes and do your very best to go to sleep, and you stop all this whining for attention that I know you don't mean, and this weekend if you've managed to be good all week, I'll take you and Ben somewhere."

She considered that. "Where?"

"You can choose, but you have to do your part."

"Hmm," she thought.

"You can think about it while you're going to sleep." He stooped down and kissed her forehead. "Goodnight Lilybug."

Luke smiled at the cuteness of it all as Alex closed the door to her room. Just next door was Ben's room, and Alex wasn't surprised to find him reading in bed. "Ready for lights out?"

Ben looked up, "can I just finish this chapter?"

"What are you reading?" Alex took the book from his hands, and was amused to see The Count Of Monte Cristo, the book Luke had told him about at the restaurant when they'd met. "This is a little grown up for you."

"But Eric said I could read it, if I could get

through it," he said determinedly.

Alex smiled and handed the book back, "fair enough, but that's only three more pages kid, then I want lights out."

Ben smiled, "promise."

"You okay?"

Ben nodded, "yeah all good."

Alex smiled, "at least you're not being a brat. And I promised Lily that if she behaves and stops being difficult, I'll take you guys somewhere this weekend, but don't let her bully you into choosing just for herself. Okay?"

He grinned, "she's only pretending to be a brat."

"We all know, that's why it's a waste of her time doing it. You're a smart kid though, and a good friend to her."

Ben shrugged, "you remember when we met in the bookshop?"

Alex nodded, "of course, I'll never forget."

"When I saw Lily I thought she looked like an angel. And I think life has been pretty great since she's been in it. I always want to be friends with her."

There was something so sincere and sweet about the boy's confession, that Alex ruffled the boys hair. "Goodnight Ben."

Luke didn't speak until they had returned

downstairs and found Christina sitting on the large couch and holding a large glass of wine and was swiping on her phone. "Knocked them out?"

"Bribed them to try and get them to sleep," Alex admitted.

"Sounds about right," she took a sip of her wine. "I can handle the overnight shift if you guys want to take off," she offered.

Something in her tone seemed off to Alex, so he just shook his head, "na it's okay. I'd think you would be sleeping while you could, before Alvin kicks off."

She sighed, "right," she agreed. "I'll take the hint," she got to her feet.

"No, I wasn't chasing you off," Alex realized that's how she had taken his comment.

She shook her head, "you weren't wrong, I should try and sleep. Nice to see you again Luke," she gave him a smile and left the room, bumping into Hunter as he was entering and spilling her wine over them both.

Hunter grasped her by the arms and bodily moved her back from him, and then took the glass from her hand.

"Hey," she objected, but she didn't try to take it back.

Hunter stared at her for a moment, then

drank the last mouthful in the glass and said, "hey."

Shaking her head, Christina stormed from the room leaving Alex confused.

"What's going on?" Alex asked, meaning what was going on with Hunter and his sister, but the answer he got was not an answer.

"Cecily Culver has just been mugged outside of Open Arms, thought you'd be interested to know."

"Is she okay? Was it Straker?"

Hunter shook his head, "unconfirmed from the footage I've seen there, but she's fine. She's with the police now, but she called Eric, who just called me. I'm going to take some pictures to her and see if I can learn anything."

Alex nodded, "do you have anyone posted at the hospital?"

"Of course I do, there's a guard on Jeanie and another at the nursery, although the hospital isn't thrilled about that one. And here you've got the standard four man team. Three once I leave."

"Alright, I wasn't implying you weren't doing your job," Alex held out his hands in a pacifying gesture.

Hunter nodded, "you staying here tonight?"

"Yes."

Another nod, "I'll let you know if I learn anything from Cecily."

Alex watched him go and was stunned for a minute.

"You still with me?" Luke asked.

Alex gave him a smile, "right here. Babysitting is fun," he laughed.

Luke laughed with him, "I have to say, you're kinda cute when you're in uncle mode."

"Cute?"

"You heard me," Luke stepped up to him. "Are you allowed to have sleepovers?"

"Yes, but you should know, it's advisable to not sleep naked. The kids tend to just burst into the room, and sex in the communal areas is forbidden."

Luke laughed, "I think I can handle that."

Alex pulled him into his arms, "how was your day dear?" he asked this as they hadn't really been able to have a proper greeting earlier.

"Boring. Although Fuller asked me discreetly to let you know that Charlie was fine and the interview went well. Apparently they were very pleased with the information they were able to get from her."

Alex eye rolled, "thanks for telling me."

Luke rubbed his back, "but let's not talk about work."

"Agreed. You hungry?"

"I could eat."

"Let me introduce you to the wonder of my brother's magically always stocked fridge."

Luke was impressed at the range of meals available. "You can just help yourself?"

"Daisy the head housekeeper, loves to cook. The security team are always helping themselves too so don't feel any guilt."

"I don't feel guilt, I'm just impressed," Luke helped himself to a can of coke.

As he was heating the cottage pie Luke leaned into the counter and looked around.

"I know it's a really big house. Jeanie inherited it from her grandfather who was some reclusive millionaire scrooge," Alex said.

Luke shook his head. "I wasn't really interested in the house, I was curious about your sister though."

Alex winced, "yeah she's having a rough time right now."

"I take it Alvin's father isn't in the picture?"

"He took off just over a week ago. But before he left things were bad."

"And she's on Tinder already? Damn that's fast work."

"Tinder?"

Luke grinned, "that's what she was doing

when we found her."

Alex groaned, "earlier she was being very vocal about how much she wanted some dick."

Luke laughed, "nothing quite like scratching the itch."

Alex placed down one portion and started heating another. "I'm worried about her."

"Well, she seems like a strong woman, and you guys are a pretty tight knit family, I'm sure she'll come out on top."

Alex winced, "she's been through so much, it's not fair."

"Life rarely is," Luke said honestly. "But I think it's all about how you choose to conduct yourself."

A beep that wasn't the microwave sounded inside the house, and Alex was confused for a moment, until Simon's stuck his head in the kitchen and just said a single word. "Situation."

Alex hurried after him, and the two other agents that were congregating in the parlor. "Terry stay here and check the feeds, Harris with me."

"What's happened?"

"Perimeter alert on the east wall," Simon's told him.

Alex knew that the east wall was closest to the road, and the most likely source of a breach.

"I'm coming," he said.

"No, please let us do our jobs. I'd feel better if you were with the children."

Alex winced, "give me a radio at least."

One was thrust into his hand, and Simon's ordered, "lock the doors when we step out, this is likely a diversion."

Alex nodded, "has anyone told Ernest and Rosa?"

"Their house has been equipped with a panic room, I told them to go in until it was clear."

He watched them go out and did as he was bid and locked the door.

Luke was at his back and frowning, "I take it this isn't a regular scenario?"

"No," he wondered if he should tell Christina or not, and opted to not. "Mind holding here while I check on the kids?"

Luke nodded and accepted the radio.

Alex raced up the stairs and went straight to Lily's room, and panicked when she wasn't in her bed. "No," he cried out, and ran to Ben's room, where he saw both Lily and Ben turned to face each other in the boys bed.

Thankfully they were both asleep already, and didn't witness the near breakdown he felt on the verge of just moments before, and he frowned down at them both.

The light was still on, and Ben was still holding the book, but it looks like Lily had crawled in to talk to him, and they'd both fallen asleep sharing the same pillow.

As quietly as he could, he turned off the light and closed the door again. Right now it didn't matter where they slept, just that they slept.

Before he returned downstairs he went to his bedroom and retrieved his gun, which he tucked into the back of his jeans.

"Anything?" he asked Luke who was still stood where he'd left him.

"A fire," Luke said.

"What?"

"Fire service has already been called, Simon's thinks someone threw a Molotov."

Alex went through the parlor to a door that led to the security office and saw Terry who was on the radio. "Simon's I can confirm there is an attempt on the South side."

He knew then that Cecily Culver had only been attacked tonight to lure out Hunter.

THIRTY-SEVEN

"I need you to stand guard over the children," Alex told Luke as he made for the front door.

Luke shot out a hand and grabbed his arm in an iron grip, "don't you dare go out there."

"It's my family."

"And this house is secure, you're only complicating things for the security team if you step outside. It's an obvious trap."

He hated that he was right.

"Have you contacted Hunter?" he called through to Terry.

"Yes, he's coming back," was the answer.

Alex didn't think he'd ever felt more frustrated. "I'm going to check on Christina," he told Luke, who gave him a nod.

He hurried to her door, but listened at it for a moment before knocking as softly as he could.

Christina was in sweats when she opened the door and whispered, "what?"

"I just didn't want you to be alarmed, there's something going on outside."

"Someone trying to break in?"

"Possibly, there's a fire at the outer wall. I just wanted to make sure you were okay."

369

"Fine," she whispered. "Although now I'm terrified."

"Sorry, I thought you'd want to know."

She nodded, "the kids okay?"

"Yeah, both asleep in Ben's bed."

She nodded again, "yeah that keeps happening." She went back into the room grabbed the baby monitor from her bedside, and took a moment to peer down at her son, who he could hear was snoring softly.

Alex felt better somehow that his sister was coming along as they returned to the security office where Luke was now sat beside Terry and listening to the radio and watching the feeds.

"He's at the wall, he obviously doesn't realize he's on camera."

Alex watched as Simon's was on another feed and nearly at the intruder. He and Harris had split and were closing in on him from two angles.

"Is it him?" Christina asked.

Alex shook his head, "I don't think we know for sure."

His phone rang then, and he saw it was Eric, so he stepped back from the feeds and back into the parlor. "Eric?"

"What's going on? The security team are

being vague but said something happened at the house."

"Intruder, we're just watching now. Simon's and Harris are about to detain him hopefully. The children are fine, I just checked they're both fast asleep," he relayed this as he knew that's all Eric would care about, and it was confirmed as he heard a heavy exhale.

"Thank God, Jeanie is asleep I didn't want to wake her with this."

"Don't. I just hope that we can finally get the bastard."

In the security room, Terry was shouting. Alex stepped back inside and saw that there was a struggle, and a flash on the screen told him that a gun had just been fired.

"What's going on?" Eric was panicking again.

"Eric stay calm I'll tell you once I know," he tried to calm his brother.

"Hunter is at the gates," Terry announced, and sure enough, on the screen Hunter was opening the gates, and a fire engine was there behind him. As soon as the car could clear the gate he was speeding up the driveway and the man was vaulting out the car towards the skirmish.

Christina gasped as she saw Hunter pulling his weapon and levelling it on the man.

Simon's was wrestling the weapon from the intruder and Harris was lying on the ground, unmoving.

Another flash, and Hunter fell back, but fired his own gun and the man stopped struggling.

Alex put his arm around Christina's shoulders, "let's stop watching." He tried to steer Christina from the room.

She wouldn't be moved, "don't touch me."

"You don't want to see this," Alex was concerned that she'd just seen a man shot and killed on screen. But her eyes were fixed on Hunter, who was getting to his feet and going to Harris.

"Alex? What's happening?" Eric was still on the phone, and he snapped himself out of the security feed they were all transfixed by.

"There was a problem restraining the intruder, he was carrying a gun, and it looks as though Harris was wounded. Hunter arrived and was wounded as well, but managed to fire on the intruder."

Eric growled, "is it Straker?"

"I don't know Eric."

Just then Hunter was on the radio, "I can confirm the identity of William Straker."

THIRTY-EIGHT

How the two older children slept through all the noise, Alex didn't know. The fire was contained thankfully, and with minimal damage to the property, although several shrubs were destroyed.

It was now 2am, and police cars and ambulances were blocking the driveway and street beyond, aside from the one ambulance that had carried away Harris who was bleeding heavily from the gunshot wound to his stomach.

Hunter was sat in the back of another ambulance, but was refusing to leave. A bullet had skimmed his arm, and he insisted that it was just a flesh wound as he stripped his shirt off so a paramedic could assess for themselves.

Luke was supervising the police officers who were reviewing the footage of the entire invasion attempt.

William Straker was pronounced dead on the scene, due to the shot Hunter had fired, which had struck him in the chest.

Christina was currently cradling Alvin to her chest and was stood on the front porch of the house and pointing at the flashing lights for her son. He'd woken about an hour ago with his teething pains again, and Christina was just currently trying to calm him while waiting for the medicine to kick in.

Alex saw with interest that Hunter quite frequently kept glancing at her, and she in turn kept looking back.

"How are you holding up?" Alex asked her.

She smiled, "glad that asshole is dead."

Alvin was mesmerized by the lights.

"Hunter is going to be okay," he said, mainly to see her reaction was what he predicted.

Christina eye rolled, "good for him." She sighed, "obviously I'm glad. As much as he's an arrogant prick, he's done his job well."

Alex laughed. "Come inside sis, you don't want to get cold."

She nodded, but shot another glance at Hunter, who was watching her as she went back inside the house.

Alex gave him a nod and followed his sister inside, where she went to the kitchen.

Luke was stretching in the parlor, and Alex gave him a grimace. "I'm so sorry about this," Alex stepped up behind him and rubbed his shoulders.

"I am feeling like whenever we're together it seems to end with squad cars," Luke joked. He leaned back into Alex. "Maybe when everything is squared away we could plan a weekend away or something."

"That sounds nice, what are you thinking?"

"Just somewhere quiet, with no other people around."

"What about your Mom?"

"I could make arrangements for a couple of days."

"Hmm, and what would we do in these two days of no other people?"

Luke laughed and turned in his arms, "nothing."

Terry left the security office with two police officers in tow, and Luke and Alex separated.

"We've got everything we need right now."

Alex had to give it to Hunter, his guys were well trained. Terry had not only recorded every moment of the incident, and provided full copies for the police to take with them, Simons had handled all the statements that were required for the inhabitants of the household.

When Hunter joined them in the parlor as the officers were leaving, he searched the room before settling his eyes on Alex. "I need to go with the police, but the next shift of the team should be here within the hour."

Alex nodded, "thank you. Are you sure

you're okay?" He gestured to the arm that was now bandaged.

"Yeah, I've had worse. Is everyone in here okay?"

Alex nodded, and knew what wasn't being said, "she's fine."

Hunter flinched, but didn't argue that his concern had been for Christina.

"Are you being charged?"

The man shrugged, "maybe, although with all the evidence I don't see how."

"Call if you need a lawyer," Alex joked, which made Hunter smirk as he left the house again.

Luke waited until he'd gone before leaning into Alex and whispering, "he's hot for your sister."

"Figured that one out for myself Poirot," he joked. "Listen I'm not gonna be offended if you want to take off and go home, you've got work in a few hours."

"Yes, you do," a female voice piped up.

Alex and Luke both turned to see Captain Markson stood in the doorway. His stomach felt like it was full of lead.

"Good morning Captain," it was all he could think of to say that was both polite and accurate.

Shaking her head she stepped into the parlor

and kept looking between Luke and Alex. "I have been told that none of the inhabitants were harmed, is that correct?"

Alex nodded, "only the security team, we all remained within the house."

She took a deep breath in, and focused on Luke, "I take it you are both involved romantically?"

"Is that any of your business?" Luke asked wearily.

"You know full well it is my business when it comes to the officers in my department and the potential for conflict of interest."

"What I think, is that although by the book that may be true," Alex said, unable to hold back any longer, "you've come here tonight because you heard the name Straker mentioned, and wanted to ensure another asshole wasn't interfered with before his time. Then you found out I was involved, but really I wasn't, so as much as you want to lay into me for this scenario, you know you can't as I literally had nothing to do with any of it. So now you're going to pick on the fact that we're dating, because I just piss you off."

She blinked at that, "is that what you think?"

"See it from my side Captain," he bit out.

She seemed saddened by that, "and you try

seeing it from mine."

They were at an impasse.

Christina came in from the kitchen then holding a now sleeping Alvin, and the sight of his sister holding a baby seemed to snap Markson out of her fury.

"See you in the morning, Carter. Steinberg, I'm glad your family is safe," she said stiffly, and turned on her heels.

Alex closed the door behind her and glowered at the floor for a moment.

"She seemed lovely," Christina whispered.

Alex wanted to laugh and he looked up to see she was smiling.

"You guys could really be in trouble for dating?" she asked, still whispering.

"Technically no, we're not partners," Luke told her quietly. "But inter departmental relationships do get monitored."

"Well tell her it's cash up front to watch," she joked, making them both laugh silently. "I'm going to bed, is there much more excitement going on?"

Alex shook his head, "you go, I'm just going to wait for the new security team to arrive then I'll be doing the same."

She gave them both a smile, "goodnight then."

THIRTY-NINE

As he'd warned, Lily came bursting into the room and dive bombed the bed, landing squarely between Luke and Alex.

Only the sound of the door banging open gave him warning to brace himself for the impact of her giggling body. Beside him Luke made an oomph sound, so he suspected he'd caught an elbow or knee to the soft tissues.

"Lily," he chastised.

"It's morning," she said brightly.

Alex blearily looked at his phone and saw that it was just after 5, "barely."

"Is Mom coming home today?"

He pulled himself up to a sitting position and blinked at her, "probably, I don't know for sure yet."

Lily decided to pick on Luke then, by poking his shoulder, "wakey wakey."

Luke didn't open his eyes, but he did start licking his lips, "so, hungry," he said faintly.

Lily poked him again, "so wake up then you can eat."

"Mmm, hungry," he smacked his lips together again.

Lily giggled.

Luke sniffed the air, still not opening his eyes, "I smell...giggly little girl... who... needs... beating up!" Luke opened his eyes and tickled her belly, making Lily erupt in laughter.

Alex couldn't help but laugh too, and decided to pin her arms down so Luke had a clear shot at tickling her.

"Stop!" she begged.

"But you wanted me awake, and you weren't carrying bacon, so this is what you get," Luke explained calmly as he continued to tickle.

When she was nearing hysterical levels, he stopped abruptly, and got out of bed, reaching for his jeans.

Just a few hours ago when they'd finally come to bed, they had been so exhausted they had both just pulled off their shoes and jeans and fallen into sleep.

Lily sighed but seemed pleased with her work so far. "Are you guys in love?"

Luke burst out laughing, "never change Lily."

Lily looked up at Alex, "what?"

"That's a very private question to ask," he explained and shoved her aside so he too could get out of bed.

"Well how will I know the answer if I don't ask the question?"

Luke laughed again, "she's not wrong." After

zipping his jeans, he sat on the bed to pull on his boots.

"The point, Lily, is that you don't have to know everything. Some things are private."

She lounged back on the large bed, looking quite pleased with herself for kicking out the two men and claiming it for herself.

"Oh no, if you're insisting its morning and kicking us out of bed, you're getting up too!" Alex grabbed her ankle and dragged her to the bottom of the bed making her giggle once more.

He shot what he hoped was an apologetic smile at Luke, who didn't seem to be mad at all, but did look tired.

"Go and get dressed, and I'll go and see about breakfast. Is Ben up?"

"Yeah, but he said it was too early," she seemed disappointed by this.

"Maybe start listening to your brother," Alex pulled on his own jeans and yawned into his hand.

"Why are you so tired?"

"Because we had to stay up late and eat all the candy and break all your toys, it was exhausting," Luke joked.

Lily giggled at his grumpy tone, "you're funny."

Luke flopped back onto the bed and scowled at her. "No, I'm mean and scary."

She grinned, "hilarious."

He intensified his scowl, "I am the stuff of nightmares and you will fear me child!" he bellowed.

Her grin flicked to Alex, "can I have bacon for breakfast?'

Daisy of course had enough bacon for everybody, and even though she was flustered to meet Luke, she quickly instructed everybody to sit.

Luke looked at his phone to check the time, and he frowned.

"What's wrong?"

Luke smiled instantly, "nothing, just dreading the day." He reached across the table and grasped Alex's hand.

Alex gave the strong fingers a squeeze, "don't take any shit from Markson."

"Yeah don't take any shit," Lily mimicked, making him groan.

"You know full well that is a word you aren't meant to use Lily," Alex chided.

Lily opened her mouth to retort but he held up a finger and gave her a look he hoped conveyed that he wasn't kidding. "Remember our deal," he said.

She considered that, then attacked the plate of bacon that Daisy placed down and focused on eating.

Luke hid his smirk and helped himself to bacon as well. "I'm sure it will all be fine," he said firmly. "We haven't done anything wrong."

After a hearty breakfast, Ernest and Rosa came in to collect the children to ready them for school, and Alex walked Luke out to his car.

"I'm gonna guess there will be baby welcoming for you tonight," Luke speculated.

Alex shrugged, "who knows."

"Well I have to take the old lady to her weekly bridge cheating club tonight."

"Fun," Alex could hear the regret in Luke's voice.

Luke gave him a look of longing then, and it had nothing to do with sexual hunger, "I feel that, we really need some quality snuggle time."

Alex laughed, "if someone had told me a week ago you were a snuggle monster I would have laughed."

"Who doesn't love snuggles?"

"True," Alex took his face in both hands and gave him a hearty kiss. "We'll work on it."

"I want you to think about places we could go for that weekend away."

"Okay, and I want you to not worry about Markson, she's got nothing on us."

Luke nodded, "call you later?"

Alex gave him another kiss and stepped back from the vehicle, "later."

When he came back into the kitchen the children were gone, and Christina was maneuvering Alvin into his chair, and Daisy was already preparing his breakfast of white looking gloop.

"Morning," he told her.

She gave him a tired smile, "morning."

"How's the cruel dictator this morning?"

Alex sat beside Alvin and took the spoon as soon as Daisy brought the bowl over. Alvin's mouth was already waiting, and he found he couldn't shovel it into his mouth fast enough.

"He's just always hungry," she said with exasperation.

Daisy patted her shoulder, "my firstborn was exactly the same. Can I get you something?"

Christina shook her head, "no I'll be fine, just coffee."

Alex wondered how often she was skipping breakfast. "I'll handle him if you want to eat and shower."

She sniffed her armpits, "yeah maybe. Do you think you can handle him for an hour?"

"I'll do my best," Alex pledged.

"Okay, well shovel that crap down him then he needs a dose of this," she placed a bottle of yellow medicine on the table and beside it a child syringe. "He has a half dose."

Alex nodded as he'd seen her administer it last night. "Got it."

"If he's still fussing give him a banana," she said.

"I've got it Christina, go and shower," he encouraged.

She smiled gratefully, "thank you."

Alex felt awful that this was exactly what her husband should have been doing for her, and wanted to strangle Tim all over again.

Daisy pinched Alvin's cheek as she cleared up the breakfast mess. "It's so wonderful to have children in the house," she observed.

Alex laughed, "it's soon to be all hands on deck isn't it."

"Have we heard anything yet?"

"Only that everyone was healthy. Jeanie was tired, but I believe they'll be coming home today."

Simon came in then, and looked grim after he'd obviously assessed the damage from the fire and he put down a stack of post, which Daisy began to sort.

"How bad is the damage?" Alex asked as he continued to shovel the food into Alvin's waiting mouth. He was banging his fists on the tray impatiently and even though he wasn't finished with his baby porridge, Daisy was already preparing to mash up a banana for him.

Simon poured himself a cup of coffee, "all things considered, not bad at all. I'd been meaning to repaint the wall anyway, and the shrubs can be replaced."

Alex nodded, "that's good."

"Oh dear," Daisy held up a large envelope to show Alex.

He looked and saw it was addressed to Christina. In the top corner of the envelope he saw the name of a law firm.

A quick search on his phone told him the law firm was based a few towns over, and they specialized in divorce law. "God dammit," he cursed.

"She's going to be so upset," Daisy said worriedly.

Alex couldn't deny that. "There's nothing we can do," which was the truth. "Let's just carry on," he said as he scooped up more gunk to feed Alvin, who was oblivious to the fact that Alex now wanted to beat the crap out of his Daddy. "You can't help your Daddy being a dickhead, can you? No you can't," he said in a baby voice.

Alvin laughed, and sprayed him with porridge, making him splutter as a chunk landed in his open mouth. "Thanks kid."

After finishing the porridge, he tackled the medicine, and thankfully that went down in without any spillages or spluttering, and then he moved straight onto the banana without waiting to see if Alvin fussed or not. One thing the kid could be reliable for, was his hunger.

When Christina came down Alex was just wiping Alvin down and was considering taking him outside. He decided to wait and see how she responded to her mail, and he didn't have to wait long.

She tore open the envelope and took a glance, her face becoming more and more stony by the second as she read. "Alex I need to go out, will you watch Alvin for me?" she stormed from the kitchen.

"Christina where are you going?" he picked up Alvin and followed her to her room where she stepped into shoes and grabbed her phone and keys.

"I need to go out, will you watch him?" she asked again.

"You know I will, but I'm worried about

where you're going."

"Believe it or not I'm an adult."

"Adults don't storm off," he pointed out.

Alvin reached out his arms towards her.

She winced as she looked at her son, "I really need to go out, for a little while. I need to breathe."

"Promise me you aren't going to do anything stupid."

She gave him a scathing look, and shook her head, "I'm not going to do anything stupid."

Alex nodded, "okay, good. Because if it was what I think it was in that envelope, then you don't need to take it as a bad thing."

She took in a deep breath, "don't. Just don't Alex."

He winced, "don't what? Be concerned? Be worried? Of course I'm going to do those things you're my sister."

"I'm coming back," she complained.

"Okay, so go," Alex didn't know why he didn't trust her to be safe right now, but he knew he couldn't physically stop her. "Just be careful."

She took that as a blessing, and turned her eyes away from her son as she left.

FORTY

Eric and Jeanie brought their new son's home just after lunch, by which time Alex was already exhausted by Alvin, and had unashamedly napped when the boy had mid-morning.

He peeked down at his new nephews who had been placed in their bassinets and smiled, "hey guys," he said quietly.

Alvin was drowsy against his shoulder, and he was hoping he was going to nap again soon.

"Where's Christina?" Jeanie asked.

"Uh, yeah she went out," Alex was now rocking Alvin from side to side, hoping the motion would make him sleepy. "Divorce papers turned up in the mail, and she took off."

Eric frowned, "Divorce papers?"

"They're in the kitchen," Alex nodded. He'd read them, and it was quite plain that Tim had filed for divorce for reasons of irreconcilable differences.

"What a fucking coward," Eric growled.

Alex nodded, "I tried to get her to stay but she said she needed to breathe. How could I deny her that? She's been cooped up with Alvin for months now."

Eric winced and nodded, "was she upset?"

"I'm not sure. I mean she was definitely feeling some strong emotions, but she didn't seem upset to me. Angry mainly, and frustrated."

"Poor Christina," Jeanie sat on her bed and sighed.

"Yeah, that on top of the night we all had, wasn't ideal."

Jeanie's eyes widened. "I can't believe the one night we weren't here is when he was stupid enough to attack. I mean I'm relieved it's over now, but I was so horrified when Eric told me this morning. Thank God you were here."

He shook his head, "honestly, I didn't do anything but check on the kids. Hunter's men were good at their jobs, they did everything."

"How is Hunter?"

"I haven't heard anything today," Alex said.

"I have," Eric said. "The police released him this morning. He was going to sleep and wash up and come by later today to discuss what arrangements we wish to make now that the immediate threat is gone."

Alvin's body took on a heaviness that he hoped meant he could put the boy down. "I'm going to try put him down," he told them both.

He'd had another dose of the medicine, and

was thankfully wiped out with all the tooth pain. Alex hadn't even been responsible for him for a whole day, and he was already worn out so he had no idea how Christina was coping with six months of doing this alone.

He vowed from then on to try and do more to help his sister, especially as her husband was officially severing all ties.

Taking the baby monitor, he went down to the kitchen and found Eric looking over the divorce papers with a scowl.

"How bad does it look?" Alex asked.

"It's mostly standard," Eric said with barely contained rage.

"Mostly?"

"He is requesting some specific items from their house be shipped to his legal representatives address but has officially signed the deed over to her alone in lieu of alimony, and he's specifically asking for no contact or details of Alvin, and in return he will pay a fixed sum of child support until Alvin's eighteenth birthday. Amount to be renegotiated through his legal counsel where required due to living costs or inflation."

Alex felt his blood run cold, "so that's it? He knocked her up and literally ran for the hills when he realized it meant he had to care for another person."

Eric shook his head, "I would have never believed he was capable of this behavior. He seemed to be so devoted to her, I think the trouble with her labor and losing Dad, then losing his leg all just came at once and he literally couldn't do anything anymore. And as much as he logically knew he was going to be a father I don't think he was in any way prepared for it. But it's not exactly something you can change your mind about."

Alex gestured to the papers, "apparently you can."

Eric threw the papers down, "if she wanted to fight this we could probably push for him to have marriage counselling and visitation with Alvin."

"I said I was done with him," Christina slurred from the doorway.

Alex turned and saw her leaning in the doorway, red eyed and bleary in a way that only alcohol assisted with. "Sis," Alex said with commiseration.

"I'm actually glad he's done it, coz I don't want Alvin exposed to that asshole," she sniffed.

Eric stepped toward her with his arms open, but she just backed up and held out her hand.

"I'm okay. I just did some day drinking and cried on a stranger who put me in a cab. I'm fine," she gave a decisive nod.

Eric nodded as well, "okay, well when you are ready, we can go through these papers together and get everything squared away."

She shrugged, "whatever."

Alex was concerned that she wasn't taking this as seriously as she needed to.

"It's not like any of it means anything anymore," she shrugged again and looked at the floor. "Best part of a decade I gave to that man, and my fertility, and he gets to just run away and pretend it never happened," the shrug she did this time was so exaggerated it would have been comical if it wasn't so tragically highlighted by the tears standing in her eyes.

"Christina," Alex tried to take a step forward, but again she backed up a step.

"He gets to start over," she said with real anger now. "He gets to just limp on with his one hoppy leg and do whatever he fucking wants. And I'm stuck with the kid he jointly decided to make with me!"

Alex winced as he knew there was nothing he could say.

"And I'm now the dreaded single mother. Bane of the dating scene. The one who has to apologize to any prospective guy that sorry, I have stretch marks now. Or sorry, I can't sleep over because my babysitter is waiting. And Alvin! The kids are gonna make fun of him at school for having no Dad, and I'm gonna get fat coz I'm just gonna drink wine and eat ice cream every night coz I'm not getting laid!"

"Christina it's not that bad," Eric said forcefully. "You have a family, we'll help you."

She shook her head, "you have your family Eric," she said sadly. "You've still got your happily ever after." She took a breath and looked at the papers again. "I hate him," she sobbed, and the tears finally fell as she let Alex hug her at last. "I hate him I hate him I hate him!"

Eric patted her back and Alex shot his older brother a look, seeking assurance that they were doing the right thing by holding her.

Eric just looked pained.

Christina pulled back after weeping for several minutes into Alex's shirt and she looked up into his face. "You know, with the beard, you kinda look like Dad."

For some reason, that made him want to cry as well. Dad would know what to do or say right now to make all this right.

She staggered away from them, and they

followed her progress through the parlor, where Hunter had just come through from the security room.

"Christina, sit down you're going to fall," Eric told her as she bumped into a wingback chair.

She shook her head and spun around, "don't talk to me like a child." She was angry again now and pointed her finger at Eric. "And I know you guys have helped me, but just because I've been under your roof, doesn't mean you can tell me what to do."

"I just don't want you to get hurt," Eric said plainly, engaging every ounce of patience he had.

She gave a derisive laugh, "bit late for that." She raised her chin, "you know what, I think it's time for me and Alvin to move out. If we're gonna do this we're gonna have to learn to do it alone sooner or later."

"Nobody is asking you to do it alone."

"Well I'm husband-less and he's Dad-less, so I think that makes us pretty much alone."

"Why are you being combative?" Eric asked, exasperated by her tone. "Nobody is against you here."

She raised her finger again, "because this family, is full of love at first sight bullshit! And I'm sick of it! Because I've been there and done that, and you know what? It doesn't work! It fails! It withers and dies just like every living thing does! Just like Dad did!"

Crack.

The room was suddenly silent as the three of them saw in horror Eric lower his hand, and Christina holding her face.

Alex felt his own mask of horror as he took in and understood the facts.

Eric had just slapped Christina.

Eric.

Eric!

It was an impossible fact.

No.

Eric was not capable of harm.

Eric would never hit a woman.

Would never hit his sister.

Their sister.

His brother. His rock. His idol – no!

The room seemed frozen in place with everyone in it locked and unable to move. Everyone except Hunter who took it upon himself to remove Christina.

No words were spoken. Nobody was capable of action right now.

He locked one strong arm around her shoulders and turned her to lead her from the room.

"Eric?" Jeanie was on the stairs and from the look of horror on her face she too had witnessed the impossible.

Eric took a step away from Jeanie as if afraid of hurting her.

"Jeanie, give us a minute please," Alex took his brother then, almost exactly mirroring Hunters move. "Keep it together," he growled at Eric.

His feet took him on auto pilot straight out the front door and around the side of the house. As soon as they cleared the corner he threw Eric down and punched him in the jaw.

Eric didn't defend himself, he didn't even seem to register the pain. He was in shock. Alex pushed his head back.

Guilt immediately swamped him as he saw Eric bit his own lip when his head smacked the ground.

"Don't," he sneered down at his brother. "You don't get to fucking wallow. You deserve your guilt but you do not get to check out."

Tears filled Eric's eyes and streamed out silently. "I didn't mean…" he whined in a tone he'd never heard from Eric before.

It was a tone of submissive surrender. A whine of complete vulnerability.

"I know you didn't dickhead." He snapped

out angrily. "When she sobers the fuck up she'll know too."

He shook his head, "how could I…" his face crumpled miserably then, and he covered it with his palms as he cried.

Alex winced, but got to his feet and turned his back on Eric.

He looked up at the bright blue sky and imagined for the briefest moment that his father were looking down on him. Giving advice and praise like he'd always done.

"You know, when Dad died, I guess I'd never truly felt the loss, because I still had my parent. We all still had you." He really wished he had a cigarette right then.

Turning back to Eric he said, "we've all depended on you too much I think. And so for my part, I'm sorry. I forget that you lost your father too, and I forget that the reason you're such a great Dad is because you've been a Dad for thirty years now."

Eric curled on his side, still crying.

"To have been a Dad for so long, and you're only just now making your first fucking mistake…I think you're owed one Eric. She'll forgive you, so you need to forgive yourself too."

"How can I forgive hitting my sister?"

Alex crouched down again so he was closer to Eric, "you don't have the luxury of another choice Eric."

Eric met his eyes, shocked again, but Alex was glad to see some cognitive reasoning now.

"That's right! You don't have a choice Eric, you're Dad! So you need to get your shit together! For your wife, and your seven children," Alex jabbed a finger at him. "And you need to do it fast dickweed, because we don't have time for rock bottom."

FORTY-ONE

Alex found Christina asleep in her bed when they returned to the house, and Hunter was stood in the doorway watching her silently. Until he saw Eric that was, and Alex sensed that he wanted to say a lot of things, but was biting them back as they still had a very clear line of employee and employer.

"I came to apologize to her," Eric said meekly.

Hunter looked at him for a long moment, "she's resting."

Eric fidgeted, "look Hunter, I'm sorry you saw-"

"What I saw, was a lot of very tired adults, one of which was very drunk and sad, and she provoked another who only really has one vulnerability that she attacked."

Eric's shoulders slumped, as if he'd been braced for an attack from Hunter.

"I know that was not you," Hunter said vehemently. "But that *is* her, and she would have blown sooner or later, she's been hurting for a long time."

Alex heard the restraint there and wondered exactly how long Hunter had been watching

Christina with more than a passing interest.

Alex faced Eric, "why don't you go check on Jeanie and the boys? I'll stay with Christina and make sure she's calm and a bit more sober before she comes out."

Eric nodded unhappily and backed away.

Alex faced Hunter as if to dismiss him too, but Hunter was already storming away in the other direction.

Christina's eyes were open when he approached the bed, and she was the picture of misery. He wondered if she had even really been asleep at all or was just trying to avoid the confrontation.

"Hey," he lay down on the bed and faced her.

Her lip trembled as if she was going to cry again, and he shook his head, "don't."

That was the worst thing to tell an emotional woman of course, and the floodgates opened as she cried, which woke Alvin of course.

Alex went over to the boy and immediately started changing his diaper, "shush big boy, we don't need more crying," he said softly.

Alvin looked up at him, "Mumumum?" he said beseechingly.

"She's a little sad right now," he explained down to the boy, "so we need to cheer her up."

Christina sat up in bed and looked over to

where Alex was changing her son, and she seemed sad, "did he just ask for me?"

"Sounded like it," Alex nodded. "Are you sober?"

"I was sober the second he hit me," she said this delicately and without recrimination.

"Did you hear him say he wanted to apologize?"

She nodded, "I don't know why I was lashing out at him."

"Because you were hurting and you wanted someone else to be hurting as well," Alex offered as a suggestion. "And because day drinking is really only for old men."

She rubbed her eyes and looked out the door, and Alex wondered if she was looking for Hunter or Eric. He also wondered if he should say anything about Hunter to his sister in warning, or should he just sit back and watch their mutual interest keep crashing on the rocks until the timing was right.

The divorce papers had only arrived today after all, so she was barely back on the market.

"I'm gonna take Alvin for a walk," he announced when he got his nephew snapped into clean dry clothes. "Why don't you freshen up and go talk to Eric? He's never going to forgive himself until you do first."

She nodded, "Alex?"

He faced her, "what?"

"You really do look like Dad," she said sadly.

It was hard to hear. Especially as he'd always been told he took after their mother with his coloring. So he looked in the mirror on her vanity, and no he didn't see his father.

But then he relaxed his eyes and pictured skin that wasn't quite so tight, with wrinkles, and grey hair and a fuller beard, and then he saw his father. And the sadness he felt was bittersweet.

Here he was, his father's son. He was living on, while his father was dead, taking breath where his father could not. "I miss him too," he admitted and looked back to Christina. "And I hate the fact that I was so stupid to cut myself off for so long, I missed so many years playing the part of super tough cop and denying anything was wrong…I'll always regret that."

Christina sniffed, "I didn't ever get to say goodbye," she said, her tears falling again, but she was stoically composed now, with no hysterics. "I miss him so much."

Alex came and sat beside her on the bed, and Alvin was delighted to see her, chanting "Mumumum," again and clapping his hands.

Christina smiled and took her son within her embrace, "hey kid, here I am."

Alex smiled down at the sight, "that day, I don't think I'd ever been more scared with so many people I loved in danger. And every day since I think of something else I should have said to Dad, or some other way to tell him that I loved him. But it's a moment I can't ever get back for a redo. And at the end of the day, what I told him was something he already knew. Same way he knew that you loved him Christina."

She looked at him for a moment before looking down at Alvin again, "I know you're right, I just can't seem to get past the regret," she said softly.

"Take it as a lesson learned then, to not hold back and tell the people you love that you love them every single day."

She laughed and bumped her shoulder into his side, "I love you Alex."

He bumped her back, "I love you too. And I'm not going anywhere, okay? None of us are. You're not alone."

She nodded, "I should apologize to Eric."

"Let's go see if he's around. You should probably drink some coffee."

The did find Eric in the kitchen with Jeanie, and they were each coaxing a bottle into their babies mouths.

Everyone except Alex had an infant in their arms as Christina stepped over to Eric, who still looked pale. "I'm so sorry Eric," she looked up at him, then down at the new baby in his arms, and she leaned up to kiss his cheek. "I didn't mean to lash out at you."

Eric's face crumpled, "I'm sorry too."

Alex thought there was nothing worse than seeing his older brother at breaking point.

Jeanie's face was pinched with worry as she looked at Alex, who tried his best to give her a reassuring smile, "it's all okay." He came to stand beside her and looked down, "which twin is this?"

Jeanie laughed, "you know, I'm not even sure right now."

FORTY-TWO

He saw his Captain, and the witness in the form of the HR director sat in the corner, and groaned inwardly.

Alex had taken his week off like a good boy, and now what? He'd barely set foot in the building before someone had told him to go straight to see the captain.

He already knew that Luke had been partnered with Fuller, and they were resuming normal duties this week, as staff downstairs were all back and fully recovered from the flu. Alex wondered who he would be getting paired off with now.

"Good morning Alex," Markson said pleasantly, although her tone was measured and deliberate.

"Good morning Captain," he said with an equal measure of calm.

She gestured for him to sit, and he did without breaking eye contact with her.

She didn't smile. "I've asked HR to witness this conversation as I feel that there have been too many miscommunications between us, and I want it to be clear that there is only ever duty of care as the priority in my actions."

He felt his nostrils flaring as he sniffed in response. "Okay," he acknowledged. "Do I need to go and get a union rep?"

"This is not a disciplinary hearing," she said. In the corner of the room came a discreet cough, and Markson was painfully holding back an eye roll as she added, "however if you would feel more comfortable you may collect a rep."

Alex smirked, "no I'm fine." He thoroughly enjoyed her discomfort. "Proceed."

Markson lifted her chin, "as I'm sure you know by now, I have reassigned Carter to partner with Fuller, as Gibson is on long term leave."

"Yes, I knew that," he said very carefully.

She nodded, "I would like to ask that you accept a relocation to the records department."

His smirk dropped, "excuse me?"

"In light of the partner swaps I have just mentioned, that leaves you without a partner."

"So I'll work alone."

"I'm afraid I need the manpower in records. Walker said that you were highly diligent and he'd love to have you on his team," she quickly threw this compliment at him, as if that would convince him this was for the best.

Alex stared at her. He was being shipped off to be a filing clerk because he'd pissed her off.

"And do I get a choice in this?" he asked with a sinking feeling in his gut.

"No, I'm afraid that it has been decided that this is for the best."

"By who?"

"By those in charge," she said. "This goes above my head Steinberg."

Alex shook his head, and looked over at the HR guy, "you taking dictation?"

The man nodded.

"Okay, in response to your kind offer of relocating and demoting to the rank of file clerk, I will of course be declining. I am a fully capable Detective, and I have not been given the opportunity to show that since I joined this precinct. And during recent events, I have been actively stopped from performing to the best of my ability, so no, I do not feel a demotion is justified or a solution to anything."

"During recent events, it was important that you be recused."

"I never argued that fact, and it was me that recognized the need for it. However it was not my fault that another operation demanded me to step back."

"No fault or blame is being laid on you," Markson said very clearly.

"So can you give me any clear defined reason

why I cannot be a Detective?"

She swallowed, "it's in your best interest's to not be on active duty, given your health risks."

"Oh now I get it. I've landed on someone's radar because of all the incidences last week where you thought I was interfering or causing trouble, and someone's looked at my file and saw the big neon sign that says HIV, and they panicked about the potential for any mishaps."

"You are a good Detective, however, it's been decided that though you are willing to take those risks it is not fair to potentially endanger others."

The HR man coughed again.

Markson blushed, "Alex, the armed man that broke into your brother's home, what would have happened if you'd been wounded?"

He got to his feet and very calmly leaned over the desk, "that is a risk every cop takes on a daily basis." So he couldn't be accused of intimidation, he stood tall and shook his head. "I'll make this easy for you Markson," he unclipped his badge and took off his gun holster and placed them on her desk. "I quit. And you'll be hearing from my lawyer."

She leaned back in her chair and pinched her nose, "I don't want that."

"You know I used to be a librarian," he told

her as he pulled on his jacket without his holster on. "That guy was dumb enough to go and talk to a gang peddling drugs outside his library and he ended up nearly dying when he got stuck with a dirty needle full of heroin. And I vowed to help people from then on. If you won't let me do that, I'll find another way, because I am not a fucking file clerk."

"Please," she said, but he didn't know what she was asking him for.

Alex shook his head, "don't ask me to be someone I'm not."

She winced but said softly, "I'm afraid this is out of my hands, if it were my decision you would be allowed to resume your duties today."

He believed her, so he decided to take it easy on her by saying, "did you get them all?"

She relaxed a little, "yes. Father Francis is behind bars awaiting trial. Mr. Miller is safe to return home now," she gave a little smile.

He nodded, "take care Captain."

He left the office and released a breath, feeling liberated.

Luke and Fuller weren't on the floor, but he would see them later, and there were no other goodbyes he wanted to say. The department hadn't been a good fit for him since he'd moved here, so he wasn't upset that it had come to this.

When he was outside, he went to his car and sat in the driver's seat, but pulled out his phone and called Ryan Miller.

"Hey man, are you okay? I wasn't sure if I'd hear from you again, Hunter said you weren't allowed to be involved anymore."

"Yeah, I'm good thanks. The situation is resolved, and I'm allowed to talk to you now. I have some good news."

"I don't know what's better than what you've already done for me. Because for all the cloak and dagger I know it was you."

"You're all clear to come home again now, it's safe."

Ryan hesitated, "really?"

"Father Francis is now wearing an orange jumpsuit and is awaiting trial."

He heard a sigh, "well, thank God for that."

He laughed at the irony of that statement. "Yeah, God."

"No," Ryan amended, "thank you. Without your help I'd probably be facing an eviction notice about now."

"I didn't do that."

"Well you arranged for someone to do that."

Alex didn't confirm or deny a thing.

"When we're back, can I at least cook you

dinner to say thanks?"

He laughed, "that's not necessary, but thank you."

"Want to grab a beer?"

He sensed that the man, much like himself, had no friends, and was reaching out. "Sure, why not. Give me a call."

Miller sounded happy at that, "I will, and thanks again."

"You're welcome, and enjoy the rest of your vacation, hope the kids are loving it."

"Yup, but if I never see Mickey Mouse again it'll be a day too soon."

FORTY-THREE

When he arrived at All Saints House, he was pleased to see Eric in his office, which now housed two baby chairs beside the desk.

Alex laughed when he saw that Eric had one foot on each chair bouncing them gently with his toes while he was on the phone speaking in hushed tones.

"This is called letting Mommy have a sleep, because she is super cranky pants today," Eric said softly once he was done with his call.

Alex grinned, "I just quit my job."

Eric blinked, "really? But you love being a cop."

He explained what Markson had said.

"Do you want to go after them legally?"

Alex leaned back on the couch, "part of me does, but that's the spiteful part. I think I just want to let it go. But I also need to figure out how I can help people now. It's why I wanted to be a cop in the first place."

Hunter tapped Eric's door then, and he was holding an envelope in his hands, "here's what you asked for."

Eric nodded, "thanks."

Hunter put the envelope on the desk and put

his hands in his pockets, "with the adjustments we agreed upon, the new arrangements will kick in tomorrow. And you've got our contact information if you need to up the numbers again."

Eric smiled, "I'm hoping we won't need to, but thank you. And no doubt you'll hear from me on other matters."

Hunter nodded and then turned to Alex, "you figured out that the law isn't always black and white then?"

He thought about it, and saw the truth. "It's still black and white, but I see the value now in some grey."

"You quit your job?"

"Yeah, I was given the option of file clerk or nothing, so I took nothing."

Hunter eye rolled, "you ever thought about security and protection?"

Alex was confused, "huh?"

"I'm offering you a job dickhead," he said with a wry smile.

"Can I think about it?"

Hunter shrugged, "I always need good people, and you're good now you've stopped being an asshole."

A month ago he would have added that comment to the list of reasons he hated

Hunter, and he wasn't quite sure when he'd stopped that way of thinking. "I appreciate the offer, I'll be in touch."

Hunter nodded, then left the office, and Alex cocked his head at Eric when he was sure the man was out of earshot. "He seem different to you?"

Eric shook his head, "no but he's right, you're not being…how you were."

"Was I really being an asshole?"

His big brother smiled, "I wouldn't say that, but I would definitely say you were being defensive to the point of aggressive."

"I never wanted to be that way."

"No, but you spent so long building yourself up to be strong and hard and in no way weak, you became quite blinded to everything that wasn't in your immediate periphery."

Pondering that, he remembered that he'd thought the librarian who had been attacked with a dirty needle had died, but perhaps he was still around buried deep within, just hiding in the book stacks in his mind and waiting until Alex felt safe enough to let him breath freely again.

Sighing, he got to his feet, "I need to do some thinking."

Eric nodded, "but you're okay?"

"Yeah, I actually am," he smiled.

He was strolling the garden twenty minutes later when his phone rang, and he saw it was Charlie. "Hey Charlie."

"Alex! Hey, I heard I was allowed to talk to you now. You know, now that my Dad's banged up."

"You sound quite chipper about it."

"I'm horrified! When Kathy told me everything he'd been doing I felt sick. I still feel sick."

"You were innocent." Charlie made a noise as if she were being sick, and Alex laughed. "How are you doing?"

"I'm good. I'm actually calling to say thanks for job."

Alex grinned, "that was my sister in law's idea and offer, not me."

"Well, I can't wait to start!"

Jeanie had proposed to install a day care at Open Arms. Not only were the majority of women who attended the services there parents with children, but the staff as well would benefit. Charlie had been offered a full time position.

"I'm really happy that you are happy Charlie. And listen, if you're still interested in working out, we can still do it together."

She laughed, "yeah maybe. Although Frankie told me you had a new boyfriend, won't he mind?"

Alex laughed too, "tell that old queer to stop gossiping."

"Yeah, I'll tell him."

By the time Alex had walked the grounds, he'd also covered a lot of mental ground too. Christina waved at him as she sat on a blanket with Alvin under a large parasol.

Alvin had several toys littered around the blanket he was entertained by, and Alex crouched down where he was laying on his back.

Christina picked up a red brick and tossed it to Alex, "hold that and waggle it at him," she said excitedly.

Alex waggled the brick at Alvin, who laughed and immediately flipped onto his belly and started crawling for the brick. "Oh my God is he crawling? He's crawling!"

Christina laughed too, but Alex saw a hint of sadness in her proud smile, "yeah, he's crawling."

He knew why she was sad too, it was a milestone that she should have been sharing with her husband.

"Good job buddy!" Alex scooped him up

and jumped with him to make him laugh. Alvin may not have his father, but he would not lack for love.

FORTY-FOUR

Tillie smiled as she admitted Alex to the home she shared with her son. "How lovely to see you Alex, I almost didn't recognize you without the beard. I'm afraid Luke isn't back from work yet."

"No I guessed he wouldn't be, I wanted to surprise him actually." Alex held out the bunch of flowers he'd brought, "these are for you though, I picked them from my brothers garden."

"Oh they're lovely," she smiled. "I always think wild flowers smell the best," she inhaled deeply, and then wheeled herself to her kitchen to find a vase for them.

"I agree," he said.

She glanced over her shoulder at Alex, "you're dressed very smartly, are you planning on surprising Luke with a romantic dinner?"

Alex laughed, "something like that." He looked down at his blazer and tie. "Will that interfere with any plans you have?"

She eye rolled, "absolutely not. I've told that boy a million times I'm a grown woman and I can take care of myself and to stop using me as an excuse. I have lots of friends who can give me rides."

"Maybe he just wants to take care you," Alex offered.

Tillie smiled sweetly, "he's a big softy under all that big mouth of his, it's true."

Alex nodded, "he certainly is."

They shared a smile of mutual love for Luke.

"With your blessing then, I'll be occupying him this evening, and potentially this weekend if he agrees to come away with me."

Tillie laughed, "you have my blessing, and also my thanks."

"Thanks for what?"

"Taking him off my hands," she joked.

Alex laughed, "I haven't taken him yet, I may change my mind."

"No, too late, no give backsies," she arranged the flowers in a vase and sniffed them again. "I'll just call my friend to come and pick me up, and I'll eat out. Are you going to hide up in his room?"

Alex laughed again, "my car is parked right outside. And I'm not intending to chase you out of your own house."

"I'm sensing something naughty is about to happen, so I don't want to get in the way of or possibly hear it," she said with a grin.

Tillie was gone within twenty minutes, and he

knew that Luke would be home soon, so he cleared off their dining table and started stacking books for his surprise.

When he saw Luke's car pull up he pulled the black rimmed glasses out of his pocket and bit back his smile as he peeked around the wall from the dining room.

The door opened and Luke pulled his jacket off, "Alex?" He looked around in confusion, "Mom? What time do you need to be at Wanda's?"

Alex put his glasses on and stepped around the doorway, "please be quiet Sir, people are trying to read." He used the best hushed librarian tone, and watched as Luke's face lit up with the dirtiest grin.

"Are you doing sexy librarian?" Luke dropped his jacket.

"Sssh," Alex chastised and stepped back to his stack of books on the dining table.

"I'm presuming you shipped off my mother?" Luke leaned in the doorway and folded his arms, enjoying Alex's performance as he read spines on books and started filing them back on the bookshelf.

Alex tipped his glasses down and peered over the rim of them, "Sir, please be quiet."

Luke actually giggled, and Alex couldn't help

the smile now, but quickly reigned it in and got back into character when Luke asked, "but I was really wondering if you could help me find a book?"

"Oh?"

Luke stepped up to him, "it's a little bit of a naughty book, I'm not sure you'll know it."

Alex blinked at him, "I'm very well read Sir."

"Hmm, I'll bet," Luke reached over and yanked his tie open. "Have you heard of the Kama Sutra?"

Alex smirked, "most of it is impossible from what I've heard and will result in injury."

Luke laughed but seemed to sober when he stroked a finger down Alex's clean shaven face. "You quit."

Alex nodded.

Luke shook his head and seemed sad, "well there goes my good cop bad cop fantasy."

"Can we focus on one fantasy at a time?" Alex suggested. "I thought you'd enjoy this."

He felt a finger stroke his eyebrow and flick at his piercing there. "Oh I am, I'm just a little overwhelmed with emotion here."

Alex loved that Luke wasn't in any way afraid to talk about his emotions, "I thought you couldn't reign in your sarcasm long enough for serious talk."

"The sarcasm is coming," Luke warned with a nod and a smile, "but Alex, you quit your job."

"Yeah, because I was being forced to be a file clerk. That's not me anymore, this little glimpse of librarian is just for you now."

Luke scowled at that, "I hate that this has happened."

"Weirdly I'm not angry about it," Alex smiled. "I am, right now, probably the happiest I've ever been, and that's including before I got stuck with that needle."

Luke's smile returned, "you're happy?"

"I am, but more important, I've let go of the anger and fear I didn't even know I was carrying. And I'm ready now, to start being alive. With you."

Luke's finger traced down his face and he felt his cheek cupped in a cool large hand. "I love you," he said softly.

Alex swallowed the lump of emotion that seemed to be constricting his throat, "I do believe I love you too Lukey."

AUTHORS NOTE

I'm sorry.

To everyone who has been waiting for the resolution to the cliffhanger I left it on two years ago, I'm sorry.

And to anyone who is potentially offended that this book focuses on a man who is bisexual and has just read man on man love, sorry not sorry.

I struggled with this book, and I won't lie about it. Not only did I start it with all the best intentions (good title pun) of writing it and releasing it a lot sooner than I actually did, but as is always the case the book went in a direction that I hadn't intended.

I'm what you call a discovery writer. So though I have an idea on what story I'm trying to tell, I just let it flow and I don't follow a strict writing plan like a lot of writers do. So if characters or events suddenly pop up out of nowhere, I let them.

When it came time to sitting down and fleshing out Alex and his story, I had all my good ideas and my intentions, but it just wasn't happening.

In part, I think it is because I used to do my

writing as a form of escapism from my crappy existence. As my existence is no longer crappy, I lost that form of motivation.

That's excuse number one.

Excuse number two, is that I am not now nor have I ever been a bisexual man. So though I can try to center myself in the character and their feelings bla bla bla…I had a genuine fear that I would misrepresent someone, or an entire community of someone's, and that is something I definitely didn't want to address. So I ignored it and hoped it would go away.

Ready for excuse number three? It's a doozy! I'm really lazy. And though the previous reasons are genuine, this one is the biggest one, and I have to hold my hands up and be honest. I was lazy.

Recent events have made me kick my own backside though, you'll be thankful to hear (or not if you hated this book). I forced myself to write every day, telling myself at the beginning that I was going to see what I could do in an hour, and there were a few blank hours where I stared at the screen and felt so frustrated that I just couldn't do it. Why wasn't this story flowing like the others had? That was when I realized that a) All of the above, and b) It was Alex's story to tell, and not mine. I needed to let him speak and choose what he wanted to choose.

I may sound like a weirdo, but that's the best way I can describe what's been going on. And as soon as I surrendered to this, the story came, and so did the surprise character of Lukas.

I'm so happy now that the story has played out the way it did, and I did my best to be true to it and not my own agenda.

Is there more to tell? Well of course! And you will be happy to know that work is already started on the follow up book which is Christina's tale; To New Beginnings. Hmm, poor Christina, she's not had a good time at all has she?!

Anyway, thanks to everyone for their patience, and I do hope you've enjoyed this book and that it was worth the wait?

All the best guys
Helen xxx (April 2022)

Printed in Great Britain
by Amazon

81893552R00246